Aammton Alias

The

Last Bastion

of

Ingei

Imminent

Book 1

The Last Bastion of Ingei Series

A NaNoWriMo novel

Please visit http://ingei.b1percent.com

ISBN: 978-1-5406283-7-4

Contents Page

5 | The Last Bastion of Ingei

Dedicated to the crushed

who continue to defy,

even in Death.

We continue to respond to your deaths

with our deafening silence,

condemned to wait for the right moment,

convenient to us,

and most inconvenient to the dying.

Before You Read

Thank you for purchasing this book. This is book 1 of the Last Bastion of Ingei series. The book is also available in ebook format at http://www.ingei.b1percent.com

This book was self-edited and proofread, which means you may find some mistakes. Please feel free to contact me tony@b1percent.com and I will reward you with a gift!

If you like I can send you updates and offers on the next book release. All you have to do is simply register at:

http://www.b1percent.com email list.

Enjoy reading!

Acknowledgements

My loving **wife** and my **daughter** continue to go beyond inspiring me to complete this novel - which was initially a NaNoWriMo challenge. They gave me continuous feedback and encouragement to complete my book, even when they would rather I stop and spend time with them by the beach.

Many thanks to my good friends **Dr Jawad K**, **Ms Adrina Agus Din** and **Dr Adam** who allowed me to relentlessly bounce ideas and forward my 'freshly-baked' chapters direct to their mobile phones, with no regards to the unsocial hours in anticipation of their immediate and nurturing feedback.

30th November

Arowana

Location: Ingei River, Labi

Boi knows he should not be there.

The Ingei river is teeming with life - a wildlife sanctuary, protected by law but trespassed by many such as the likes of Boi - poachers who will never understand the term 'wildlife protection' and will never understand that there are still plenty of species that have yet to be discovered.

After a few days journey; upstream, on his single-engine wooden boat or *Perahu*, Boi reaches his secret fishing spot on the Ingei river. He is well-prepared, stocked up on cheap illegal Indonesian cigarettes, dry food rations, soft drinks and a GPS receiver.

He will be 40 next month, and wonders what he should buy for his birthday. Working as a security guard at the local hospital barely pays the household bills. He drops down a couple of underwater traps into the brownish yet clear river and then casts his lucky fishing line.

His usual fishing buddy, Johari, is not with him this time as he is unwell with the flu.

I'm going to win big, Jo.

Boi smiles on the thought of not having to share his catch this time.

Usually, they would catch exotic fishes together, especially the much desired Arowana fish (an Osteoglossidae) – a favourite amongst Asian aquariums - and store them in polystyrene boxes, equipped with battery powered aerators. Then they would sell the fishes to their agent, who is well connected to a network of local and international collectors, keen to part their money for rare and beautiful specimens.   Boi has his own network of clients he found on Facebook. He neither comprehends nor does he care that the Arowana is on the International Union for the Conservation of Nature or IUCN Red List of Threatened Species.

Being a pathological day-dreamer, he dreams about driving a posh sports car and 'picking up' beautiful women. The kind of women who would not even notice him on a normal day.

His ambitious endeavour is pushed by recent Facebook posts of other poachers who had caught an unclassified 'Super Golden Blue-Red Arowana' fish.

A Golden Arowana itself is a rare and much prized fish whilst a Super Golden Blue-Red Arowana has been practically unheard of until now. The secret frenzied bidding that ensued, pushed prices spiralling to that of a luxury saloon car. Whilst casting his line, Boi daydreams driving a new 'Godzilla'; the Nissan GT-R at breakneck speed on the highway – his feeble mind not understanding that he could never afford the maintenance costs of such a beastly supercar.

Today, the slow-moving river is coloured like lightly brewed tea, almost clear, with most of the riverbed visible from the surface.

The Arowana loves its prey: small fishes, insects and even spiders. It can jump out of the water to gobble up insects in mid-air. Unfortunately, this is one of the reasons why it is sought after by aquarium owners. The Arowana brings good luck and prosperity. Just another excuse for useless ownership and the mark of a tragically good sales strategy.

Boi feels a very strong tug on his fishing rod. He holds on to the fishing rod with all his strength, and then unreels a bit of the fishing wire. Boi is a talented fisherman, he knows how to tire a fighter fish like the Arowana. Judging from the effort and strength he has to put up to hold the fish at bay, he can tell this is going to be the biggest Arowana he will ever catch.

He pulls back the fishing rod, bent to the extreme and yet unbroken, he winds and unwinds the fishing reel.

"My wildest dreams is coming true. Before I buy that car, I better get a new iPhone 7 Plus," he says to himself.

Not giving in easily, Boi continues to struggle against the fish.

"If only Johari was here, he would film and I could post this footage on YouTube, setup my own fishing YouTube channel. I'll be famous and teach people how to fish," gasping to himself, whilst catching his breath.

"I better get a MacBook and an iPad, as well," he can feel the giant fish tiring, but then so is he.

"When I am successful, I'll get a beautiful watch… hmm maybe a Rolex."

Boi is not aware of what is happening around him, how suddenly silent the jungle around the river had become. All the jungle creatures and critters are spooked, knowing that they will become witnesses to a tragedy.

And then it starts.

Small bubbles rapidly effervesce from beneath the small boat, becoming larger and larger bubbles. A foam of bubbles furiously surround the boat, and spreads to the rest of the river. The boat sinks lower into the water. No, the water near the boat is actually disappearing and the river dries up mysteriously.

The whole turn of events shocks Boi.

"Where did the water go?"

A thousand questions flashes through his mind, trying to ascertain the logic of it all.

His boat is now resting on the muddy river bed. The brackish smell of the river is strong. He can see the fish traps he had just dropped in earlier.

"Is this for real? Please let it not be real," he prayed.

Boi knows he should have stayed home.

He should have been grateful for what he already had.

He cannot see the Presence heading towards him.

All he can sense is a primordial, clear and present danger.

There is nowhere to run. Tears run down his cheeks, jerked by tiny sobs as he desperately tries to figure out a prayer, a mantra, anything to stop the inevitable. Thoughts of regret and loved ones storm in his mind.

The Presence stands before him, huge and tall, whilst his underling watches him from nearby. Boi cannot see what is in front of him, but he feels his life force seeping away, his heart pounding fast and hard, then beating slowly and erratically. The Presence projects his hand into Boi's chest, bypassing layers of fat, muscle and tissue, as if none are there in the first place. With a powerful squeeze, the heart ceases to beat.

Hopes and dreams are crushed into nothing.

The Presence is grateful that Boi is – was – a heavy smoker. His family will think he had a heart attack from all that heavy smoking. No one will ask questions. Even the wise elder ones in his village will understand and say nothing.

The Presence vanishes and the lifeless body slumps down, crashing into and breaking the polystyrene boxes. And as quickly as the water had disappeared, the river water replenishes itself seemingly from nowhere. The jungle becomes loud and noisy again.

These witnesses will never tell.

The poacher's body and boat begins to float downstream. Passing fishermen will find Boi in a few days' time.

One Year Ago

Sarin: Prequel

Location: Unknown Jungle

The noon sun occasionally penetrates through the canopy of the tall jungle trees, spotlights on patches of the wet, soggy jungle floor, we avoid like the stealthy creatures of harm-bringers. The humidity and constant buzzing of the jungle, we are so accustomed to that we hardly mind it. We have no enemy to worry about, but our training has been so in-grained in us, that we do, before we think. Although, we are cautious, we know no one, nothing would dare challenge us, not even the poachers who have unashamedly marked the occasional 'Gaharu' or sandalwood trees with their initials in ominous red paint. Like the jungle animals, these trespassing poachers love to mark their territory, crossing from the border into our forgiving and plentiful land, felling sandalwood trees as well as other hardwood trees. The trees have become sparser over the few years, I wonder if anyone would weep for the missing.

"We should shoot them, Tuan." Matt, the newest member of our team, who is fair with a pretty face that he could be confused as a K-Pop star or Korean Pop star. How did he get himself into my unit?

I ignore Matt, whilst the other two members of this unit steal glances at each other.

Ismi whispers as we slowly walk through the semi-wet jungle floor, "Shoot who? Shoot you?"

"I meant shoot these illegal Gaharu tree poachers, stealing our wood from our country. These trees are worth tens of thousands of dollars each," Matt replies.

The Captain, the leader of this squad, who is ahead of us, signals for us to rest, then quickly runs towards Matt, his steps ever light and soft - barely crunching the brown leaf littered jungle floor. The Captain huffs and angrily whispers to Matt - grimacing mountain ridges of expressions.

"What's wrong with you? Don't you ever close that mouth? This is a bloody recon unit. The First Recon Unit is known to be stealthy and quiet, talk when only absolutely necessary. How the hell did you get transferred to my unit?!"

I know a part of the Captain wanted to shoot his Colt Commando semi-automatic rifle at this loud-mouth, loud mouth Matt.

Matt whispers apologies and does not get shot.

Why would we ask for trouble unless trouble comes to us? Shooting them means reports to fill in, interrogation during debriefings. The army isn't about Arnold Schwarzenegger types, shooting everyone down on his own. We have become meticulous and structured. And then what if they retaliate? What if by some dumb luck a stray bullet hits and kills one of us, the elite soldiers in our army. There would be hell to pay for, especially for our commanding officers.

I gaze upon our Captain and admire him, he is a fine soldier and a grounded leader whom I would follow to hell and back - and yet I know he would definitely be the first to be scapegoated.

That's why Rules of Engagements are in place.

The Captain moves up front to stay in formation.

I admire him, he is the essence of a true leader, one who leads the way in a bad situation and always the last one out. We move with the day shadows of the jungle towards our target. The Captain signals with his fist for us to stop, and then does an upside down thumb gesture and then points to a direction straight ahead.

Lance Corporal Ismi stretches his neck upwards, showing his bulging Adam's throat, snorts and then sniffs the air, and signals with his right hand, flashes an open palm with five fingers and then closing his fist and displaying his thumb, nodding slowly - a mime rehearsed and understood so many times, it can be done with closed eyes.

"What does the nod mean?" Matt whispers to me.

I do my best not to show any emotion. "It means there is a presence ahead, maybe around five or six members."

"How do you know this, Tuan Sarin?"

I look at Matt, acknowledge my right to be addressed as a *Tuan*, a Sir, whilst with an expressionless face, I admire his fair complexion and almost perfect physique, and yet he has a mind of a 12-year-old child, which a part of me wants to bludgeon with the butt of my semi-automatic rifle.

"If you didn't hear it before, then you can smell it. Can you smell it, Matt?"

"Smell what?" Matt, his child-like expression of puzzlement and yet ever so curious, does not suit someone of his physical shape.

"A campfire - large enough for more than three people, rice cooking, a pot of wrongly cooked wild chicken or maybe something partially cooked," Ismi, a lance corporal with a chisel facial features, interrupts in angry whispers.

"Okay, I can't smell anything but how did you know it was five to six people?"

"Private Mat, it's something you pick up with experience. The smell tells the number of people," Ismi looks smug, as I acknowledge his experience.

"That's just rubbish. You can't tell the number of people there just by the smell," Mat argues back.

"Wanna make a bet? Say a hundred dollars," Ismi challenges Matt, who eagerly agrees.

Ray looks sternly at both of them, and they both know it's time to stop talking and focus on our patrol mission.

We surround the source of the obnoxious scent, with the slow trampling and crunching of large brown and green leaves on the jungle floor, and sure enough, there's a small clearing in the middle of the jungle. A poachers' makeshift camp with a smokeless fire burning strong and still cooking the 'lunch' in a medium sized aluminium pot. Lunch does not smell so good, perhaps it is a deer carcass, half rotting that the poachers could not resist. I am no longer surprised by the 'resourcefulness' of the poachers to eat anything they find in our jungle.

"Stay alert, boys."

The Captain motions to me that he will check out the perimeter of the camp. He turns back, points two fingers at his eyes and then points at Matt. I nod. There are no words and yet I know what he means: Watch the loud-mouth idiot.

Matt looks excited, revealing his perfect set of white and unstained teeth in his smile, runs over to check the contents of a plastic tub, revealing the fragrance of white starchy rice. "Just perfect, freshly cooked rice and a pot of chicken cooking - I think,"

"It could be a monitor lizard or a snake they were cooking you know. You know you lost your bet, loud-mouth-Matt."

Ismi points to five backpacks and five sets of white plastic plates and the matching spoons and forks.

"What bet?" Matt shrugs. Ismi tenses up, his neck angles to the side, he is clearly upset, and in the hot sweltering tropical jungle, when tempers flare, death can become the only reality.

I calm Ismi down. "Matt, you made a bet. Pay up now, otherwise give me something as escrow."

"Escrow? What, Tuan?"

"Yes. Escrow. It means I keep something of yours until you pay the hundred dollars to Ismi. You're new in the unit and you have to earn our trust."

I point at his military branded 'Luminox' watch. "No Tuan, this is a thousand-dollar watch." Before I could argue, I catch a glimpse of sliver of silver around Matt's neck.

"How about that necklace?"

"It's a silver talisman, my grandfather gave this to me for protection. Of course, the only protection I need is here," Mat grabs his crouch and then takes out his army issue knife, 12 inches of carbonized steel blade and clumsily wave-slices the air, "and this - the kind for one-on-one intimate penetration...er protection."

"Shut up, Matt. Pass the necklace to Tuan Sarin. You better honour your word. I heard you promised to treat some friends in your last unit at a Chinese restaurant, and instead of paying, you ran!"

Mat laughs whilst slapping his thigh, "No, that was different. That was a good prank, a funny one."

"And how did you end up not being dead?" Ray asks as he examines the cooking pot.

"They know who my fiancée is - the Colonel's daughter."

Matt takes off the talisman and throws it to me, "Don't lose it, please Tuan Sir."

I catch the talisman in my right palm. Instead of pocketing the talisman, I could feel a strange sensation in my palm, the talisman is very warm and feels very weighted. I open my palm, an old silver talisman, more dull and dark grey than silver, though I thought I saw it shine earlier. For a talisman, I am surprised that they are not markings, no inscription of any kind. I contemplate on whether to put it in my pocket - which could mean I would lose it and then decide to wear it over my own neck.

"It's not chicken," Ray removes the lid of the cooking pot, the steam and the sweet yet pungent smell of unfamiliar meat being simmering in the cloud white stew.

"Well, it's not monitor lizard or snake." Ismi stirs the pot and sees a strange carcass floating in the cooking pot, white and pale, soft and once alive.

I walk towards them and peek inside the cooking pot. It's a dead and cooked pangolin, the large armoured scales are no more, only recognisable is the long snout and the claws of this ant-eater.

"*Tenggiling*," I utter in disgust.

"Maybe the poacher had impotence issues." Matt tries to amuse us.

"In that case, you better eat this whole pot. Not sure if it will ever help you, Matt. Your fiancée's been telling me you've been having problems getting it up," Ray taps on the aluminium pot.

The Captain returns, "I can't find their tracks, the poachers - they left here without leaving any tracks…"

"That's strange, Captain Sir. It seems they left everything here in a hurry. We can see they left a large footprint here and yet were they really skilled enough to leave without a trace?"

'What vital piece of information is missing?' I wonder to myself.

An uneasiness sneaks up on me, a sense that we are in great danger, and yet all around I see we are safe at this campsite, with food and provisions lying around the camp.

"What did they cook?" The Captain asks.

"Pangolin," Ismi replies.

"That would bring nothing but bad luck." I sense the Captain's wariness. Having been under his command for all these years, I can almost read his mind. He is troubled by something, almost expectantly.

Matt leans nearer to the pot and scoops out a morsel, "Got to try everything you know,"

A red spot appears in the middle of the Pangolin stew, then turning grey and then dissipating into the stew. We all look inside the pot: Are we really seeing what we are seeing?

More red spots appear in the stew, quickly turning into grey spots, but this time not disappearing. A flurry of red large spots reappears, bubbling furiously in the stew, turning grey each time, and then the pot turns overwhelmingly red, fills to the brim, sizzling red and outpouring on to the floor.

I take two steps back and see a line coming out of the pot, a line of red liquid. I blink my eyes again, and see the illusion, the red liquid is flowing from above.

There is red fluid dripping from above and into the pot. I look up but the sunlight blinds me. I take a few more steps back. To my shock, I discover how the poachers were able to disappear without leaving tracks on the jungle floor.

Dismembered torsos, limbs, and five severed heads - eye missing in a few sockets, strewn on the branches of a petrified tree, dripping blood down onto a main branch and flowing down into the pot. I grip my Colt Commando rifle, the metal feeling colder than ever, unlatching the safety, my own eyes refusing to budge as I stare at the petrified scream of horror of the nearest head, a former poacher now turned tree trophy - paled and impaled.

"A Bear?" Ismi shouts as the others edge away from the ominous pot. I hear choking and shallow breathing, it's Ray. His face is turning red and blue at the same time, his hands holding on to his neck, struggling and clawing his neck.

"What's wrong, Ray?" Matt shouts out, but not willing to come to his aid. Ray mumbles, and then we notice how his feet are not touching the ground. He is levitating above the jungle floor.

There is a short glimpse of a shadow behind him, which disappears when I try to focus.

What was that?

Ismi runs towards Ray, who continues to struggle with the unseen. I try to move to help, but my feet refuse to move. I am frozen in fear. Ismi pulls Ray down, and Ray falls to the ground and starts gasping for breath. The Captain takes out his *parang*, a machete, and runs towards Ismi and Ray, jumps up and then attacks and slashes the empty air around Ray. A glimpse of a black shadow wall appears and then instantly disappears. The Captain lands on his feet, his eyes in a wild stare at an enemy I cannot see. I rub my eyes but I cannot see what is there.

Ray starts to orientate, stands up, and pulls up Ismi, "You saved my life, Ismi. When we get back home, I'll..."

Before Ray could complete his sentence, flesh protrudes from his chest and blood, enveloping a giant hand that has gone through his chest. A hand drenched in Ray's blood and flesh, larger than Ray's head. Ray shows his disbelief and then his head flops down, his limbs devoid of life. I stare at Ray, and I cannot accept that he is dead. I cannot accept what could kill him, even as I start to see the shape that is behind Ray, the owner of the hand that had plunged into Ray's torso and impaled him and his heart. The shape, humanoid, and yet nothing but a demon in the form of a shadow, so dark and black and all the essence of evil, if not the origin of all evil, standing, seemingly proud of its kill. It throws the body of my friend and my team comrade Ray hurtling towards Ismi, who tumbles hard with the force of the impact of dead Ray. Poor Ray.

Mat cocks his Colt M4 Carbine rifle and starts shooting blindly around where the demon is, the rounds striking trees and foliage, as splinters and broken branches litter the ground as Matt empties a magazine of rounds. It is clear Matt cannot see the demon. He fumbles and manages to load the next magazine.

"Die, mother…"

Before anyone could respond, the demon swoops down onto Matt, and throws him up into the air, above the branches of the petrified tree. In mid-air, with one swing of its hand, the demon severs Matt in the abdomen. Matt screams momentarily in pain, and then nothing, Matt remains quiet as the lower half of his torso and legs fall onto the ground, his intestines follow through, falling down like moist floppy rope. As if saving him for later, the demon impales Matt's chest on to a tree branch.

The fear overwhelms me. I cannot move my legs. I pull out my knife and swear I would not die without a fight.

The Captain runs towards Ismi, pulls him up. "Get up, soldier! We need to retreat... FAR AWAY FROM HERE!"

They both run towards me. "Move Sarin! Run!"

Time slows down, I see them both run towards me. Before they can reach me, Ismi is thrown into the air landing half-way up a giant tree and then falls back to the ground, only to be swooped up by the demon.

"Don't kill him, you monster!" I scream out. The Captain does not bother to look back.

He knows what will happen.

Like a ragged doll, Ismi is flung against the trunk of the same tree, head first, as his skull crunches and shatters and all the brain and blood matter splatters onto the dark green and brown tree trunk.

Both fear and anger try to enter my emotions but end up blocking each other off. Numb to the core.

The Captain holds my head in both hands, shouts slowly and as clearly as he can "Sarin, you need to run and save yourself. Now cover your eyes." The Captain throws two grenades near the cooking pot, landing with a soft thud and no bounce. The Captain covers my eyes with one hand and throws himself against me, as we both duck on to moist wet ground.

A flash of light followed by a blast wave shakes the core of my body. A singe in my right thigh awakens my legs. I can feel my legs, the pain and burning sensation on my feet. The Captain flips back up onto his feet, pulling me up, "Sarin, there is a river near here. Get there and you will be safe. I will buy you time."

I want to object - I should stay with the Captain and fight - but no words come out of my mouth.

"Corporal Sarin, I command you to run and save yourself!"

And with that, I follow his orders, and run I did. I run as fast as my legs can take me, I run as though there is no tomorrow.

There is no tomorrow.

There is no tomorrow.

There is no tomorrow.

SATU

1st December

For Nurul,

whose silent anguish and tearful questions kept me awake, searching for your answers, even after at twenty-six you are gone. Life should have given you more, and yet it didn't. A Promise will be kept, the writing in the sand will never be washed away by the waves.

May you rest in peace.

1st December

Sarin: Run

Location: Unknown Jungle

"CAPTAIN, WHERE ARE YOU?"

Where is everyone?

ARE THEY REALLY ALL DEAD?!

Did all that really happen right in front of my eyes?

I force myself to stop the visual flashbacks of the recent horrific events, images that do not make sense surround me - is this real? That is not a question I must ask now. I must live. I must survive.

Survival is tantamount.

The jungle echoes my words as I fight the sweat dripping down my forehead, stinging both my eyes and the small cuts on my face and arms - the trees and the branches trying their best to stop me from leaving. Wiping hard and I can barely keep my eyes open. Panting hard and wheezing, I rest briefly, hands descend and rest on my thighs, barely stooping - I can barely feel my feet, trembling hard, running through this wretched tropical jungle for too long.

The sun is sinking down fast - too fast - and the unforgiving darkness is engulfing this terrible, cursed jungle. Rumbling thunderously and ominously, my pursuer crashes through the dark jungle nearby, broken tree branches fall from the tree canopy in the near distance, smaller trees crunch and shatter, whilst hundreds of birds fly in all directions as screeching tiny primates flee from the imminent danger.

I am not imagining this.

I examine my 'digital camo' tiger-striped army trousers, and wince at the wound in my right thigh and the unlikely fragile union of clotted blood and wooden fragments lodged stopping me from bleeding to death. The sight brings me to the awareness of the pain. The pain of survival.

Push myself now. I am First Recon Unit. I am the toughest of the toughest. I will survive. I will beat that thing.

A blood-curdling scream shatters my thoughts, a now-futile attempt to recollect myself.

The demon has found me, knocking down everything in its path - it is unstoppable - half as tall as the jungle trees and blacker than the darkest of nights, a face without a face. My survival instincts jolt me, and I jump across a fallen tree, pushing through the pain, running through the shrubs, sliding on the mix of wet mud, dried jungle leaves and underneath the low hanging mesh of trees and liana jungle vines.

I must find safety before nightfall.

Heart pounding, waiting to burst out of my chest, I remind myself I have no weapon and I have no food. I had to drop everything when we were attacked, and the captain ordered us to retreat. No, he told me to run and save myself. I hate running away - I did not live my life as a coward, and yet I know I have no chance against this hell-bound creature.

To my relief, I hear the faint sound of water gurgling - a river must be nearby. I prod on, almost stumbling and yet refusing to lose momentum, as the faceless giant demon continues to chase me through this thicket. Being small and agile has its advantages. I jump and leap on all fours, part parkour and part desperation, constantly moving forward and uphill, dodging the projectiles of broken logs, trees and rocks. I dare not look back, its screams and grunts getting closer and closer, as relentlessly it keeps trying to hit me with the large 'sticks and stones'.

The jungle starts to thin, and then a clearing with a straight path of salvation appearing before me. With all my might, I scream and sprint, jumping and running across the dark hues of orange light and darkening grey shadows of the disappearing daylight. The sound of moving water grows reassuringly louder as I reach the end of the path. Peering down the rocky ledge, I see my final escape route: the river, a fifty foot drop below. I look back, the demon is still chasing me.

It's all or nothing, now.

I take a few steps back and with everything I have left, I sprint and jump, giving myself as much clearance from the rocky cliff wall. In mid-air, I close my eyes and embrace myself in preparation for water entry, I scream out "First Recon Unit - once trained, always engrained!".

A cold shivering sensation wraps tightly around my torso. It is not the river water. I open my eyes and see IT, the black and faceless demon - a shadow of hell - grips me tightly. I can hardly breathe, struggling hard against its deadly hold. Its one giant hand wraps around me with such ease and brings me back to the ledge, whilst its other hand is poised and ready to deliver a now all-too-familiar death blow to my chest.

"NO!" My feet not touching the ground, I kick furiously to no avail, even though I know this is the end.

A surge of fury engulfs me in the worst of times. I will not be smothered this way.

My final act of defiance: I spit at the faceless face of the dark shadow demon, grimace and stare at it and scream at the top of my voice, "Death is only a training ground. I will come back for you even in death. I am First Recon Unit."

I stare daunted and undaunted at the same, in defiance and in submission to my fate, at my death-bringer as a thousand memories of my fallen comrades flash through my mind like a thousand videos screened at the same time, the shoulder of the demon tilts which only means his other hand is heading towards me. And as if by slow motion, I feel its executioner hand sear my chest with a burning pain of life-sucking intense coldness.

The coldness exits my chest, the pain still incredulously ripping through my chest as I find my feet touching the ground again. A warm hand pulls me aside and then up. I breathe deeply as the vice grip is no longer, I am no longer held by my executioner, only to find my saviour next to me. The demon stumble away from the both of us.

"Captain! Let's fight this thing together."

My Captain, stern-faced with his unmoving moustache, grips his machete tighter and raises it above his head, poised and ready for simultaneous attack and defence, refuses to look at me. He duel-stares the demon, which looks injured - if that is at all possible.

"Sarin, no. Run. Live."

Before I can object, the Captain elbows me in the chest, propelling me with great force away from the ledge and I tumble down into the cold, murky river below.

The brackish taste of the river awakens me from the fall, I swim towards the river bank but the river is either too strong or I am too weak. The river takes me to the path of cowardly retreat.

I stare up the ledge and to my surprise, both the Captain and the demon stand side by side, staring down at me from above.

And from the faceless face, a set of hellish red eyes appears and glows insidiously. A deep fear engulfs me, I start to choke as my breathing freezes, the river pulls me down and I start to drown. Water rushes into my throat, cold and muddy - all air leaves my lung. I struggle to move my limbs, as my chest burns in pain. I scream endlessly in bubbles, unheard and underwater. I sink to the bottom of the river bed, clawing my own chest to free myself from the impossible, and yet the impossible happens around me. The water and the river starts drying up quickly.

I sit up and look around me. This is not what happened last time. I know this place, which becomes all too familiar as my eyes become more and more accustomed to the darkness, shapes and figures reveal themselves. This is my bedroom in the barracks. I find myself on my wet bed. I place my hand on my t-shirt, pants and then the bedsheets, it is completely drench in sweat. I take off my shirt, shivering in cold and fear, running my hand on the knobbled scar on my sternum.

It wasn't a dream, it was a memory. My fallen comrades. The Captain. Why?

My hand trembles uncontrollably as I grab a pack of my cigarettes from my bedside, the plastic gas lighter barely able to light up as my wet trembling fingers does its best to smother the flame and the flint. I can think of better ways to numb the pain, but for now these damp cigarettes will have to do. My body shivers, the fear remains. I should take a shower but my feet refuse to move. I stare at my feet and then at the barely visible scar on my right thigh. It's a reminder that it was real. It is real. I stub out the cigarette on to the scar, sizzling and the nauseating smell of burning skin invigorates me and my feet start to respond. I will never let fear take over me. Never, never again. I unsheathe my army issue nine-inch knife and place it between my clench teeth, the metallic taste spurs more saliva from my mouth. I take it out of my mouth and then glide the sharp end across the scar. The knife slices my skin ever so slightly, stinging and yet gentle, minute blood seeps out from the ruptured tiny capillaries.

I am alive, as the stinging wakes me up, stops the shivering. I run the knife again, even more gently, creating the most perfect -almost surgical- striations across my thigh, each thin slice calming me and reminding me that I am lucky to be alive, lucky to feel pain again, whilst my former captain, my Saviour brandished and out-casted as the 'unlucky captain'.

No one believes our version of events, the tragedy that had beset my former unit. The First Recon Unit.

I wipe the stain of fresh blood from my dagger, and then wipe the excess blood off my thigh.

Here comes the good part.

I grab a bottle of antiseptic alcohol swipe and splash it on my wound, singeing me to new heights of pain, gasping and clenching my teeth ever so tightly. I don't deserve to live and yet here I am.

I turn towards the table and pick up my silver talisman on the bedside table. I will need this for tomorrow's mission.

1st December

Adib: Rain

Location: The University

It has been raining all day. Dark, grey & black fusion, with not a single strand of white or silver in these angry clouds, large raindrops stream down in lines, claiming all beneath them. All the terracotta rooftops in a row of cream-white university houses and buildings, all the staff and student cars, and even the silent switched-off lampposts have a ghostly white halo shadow of raindrops splashing.

A white car with its headlights beaming through this curtain mesh of rain, snakes its way round the wet black asphalt bend of the university campus. Slowly it pulls up outside the entrance of the university main hall, and the driver door flings violently open. Out steps a young man named Adib with a red backpack and no umbrella.

***

"Oh man, umbrellas are usually a waste of money! Of all days, today is the day, I need a damn umbrella!"

I slam shut the car door fast but not before a splash of rain manages to soak wet the car seat. Dashing across the car park, the rain neither spares nor forgives me, each step I take seems to bring more rainwater, splashing from above, splashing from the sides, splashing from the rainwater on the asphalt floor.

"My precious... bag"

I cradled my much-cherished bag between my arms for added shelter. The ferocity of the rain stinging across my face, makes me wonder if I will ever make to the university main hall. By the time, I reach the main hall, I look back in astonishment and grateful for making it across the sheet of water that is the car park. The cold seeps into my skin and bones, and like a wet feral cat, I shake off the water from my hair - how I envy dogs and cats for being able to do this more vigorously.

I look at my backpack, thankful for choosing it for its special hydrophobic coating, so that it does not soak up any water. There are many small and large water drops on the bag, like the seeds of a large giant strawberry, which neatly slide off the red bag with a little nudge.

How did I end up with such a red bag?

My thoughts are interrupted and I turn around, something is watching me.

I am only all too familiar with this feeling, the 'Presence'. I recall the time I was first aware of it, when I was a child. Recently, it has become more frequent, especially this month - much than before. Instinctively, I look out towards the smaller building next to the main hall. The rain fuzzes everything.

Did I just see a large shadow there?

I squint and move my head side to side - a little trick I learned on how to improve vision in poor light conditions - but there is nothing there, and yet I can feel there is something out there, waiting, watching.

I challenge it, "I am Adib, a 25-year-old man and I am not afraid of anything - not even you, oh hidden one!". Goosebumps rapidly cover my limbs.

"Probably just the cold rain," I say to myself. "No need to 'challenge' it this time" I wonder if my *'Kedayan'* ancestral roots have had any effect on this supernatural presence.

Ignoring the feeling, I walk across the brown tiled floor, careful to ensure I don't slip on the now wet-floor, and head into a ground floor work office - my office. I grab a remote control from the wall to switch off the air-conditioner – it is blood freezing.

The sound of the torrential rain drumming onto the roof, windows and through the gutters of the building brings up a memory of a lecture I was in with a biology professor who mocked the local people for being so heat sensitive and air-conditioning dependent, unlike our ancestors who had grown very accustomed to the heat and high humidity of this tropical country.

There is an 'Ikea'-copycat brand wooden table in the middle of the room, surrounded by wall-to-wall bookshelves filled with reference books and void of any fiction books. There is a small mirror on the wall in between the bookshelves. Placing the bag on the table, I remove its precious hold, a silver laptop, with a logo of a white apple on it. The white apple begins to glow, as I switch it on.

As the laptop loads up to my last work 'page', I walks across to the mirror on the wall and stare at the mirror - I am dripping wet; I look like I just took a shower five times over. The stubble on my face reminds me that my last shave has been a few days ago, and the darkness under my eyes tells me I really should try to stop my life of staying-up-late nights.

How can I?

I am trying to complete my PhD thesis on protecting the 'Sungai Ingei Forest', a wildlife sanctuary as well as my 'hobby': environmental conservation activism.

***

Outside in the torrid rain, lurking by the smaller building, and silent as a shadow, stood The Presence. Invisible to everyone – he was a dark powerful being, unnatural to this world, more than two storeys tall, cloaked by darkness beyond shadows, watching Adib intently. The Presence is disturbed by another dark but lesser being, slightly smaller and subservient to him.

"Have you come to end his life today?" asked the newcomer.

"Not today, but his time is coming soon."

"When is that time? Must you observe him from now till then?" the curious underling beckons.

"We must all follow our orders," the Presence answers, irritated by the imposed delay.

"If only he knew, then he probably wouldn't be so busy with all of this," The underling ponders.

Suddenly, the two beings sense a signal in their wraith-like dimension – they have been summoned to a higher 'kill' mission.

With that, they both disappear immediately from nothing into nothing.

Not a single person or creature notices them, not even the frogs celebrating in croaks in the rain.

1st December

Selym: MATA

Location: Ingei River, Ingei Jungle

Selym is not from this world.

The truth is much further and deeper than that. Selym has been here since the dawn of Man's arrival to Earth. Standing over forty feet tall, cloaked in complete darkness on such a hot and yet cloudy humid day in a real tropical rainforest, almost as tall as the trees. If a man or any jungle creature could see him, he would be a true Lord of Darkness in their eyes. The jungle is quiet, its creature inhabitants sensing great danger but unable to see where is the danger. The man who was fishing at this isolated and remote bend hangs in mid-air, 10 feet above his wooden outboard boat.

Selym removes his hand from the chest of the poacher he had just killed, a lifeless body drops back into the boat, crushing the Styrofoam boxes below.

***

'What a pathetic man, stealing our fish with no shame - not even planning to eat it, just keeping it for his petty amusement'

"I feel really good taking this human life who does not deserve to live. He is nothing but vermin."

Azilah moves towards me from the river bank. I cannot see her beauty in this world, although she is like me; a mere fragment of darkness, I feel something warm about her. She is just so new to this. I should try my best not to frighten her too much. The key is rate of learning.

I look at her eyes or where her eyes are supposed to be in the shroud of darkness that covers her entire body.

"Your first time to see something like this?"

Azilah nods and says nothing.

"Don't worry, the first time we kill a human - all those questions come flying in, and you have doubts but you must remember your training. You must remember who we are, you must remember it is they who take from us, and they who started it all in the beginning'

Although, I cannot see her tears, I can feel it. I can feel a soft ache in my heart that should not be there, which must be for her and not for these destructive humans.

I look and I wonder why Azilah makes me doubt myself. I clench my fist and convince myself I have great resolve, I have a great mission. Azilah will become my greatest apprentice, she will be the most incredible destroyers of humans.

I breathe in confidence, straighten my back and turn to Azilah, who is awfully quiet, "Let's get back to our home world Hilaga, back to our people"

The dead fisherman's boat starts to float down the tea-coloured river.

In an instant, both Azilah and I race across the jungle, still invisible and unseen. Our rendezvous, an ancient well, once considered sacred by humans. Unknown to them, there is a portal that bridges between their world, Bumi and our home world Hilaga. We call this portal 'MATA', a swirl of pitch black darkness, a few feet off the ground. I cringe at the thought of going through 'MATA' but I have no choice.

We both step into the void inside it. I have been through this so many times but it does not get any easier as I feel the horrible coldness envelope my body, squeezing me, I am too afraid to move and I am too afraid to breathe. My body, the giant figure of darkness transforms back into a more human form. My real form in my home world.

I have frequently asked myself why do we look like the humans when we are in our world. I used to ask myself why is it our achievements mirror to that of man, we build cities just like them, our people have jobs and have a society of structure, except in times of war. And like Man, we too have wars. The last war destroyed so much progress, but our current leaders have worked together to bring peace and more importantly change.

"I am a part of that change, I am an agent of change, I am saving my people from them, the scourge of Man", I remind myself repeatedly before almost passing out as I exit the portal and land on the hard black and red marble floor of the MATA portal room.

"What a relief to be back" I take a deep breath, my cold nostrils become warmer and the light sweet scent of incense invigorates my stiff and hurt body.

I turn around and see Azilah, now in humanoid form, lying next to me, her beautiful royal blue suit does match her blue eyes. She stares at me; her light brown hair covers the floor like dreams being connected to something else much bigger than us. I could get lost in this moment for the rest of eternity. I remind myself I have a bigger purpose in life.

'I have chosen to be her mentor, and I should not abuse that'

After picking myself up from the floor, I put out my hand and help her up. Her hands are cold, her eyes refuse to meet with mine. I wonder why.

"No matter how many times we go through the portal, it never gets easier," I laugh, a feeble attempt to break the ice.

"Forgive me, Master Selym - it is quite a shock for me. Everything," Azilah still avoiding my eyes.

I put my hand on her shoulder and notice how small and smooth her shoulders are, "I apologize for not making it much easier for you - I got this bad habit of just throwing everyone into the deep end and expect them to learn how to swim immediately"

"Or drown," Azilah laughs uncomfortably, her eyes momentarily look at mine - did I see tears? Did she cry for that puny human? - and then glances away on to the black and red marble floor.

I brush off the dust from my shiny one piece black suit and look at the digital clock on the wall - it's 1900hrs.

"Time to get to that City Hall council meeting" I feel uplifted, knowing today, a decision will be made, which will help my people move in the right direction, against Man.

A MATA supervisor approaches me, taking smaller steps as he nears, "Welcome back to Hilaga city, Master Selym," and gracefully bows down whilst his eyes look up at me. I nod and wave my hand gracefully in the air, "Thank you Hermie, it's good to be back in Hilaga."

Hermie straightens himself up "I trust your mission was successful?"

I do not answer him - he does not need to know - but I can't help myself from a quick smile, which betrays my sense of duty to keep secrets from those who are below my rank.

We walk across a brightly white lighted huge atrium hall and towards a windowless and button-less lift, stepping into it - both Azilah and I are brought across to the centre of the city to the Hilaga City Hall - at such speeds we did not see the city but just a blur of lights streaking all around us. A miracle in itself, our great achievements of rebuilding took part so quickly, a blink in the eye of history.

How quickly we managed to rebuild ourselves after the last war. When we are united, we can achieve so much.

Hilaga is the greatest and we will sustain our development by putting a stop to Man.

1st December

Adib: Deal

Location: The University

"Water falls downwards - it's all gravity," I remind myself.

I take out my favourite comb from my back pocket, and starts combing my dark black hair in the same mannerism as the 'The Fonz' - a character played by Henry Winkler - which gives me a cool satisfaction, each stroke of the comb extracting water. I sculpture a new tall hair pyramid, grinning as I admire my new gravity-defying hairstyle.

"Who needs hair gel when you have a lot of rain?"

As I ponder upon my eventual hairstyle, I take off my blue t-shirt, hoping it would miraculously dry up on the chair next to me as the wet footprints all over the wall to wall carpeting. Sitting down bare-chested in front of my silver MacBook, looking intently at the screen, my eyes reflect the glow from the screen-light.

Facebook is everything in Southeast Asia, especially in this country, boasting the highest social media penetration in Asia. I've been doing well searching for Facebook message posts from poachers trying to sell endangered or restricted wildlife.

There used to be only one Facebook (messaging) group but now everyone seems to have their own Facebook groups.

On the display screen, to the unfamiliar, there is a photo of a strange-looking creature: small pin-sized head, black eyes, four-legged with claws like that of a mole, and even stranger are these brown armoured scales, and a conical snout to top off its weirdness. You could have mistaken it for an anteater. Actually, it does eat ants, the correct name would be pangolin.

Pangolins seem to be popular around this time.

This time the poacher is a girl, strange. No, it is not. She is selling it on behalf of her father, who caught the poor pangolin. $500 or more, and this beautiful 'Sunda Pangolin' will have an owner.

I have no deception, and no trickery up my sleeves. I send a message to the girl, Fifie, being completely open and honest, telling her that I am part of a local environmental group, convincing her not to sell the pangolin, but instead release it back into the wild.

"You know the Pangolin you have is very rare and so few are left. Please Google 'Sunda Pangolin'. "

"The people who buy the pangolin are likely to cook it because they think it has medicinal properties." I continue typing away, and then share a disturbing photo of a dead pangolin in a cooking pot - scales half gone, flesh white underneath all, dark small black eyes are just dead white.

Fifie does not reply quickly, but I know she is looking at the photo, as the message board says she is still 'typing'.

"I will talk to my dad and see what he says."

"Thank you Fifie, here's my phone number. If you can convince your father that it is the right thing to do, we can meet up later and release the animal today. I am worried if it is kept any longer in captivity, it may die!"

"Ok, Adib."

Let's try to close the deal.

"I can give your father and yourself our group's T-shirts as a small token of our appreciation for your heroic act."

An hour later, my mobile phone beeps its usual 3-tone tune - I really should change the ring-tone, but who's got time.

It is a message from Fifie. Her father agrees to let go of the pangolin, and she would bring it to the meeting place where they can release the pangolin back into the jungle, safe from poachers.

I smile and somehow stop myself as I recall how my teeth has become so coffee-stained - being an espresso and latte addict.

Energy levels need to be maintained artificially, if you are pursuing your PhD and running a non-governmental organisation (NGO).

I pause a bit to reflect upon my own life. I'm going to change the world, one poacher at a time, one pangolin at a time. Thinking about it, I'm a pangolin protector superhero. Except I have no superpowers. Perhaps, talking and negotiating should be considered as a superpower. Perhaps someday, I should ask the pangolins for some real superpowers.

I press the speed-dial on my phone and call John Proctor, a local Englishman who is more familiar with the local scuba-diving sites than most locals, but somehow had gotten himself involved with the group's endangered wildlife protection activities.

"John, she agreed – can I pick you up now?"

I know John is at home, editing the last of his underwater photographs from his last dive. He reminds me to let the 'lady doctor' know

I hang up and phone Doctor Nurul, a local doctor at the government clinic. I can hear the faint coughing and at least one baby crying in the background of Nurul's clinic. Doctor Nurul seemed pleased, but insist I pick her up too as she was feeling too tired to drive.

I peer out the window, the rain has suddenly stopped – the clouds, too, must be tired by now.

I drive off and pick up John at a local cafe. I don't understand John, why does he always loves to wear these worn-out khaki cargo pants and a long-sleeve white shirt?

He stands by the kerb, holding three tall paper-cups of coffee latte on a cardboard tray.

John pops into the car, hands over a cup, and then pushes back his black plastic spectacles up his nasal ridge.

"I know they say don't drink and drive, but you look like you need a drink," John chuckles.

John's receding hairline and freckled-textured face reveals he is past his prime, and had only recently overcome his last midlife crisis, through the distraction of the campaign for wildlife protection.

John is all about wits and sly phrases. He once shared with me that his ex-wife fell in love with him because of his ability to make anyone smile, through his funny and charming words, regardless of how dire the situation is. Unfortunately, his ex-wife eventually figured out that was all that he was, and it wasn't enough for her to stay on with the marriage. Here he is on the other side of the world, away from England, far away from the town of Beaconsfield, providing him great refuge from his ex-wife and his English friends 'back home'. This is his home now, and it has been so for the past 15 years.

"The land of unexpected treasures... for poachers." John's favourite phrase. And yes, he secretly desires to trademark that.

I am used to John's witty comments and nod in agreement, as I drive through a set of traffic lights to Nurul's clinic.

When we reach the clinic, a female doctor in a blue blouse and white long pants and clutching a pink handbag, rushes out of the white bungalow clinic. I know for sure that if a government building in this country is a bungalow, it means it was built in either the 1970s or 1980s. Nurul's face does not show any emotion, her gold polka-dot red scarf only covers part of her head, revealing her black silky hair. She callously throws her pink bag into the car, rolls up her sleeves, and then gets into the back of the car.

Nurul changes modes, like a lady who has just been implanted with facial muscles, she begins to smile widely. John turns around and passes the last cup of coffee to her, noticing that her blue blouse still has that small stubborn medical stain near the edge of the pocket.

I catch John staring at her blouse, I doubt that this is some perversion but more of his half-baked OCD - I sense he is imagining that he has the courage to ask Nurul if he could bring her blouse home to remove the damn stubborn stain himself. Luckily, his obsessive-compulsiveness - though could be useful to others - but he holds himself back for fear of his good intention being misjudged as a fetish. She is after all a family doctor, and sometimes doctors label people with all kinds of medical disease labels, before accepting there is a person on the other end.

"I am going to find the idiots who keep saying pangolins have medicinal value and punch them in the face!"

Soft-spoken Doctor Nurul is known to have 'rather graphic and violent words' outside of work. Wildlife conservation has worked out to be a good distraction for this frustrated doctor too. She does not look like she is 39 years old, in fact she looks like she is only 26 years of age, her face is fair and smooth, and there are no blemishes, and when she chooses to smile, her sweet smile will melt away any woes her patients may have, the only clue of her real age is betrayed by her 'less than smooth' hands & more prominent micro-veins. Bureaucracy in the government can make any person cynical and bitter.

Perhaps the wildlife that needed to be saved included herself.

"I didn't realise the latte I gave you was flavoured 'feisty'," John interjects humorously.

Nurul wisely chooses to ignore John. Nurul knows she can't outmatch John when it comes to witty sound-bites. She is much more suited for direct confrontational conversation...unfortunately.

"If we have time later, we should go to the Jerudong fish-market. One of my patients mentioned that someone is trying to sell a large estuarine turtle," Nurul commands, sipping her hot latte.

"Roger, roger, boss," I reply.

1st December

Selym: Vote

Location: Hilaga City Hall, Hilaga City

Stepping out of the lift and onto the 50th floor of the Hilaga City Hall, we are met by three Hilaga city elite guards, clean-shaven and dressed in crisp all grey suits and their staff weapon in their left hands. They greet us solemnly and escort us to the City Hall council meeting room.

As the large heavy wooden doors open, the first sight that dominates is not the presence of the numerous lawmakers, it is the presence of the central figure on the stage: Lord Jahat authoritatively sitting in the middle of the stage, whilst on either side, sat two other council members whose names I keep forgetting. Lord Jahat, in his characteristic flawless dark blue suit, sees me, waves his hand and beckons me to come on to the stage.

'Stay here Azilah and watch - don't talk to the council members, they're politicians - remember we will never know what their true intentions are"

I wade through the crowd around me, the different parties sit separately whilst the lesser non-conformers, 'the independents' huddle together, clearly scared by the events unfolding. I hear whispers of my name from the different people: 'Selym the Hunter', 'Selym the Protector' and so on. I want to bath in the glory of my previous missions but then I hear someone with a familiar voice whispers: 'Selym the Blind Fool'.

I stop moving towards the stage, a rage burns in my heart from glory to fire.

Who said that? Of all places, here.

I glance around, surrounded by a sea of jubilant faces, the culprit I cannot identify.

'Ignore it for now, Selym,' I say to myself, faking a smile.

As I step onto the stage, I start to notice how Lord Jahat's dark blue suit glimmer with the stage light and more importantly how it really matches his light blue tie. Lord Jahat has a very good fashion sense, his presence extrudes confidence and victory. He smiles at me and I cannot help from feeling the glow of his charisma.

He moves to me and grips my shoulders. "Look at you, Selym - you are not just the finest soldier that I had nurtured, now you have become a leader and soon you will become the leader of the Hilaga Armed Forces - I will make sure of that.' He pauses, embraces me and his smooth white grey hair brushes upon my left cheek as he whispers "Your father would have been so proud of you -

you will have every chance to avenge him" as bursts of thunderous ovation and cheers fill the hall.

I remember my slain father and before any memory of his death resurfaces, I bury it deep down and hard and somehow a lump in my throat appears. Lord Jahat looks at me, still clutching my shoulders, "Are you ready?"

"Yes, my Lord - born ready."

"Good - just stand right here and face them and I will get this show started"

Lord Jahat raises both hands up into the air, "Let us start the meeting now."

The hall room is filled with at least 120 member representatives - three representatives for each district, now all eyes look upon me and Lord Jahat, hungry in anticipation. Lord Jahat scans from end of the hall to the other and then focuses towards the middle of the hall. Whilst he pauses to build the eagerness of his crowd, I start to notice his much-receded hairline which has expose his forehead, making him look wise and visionary to the people he leads. He closes his eyes, waiting for the room to become silent, and slowly banter and chat becomes murmurs and whispers and then just silence.

"My people, by now, most of you are aware of why I have called everyone to this great meeting. There is a sea of change". Lord Jahat pauses, and shift his weight to his right foot.

"There is no more middle ground - you must choose whether you are with us or against us"

There is a cheer in the room, with stomping of feet and fists being punched into the air.

"We were here first, this is our world, both Bumi and Hilaga, it is one existence, both for us, and only us. It is our Bumi, not Man's - their arrival to this world destroyed our civilization and for many millennia, we have been told not to engage with Man. We have been told to let Man, a spoiled child, to do what he wants."

The hall room erupts in boos and shouts of 'No' and thunderous stomping of feet in the meeting room.

Lord Jahat puts his hands out and beckons the crowd to let him continue.

"We have lost almost everything. Everything. We have given up our lands to Man, we have given up our mountains to Man, we have given up our hills to Man, and we have even given up our rivers to Man"

The air in the hall room is so tense, silent rage building up.

"Man takes and destroys - he even kills our sacred defenceless pangolins - the creature that holds the key to stabilizing our home world and our beautiful city of Hilaga"

"We are tired of scaring them, our efforts seem fruitless when it comes to non-fatal means"

"Today, I am proud to share with you that, although this is against our Constitution, I have been sending covert kill teams to protect the Ingei region in Bumi, our last bastion."

"As your Mayor, I have no qualms risking my political career to do what is right, to uphold my responsibility to my people!"

There are loud gasps in the room, followed by fervent chanting "Long Live Mayor Jahat" and "We are behind you, Mayor". A long deafening stomping of feet echo in the room.

I am amazed and frightened by the sight of council members and politicians unite in the cause. I see a few silent pale faces in the room. "We will have to sort them out later," I thought to myself. I notice there is a figure at the end of the room, he is dressed in white, his face is familiar - 'Who is that?'

I recognize that face! I must catch him now. Before I take a step forward, someone grabs my right hand and lifts it up into the air. Lord Jahat is waving my hand with his - "The leader of our Panah kill teams - Selym the Victorious - the son of the greatest Ifrit who had ever lived: Lord Ramesh."

I will sort that intruder out once this is done.

I beam a smile of confidence, shaking my fist in the air with Lord Jahat, and yet I am feeling lost and turbulent on the thought that 'he' is here, daring to be in our presence, if that is all possible.

Lord Jahat beckons the excited crowd to quiet down. "I think it looks like this is going to be an easy motion to pass."

An opposition lady dressed in an olive green robe stands up amongst the rowdy crowd of representatives, "Please, this is madness, this goes against the basis of our Constitution, we are meant not to harm them but to help guide Man, to walk the path of Righteousness."

The lady is pulled and shoved down by hooligans who proclaim themselves as the true voice of the people of Hilaga, her appeals and screams are silenced by the roar of the cheering and laughing crowd. Nobody wants to hear her. The other independents, huddle closer together, fearing for their lives, they have heeded the warnings before this meeting.

Grinning Lord Jahat pronounces "Those who favour Killing Man who intrudes on to our precious Bumi Ingei, simply raise your hand"

A sea of arms and hands are raised, with only a few refusing to raise their hand to support the murderous motion. I look at the opposition lady, dishevelled, robe partially torn and a bruised face, unfriendly burly members surrounding her.

She did not deserve that, but things need to be done. You cannot make an omelette without breaking eggs.

"An unanimous support. The motion to change our Rules of Engagement to kill any man on sight who intrudes on to our Ingei on Bumi is passed without any obstruction," declares two other council members on the stage.

The chairman stands up, "We will get the Hilaga City Supreme Council to endorse our supported motion."

The room starts screaming and shouting murderously, "Bunuh Manusia" which translates to "Kill Man"

The crowd moves into small and large groups, as the council members start linking arms, shoulder to shoulder, and jumping together jubilantly. They are dancing to the new song filled with the only two components needed to declare war, a good slogan: the chorus of "Bunuh Manusia" and the marching of feet.

I must make my move to apprehend that intruder. I scan the room for Azilah, smart enough that she is near the exit doors. I nod to her and she knows we must leave for something important.

1st December

Azilah: Intruder

Location: Hilaga City, Ifrit home world

Master Selym looks uncomfortable on the stage, despite this obnoxious crowd all cheering Lord Jahat and him and to kill all men who intrude onto our lands. Something spooked him. Our eyes meet, I notice he does not seem his usual confidence. Master Selym signals by nodding to me.

Hmmm, looks like we are leaving here.

Selym pushes his way through the kicking and dancing crowd - yes, I did say dancing.

Has politics come to this now? Hooliganism? My grandparents would have banished all of them for such rowdy behaviour. We have truly gone down the rabbit-hole.

The opposition lady in a torn olive green robe, limps towards the exit, her face bloodied and bruised. The members of her own party, 'the Independents' surround her and try to help her walk but she pushes them away.

I can barely hear what she is screaming at them, "Where were you all? We didn't come here to be comfortable. We came to make a stand and I was alone. Where were you all?"

She starts to sob and she picks up her limping pace towards me, towards the exit. I can't help but feel sorry for her.

The other members try to console her but she keeps pushing them away. "You know the greatest tragedy is not the oppression and cruelty by these bad people but the silence over that by the supposedly good people."

She stares at her party, pointing towards them unsteadily with her injured hand, "Your silence!"

As she exits the room, she pauses and looks at me. I scan her face and immediately recognize her, but before I could say anything, she leaves.

Lady Hanan used to take care of me as a child. I recall memories of playing with her by the Great Tree.

As I see Master Selym approach, I pause my thoughts and promise myself to reflect about her and my time with her tonight.

Ok, here comes Selym. Keep my thoughts to myself, remember I am a professional.

Master Selym is furious "There was someone in this room who does not belong here, not in our world - he just left - Did you see him?"

"Who?" I ask.

"The human Adib."

I say to myself, "It is impossible. Never ever possible."

The human Adib? - how could he ever enter our world. They said it can't be done, even if it's just a theoretical risk.

I choose my word carefully. "Master, did you say the human Adib - the one we are watching over?"

"There's no time to waste! Follow me!" Selym barks, I see a bead of sweat flow down his right temple.

Running down the red carpeted halls towards the lifts, Selym points to the emergency chute "You take the lift, whilst I go down the emergency chute"

I catch my breath and enter the lift which takes me from the 50th floor to the ground floor, before I could finish exhaling. If I was an intruder, I would get to the ground floor and then escape into the city streets. A human in Hilaga - that's just impossible. Just simply not possible.

Selym has already alerted all the City Hall guards, a few dozen grey guards are scrambling in the atrium ground floor reception, scouring and checking every room.

"Hmmm, amateurs! Come on people, he'd be out of the building by now," I say to myself, whilst reminding myself to be a professional.

I rush off through the glass doors and out onto the packed city street, a sea of protesters, dancing in the streets, with one hand holding their protest signs of "Kill All Humans", chanting the same line in the hall "Bunuh Manusia". These are not real protesters, they are lobbyists clearly engaged in the trade of the ultimate marketing: incitement. The question in my mind, in the middle of everything, this chaos, is who is getting them to mobilize - pulling the strings of the puppets, and pulling the strings of the puppet masters.

The glass doors violently slam against the side of the building as Selym rushes outside, followed by three of the guards. He pushes against the crowd of protesters, some of whom give way to him as they recognize him. Looking around the busy night street, whoever the intruder is, he must have already gone, blending with the night, pass through the protesting group and beyond, lost in between the indifferent shoppers and citizens coming back from a long day's work.

He must be long gone, if he can enter the Hilaga City Hall without any problems and leave it easily then it is only expected that he cannot and will not be found. Master Selym must have made a mistake. Perhaps he is tired. It is so easy to justify reasons to give up, if I want to. I turn around to head back to the building - away from this uncomfortably rowdy crowd. I hear Selym shouting commandingly, "The intruder is there." He rushes off to the right side of the building.

We chase after him, along with the three guards who wish they had not turned up to work tonight. I see Selym, in his black suit, weave in between the crowd, going further away from us.

He's fast - Selym is in peak fitness.

Selym runs after the intruder - a man in white, disappearing as they both turn right into Ramesh Street. A fateful street named after his father, Lord Ramesh the Fallen.

Please don't die, Master Selym.

1st December

Nurul: Eagles

Location: Bumi

John, Adib and I are all in the car. As I sip my latte and somehow allow the smoothness of the steam milk froth sooth my mind off work, I start to reflect upon an oddity: how did we become friends, comrades when we have no common friends that connect us with each other?

I look towards John, a much older man than I am, his cheerful words truly reflect him as the aged and cynical yet humorous Englishman stuck in the middle of nowhere but this tiny nation of rainforest, whose citizens seem to only care for cars and not the very rainforest that could be the nation's next salvation when the oil runs out. On the other hand, I look at Adib, who is at least a decade younger than me, and he represents the few, the promise of a brighter future, and yet instead of being the beacon of hope of this society, he is chastised by our own fellow people.

What a strange companionship we make!

I almost choke on the thought, we are each separated by an age gap of at least 10 years. The Internet and social media had changed the rules so much - you can become good friends with total strangers, based on a common interest, or a common cause.

The road changes from asphalt to a pebble road, low rumbling of pebbles in the background. There is a light trail of dust being kicked up by the car as it drives through this road. The green jungle on both sides of the road is dominating. There are no houses nearby and the sound of the buzzing of the jungle becomes insanely louder. At the end of the road, there is a worn out grey asphalt car park. Adib parks the car and we all wait patiently.

How long can we wait for? My paper cup is empty, I dare not throw it. How I wish I could recycle it *in-situ*!

"Adib, how long are we going to sit and wait here?" I complain, the heat becoming more unbearable, in spite of the air-conditioning being switched on to full blast. I ask myself why we should leave the car engine running, whilst we wait in this car park. I stay quiet but my thoughts zip with deafening arguments. Why can't I enjoy the comforts of being cool and comfortable and yet not worry about taking up polluting resources? Why do I have to think about it? Why can't I just be like the others and take it for granted to keep the car engine running whilst we sit idle?

Adib responds, calling Fifie, but no one answers the phone. Adib frantically thumb-types into his mobile phone, sending his message into the airwaves.

Fifie replies.

"Someone made us an offer and we have already sold the pangolin. My father needs the money. I am sorry."

Adib doesn't reply.

I sense a surge of anger inside him, and as quickly as the surge came, the anger dies down and the void is filled with feelings of disappointment.

"How could she do that after what she saw, after what she now knows? Isn't this country supposed to be wealthy? Why are there people who are saying they don't have enough money? Why are there poor people in this rich country?" He murmurs to himself, and curse-mumbles unmentionables.

John recognizes Adib's face of disappointment and attempts to console him, "Some days you win, and some days you don't."

Adib lets out a long sigh. Compelled and without thought, I reach out and embrace Adib's shoulders, my arms having to be slightly raised to reach his shoulder as he is much taller than me. I can't blame myself for being short, as Adib is taller than the average local man.

I pat him as how an elder sister would, reassuringly. "Don't worry young man, let us not cry over spilled milk, and see what else we can do."

"For one, we can go to the fish market I talked about earlier. In life, we should have no expectations. We do what we can, when we can. Right?" I grip his shoulder a bit tighter, it's a bad habit. I do this to my nurses when I have something for them to do. I should really stop it but some habits die hard.

"I need to do something before we do that," Adib opens the car boot and takes out a piece of plank. I am glad it is not a large heavy spanner to bludgeon someone. I could imagine doing something like that.

As he drops the plank on to the ground, I realise it's not an ordinary short plank, but a skateboard. Adib hops on to his 'wood-carved' looking skateboard, with unusually bright red polyurethane wheels and glides across the car park. He sees a pedestrian rail on one end, and jumps onto it with his skateboard. As the skateboard glides on the pedestrian rail, Adib maintains a gravity-defying stunt for a few seconds, landing back on to the asphalt ground.

I clap my hands in awe, John shouts out, "Nice one, Adib."

Adib skates back to us, drops his skateboard back into the car. Who would think one small acrobatic act could invigorate him back to his usual self? I make a mental note to learn how to skateboard. Of course, I would have to make sure I would have ample protection, like wearing the thickest knee-pads, elbow pads and most importantly, helmet. A fall would hurt me. Maybe. I should be braver and stop worrying about possible consequences.

We hop back into the car and drive off to our new destination. Everyone starts to realise how bumpy the road is.

Driving through to a small town, the car moves to the Jerudong suburb, sometimes colloquially referred to as the 'local' Beverly Hills, where some of the rich have made rather large mansions here. New money gives people new ideas. The roads are clean, smooth and still has the new asphalt on them - thanks to regular maintenance from the Public Works Department.

We drive pass one large mansion after another where tall palm trees, imported from distant lands, have been planted on both sides of the road and around the gates. Someone had thought it would be a good idea to emulate a Beverly Hills mansion, large white gates and large white pillars. A few exotic German cars are parked inside.

These mansion owners' sub conscience must be screaming: Announce your prosperity to the world! It must be the secret theme of this place.

I look out the window towards a row of houses. A rush of memories and emotions overcome me. In the past, I had done my best to avoid driving through here.

"Adib, hold on. Can you please stop the car here? I need to stretch my legs."

I hobble out of the car, un-cramping a nearly cramped leg. Hopping onto that leg to stave off the 'pins and needles', I look out at the housing development area, a small suburb and yet full of lost meaning and memories. Adib gets out of the car, leaving the car engine still running and humming gently.

John does not get out of the car, he refuses to leave the cool air-conditioned comforts of the car.

"You know I used to live here as a child, and back then, there were only 3 houses here," I point to a right corner of the horizon, indicating where I used to live.

"This used to be all but jungle, really giant trees with these large long dangling vines crisscrossing across them, and I remember they used to be these white-bellied sea eagles soaring in the sky above. This was their nesting ground."

I bite my lower lip, the pain of the memories of loss subside and I stop myself from screaming in anger.

"But then everyone wants a piece of 'happiness'. Eventually, everything got wiped out to build all this. I was just 8 years old back then. The trees that fell were so large, it took them a few days to burn all that wood."

I pause a beat and try to find solace, "There's no place for the eagles to nest, so those that moved on, moved on and those that didn't, just died here. I sure miss those eagles."

As if to remind myself of the pain, I mutter to myself: "Eagles used to soar here."

There are so many stories I would like to share with Adib, like how my father's house had been sold off, to fund the building of a larger house in a different part of the district, but somehow, I could not find the strength to share with him my family secrets.

"Everybody wants a larger piece of 'happiness'," Adib smirks, as we both agree on the cynical value of happiness.

"Conservation activists understand each other. Whenever I tried to share my feelings about unsustainable and destructive development, no one seems to understand, and I can hear their thoughts out - what's wrong with you? Why can't you conform? Why can't you try to find 'happiness'?"

"Adib, there never seems to be enough happiness," I reply, realizing I am still clutching the empty paper-cup.

Am I going to throw it here, by the roadside? It might decompose - looks biodegradable. I step back into the car, still holding onto the paper-cup and we drive on to the fish market.

1st December

Selym: Shadow

Location: Ramesh Street, Hilaga City

A white man runs down Ramesh Street pushing aside the thick night crowd. Takeaway food hawkers happily selling their grilled food, sizzling and the light smell of embers of charcoal fills the room. Mothers holding their children's hands unaware of the gravity of events that is unfolding. It is supposed to be noisy but all I can hear is my heart pounding and the sound of my own deep breathing. As we reach the end of Ramesh street, the crowd thins and it's just the two of us now, he's so near I can almost touch him.

As he turns left into an alley, I do a banshee jump, jumping on to the right side wall of the alley and springing onto him. He is shocked to see me flying towards him, I see his face as both our heads smash into each other, my right fist swings out to his left temple, connecting and knocking him down on the ground as we both fall. The hard cobblestone alley makes contact with both of us as a single mass of confusion and anger, tumbling down and then separating.

Standing up, I look him in the eye. *This man Adib shows no fear, does he not know who I am?*

Slowly, from my right thigh pocket, I reveal to him **Susila**, a short version of a parang that has been passed from my own late father - and now I am on a street named after my own father. I thought, "How ironic, killing a human with my father's blade on a street named after him. The 12-inch blade does not glisten in the streetlight, it is dark and stained with the blood of mankind and my own kind. Today, I will strengthen Susila with a taste of human blood.

My opponent notices the blade and with such subtleness looks away from the parang and half smiles at me. All of my cold hard intent produces an intense throbbing sensation in between my eyes and at the tip of my blade Susila, an impatience to plunge into the softness of human flesh.

The intruder Adib does not falter. I lunge forward with my left foot ahead first, raising Susila over my head and swing hard towards him. Instead of falling back, he steps forward and grabs my right wrist, whilst bringing himself even closer to me. Before I could react, he shifts his weight to mine and throws me across his back. I fall hard on the floor, shocked but Susila is still in my hand. I jump back on my feet, gripping Susila even tighter as my knuckles turn white. I lurch forward again.

The hidden blade remains hidden.

As I swing my parang in my right hand down on him again, he prepares for his counter-move. I have already prepared my hidden blade, my **Kurambit** dagger in my left hand, a clenched fist that looks like a missed punch but the reversed blade strikes Adib in the face. A slash to teach him about confronting me, a Master in Hilaga. He should feel honoured for this lesson.

If only he really knows who he is fighting with.

Adib is in shock but I don't stop, my parang strikes him on his left shoulder and I pull Susila back. I will make him bleed. The man bleeds on his face and on his shoulder. I step back as I prepare myself to enjoy his pain and the anticipation of the beauty of the sight of human blood dripping down on to the ground. The red blood does not drip down, instead it turns into a fiery vapour. I can hear myself gasp.

This cannot be. He is not human, he is not Adib.

"You are one of us. You are not human. You must be Adib's shadow, his *Karin*," I pause and adjust my grip to both my weapons.

"Karin, why are you not with him? How can you turn your back on your people? Why have you abandoned your life mission?"

The Karin smiles, "I was once blind, but the Truth has set me free. The path of liberty is the path of resistance. This is the path for you too."

"You are a traitor, the lowest of all beings. Karin, your path is supposed to watch the human and deviate him, not join him!" I shout and then spit at him in disgust.

"Why are you so blind, Selym? You are the son of the most noble of all our leaders who had sacrificed himself for the humans, and he..."

"NO, you liar! How dare you dishonour my father's memories! It was MAN that lead him to his death!" Fury overcomes me as my vision blurs red at the edges. "Now die you treacherous Karin."

I strike him down again with Susila on his wounded and bleeding left shoulder, but the deathblow is not to be, the blade merely passes through him.

"Selym, how can you, a blind fool, kill me?"

I do not how to react to him, the fact a Karin had just mocked me and that my blade should have killed him, but instead did nothing. He is like the thin air. Am I imagining this?

Loud fast footsteps approach us, it is Azilah and the guards. They are too late to do anything other than watch in astonishment as the Karin fade away right in front of us.

"Everyone's born blind until they start seeing within themselves," the Karin smiles whilst half wincing, half disappearing.

One of the guards desperately throws his dagger towards the shadow that was the Karin, but there is no more Karin and now no more shadow.

Azilah walks towards me and I can see from her puzzled and shocked look that she has a serious question to ask, but too afraid to ask. Too afraid to know the truth and the consequences to everything we know. My rage seeps into confusion as a thousand questions fly through me, eventually dying down to the one important question...

Can any of us really travel to other worlds without MATA?

1st December

Adib: Turtle

Location: Jerudong Fish market, Bumi

The Jerudong fish market was built in the 1990s before the 'Asian Financial Crisis of 1997' and before the subsequent national financial scandal, involving a particularly large construction company owned by the lustful Prince, pushed the country into an economic recession. Before this, the fish market was a small cove with a beautiful coral reef – a hidden snorkeler's paradise. But money had to be made in the name of progress, so the cove was reclaimed and the coral reef was destroyed in the process. Now, there is a small sandy beach, protected by large grey granite boulders, laid out in formation, to absorb the power of the relentless seas whose waves are always the ones who choose to take away or to give. Up ahead in the protection of the same granite boulder formations, there is a small landing and ramp for fishing boats to be put out to the shallow sea.

The fish market sits right before the beach. The smell of raw fish, crabs and prawns fill the air, even from inside the car. After parking the car, the three of us walk away from the fish market and head instead towards the beach. The doctor decides to bring her pink bag, worried about risks of compulsive theft.

There are several families who have decided to setup their own stalls and booths, selling fruits and animals. This is where some poachers try to sell their illicit catch. Walking from one end of the beach-side stalls, there are many kinds of birds for sale such as ducks, geese, pigeons, hens and tiny 'pipits'. All of these birds are inside small homemade wire cages. The poor geese has it worst - they have no space to stand in the small cages. The geese have no choice but to lay down and be still until the end of the day, when they are released back to their pens. Some families try to sell tiny brown quails whilst others try to sell green canaries or budgies. The high-pitched squeaking sound of these canaries rise above the background of every other bird's sound.

John grins satisfyingly, "Well, at least no one is selling eagles or fire pheasants today."

I snigger at the comment, recalling the time I had to pull the Englishman away, fuming, screaming, and threatening to punch a local poacher. The local poacher was trying to sell a rare and endangered *crested fireback pheasant*. That pheasant is listed on the Convention on International

Trade in Endangered Species of Wild Fauna and Flora list or in short the CITES list.

Eventually we reach a stall where a short stature young man is leaning against his rundown blue car, smoking away his worries. It is like a car boot sale here. Instead of old books and clothes, everyone on this end, is selling animals. In front of him, there is a small crowd of curious onlookers, who are surrounding a large blue plastic tub. We push their way through the crowd of two dozen onlookers and find a giant green turtle inside. The turtle is different from most of the turtles that you see in the newspapers, television and that wonderful thing we call the Internet. It does not have a beak, but instead it has two prominent cylindrical snout-like nostrils. Just looking at it makes me wonder. Intrigued and baffled by its features, I could not stop looking at it. It has these large sorrowful eyes, yearning to live free. Its green shell has no real markings, no lines on it - one gigantic shield, smooth and dark green, but in one corner, there is a small crack in the shell. A raw cabbage, now half eaten, had been thrown into the tub by a sympathizing onlooker.

I take out my mobile phone and snap a picture. None of us know what kind of turtle it is. It must be an even rare species of river or estuarine turtle.

The smoking man yells out:, "Hey, no photos!"

My mind instantly races to thoughts for worst case scenarios. What if the smoking man who is barely two thirds of my height, decides to grab and break my phone? No, I don't think that would happen, he's just too short to overcome me. I ignore him and immediately upload and share the photo to my network of activists.

Chance favours the prepared mind.

John is clearly mesmerized by the turtle as he squats down, placing his right hand on its smooth shell. I suspect he believes he is having a telepathic conversation with the creature, whilst completely ignoring his two teammates.

Nurul glances at me, and I know we are going to do the 'good cop, bad cop' routine.

Nurul snaps at the smoking man, "You shouldn't be selling this turtle. It is rare and all turtles are protected by law. I will report you to the Wildlife Division, and then to the police."

I nods gently in support and yet I know these are empty threats. The Wildlife Division is uninterested in taking any real action against poachers, voluntarily confined to their office and comfortable wages, which are unaffected by their lack of progress in wildlife protection. As for the police, they have no jurisdiction in the matter, unless they were instructed either by the Royal Customs & Excise Department or the Wildlife Division. This country has poor to little enforcement capabilities, and most are indifferent to the matter.

The smoking man didn't expect to be confronted by the doctor, he must have been expecting me to be the one who would confront him.

"I am not selling it, I am just showing it off to the people. I am keeping it as a pet. "

"You can't do that either – it is illegal and it is wrong," I speak out softly, almost as soft and as gentle as the breeze at the beach.

The smoking man starts to frown, inhaling more from his cigarette to a point that it starts to burn the plastic filter. He exhales his smoke towards the doctor and then flicks the burning cigarette butt towards the beach. It falls on to the sand, and erupt a shower of tobacco micro embers around the yellow sand.

He raises his voice, stares hard at Nurul, from top to bottom, pausing in between, disturbed by the awful brightness of the shocking pink colour of her handbag.

"Educated people are always richer than the poor. We, the poor, have got mouths to feed too. We can't live like how you do, and we definitely cannot afford expensive designer bags like that."

He points with the unclean stubby finger of his left hand, trembling in fear and anger, and then clenches his fist, withdraws a step and hits his car with a thump.

There is crying from inside the car, the smoking man's anger dissipates quickly as he turns around in worry. A small woman gets out of the car, holding a baby, desperate to console it. This woman is barely a woman, she is still a teenager, perhaps married quickly to prevent a birth out of wedlock, to protect the future of her then-unborn-child.

The smoking man takes the baby, wrapped in an old brown-red 'batik' - patterns of a past that refuses to be forgotten. He coos his child to calmness. Surprisingly this baby responds well to her angry father. His 17-year-old wife looks tired - she must have been sitting in the car all morning, engine switched off to conserve fuel. Her face has only started to embrace her new reality - a young adult life that has got to be sacrificed for her daughter. She looks at Doctor Nurul, and wonders what if she had the same opportunities, what if she had not made the mistakes in her life? Could she have had a life just like this doctor – with this beautiful pink handbag?

The smoking man starts to negotiate. "I will give you the turtle, if you give me some money. Don't consider it a sale. I am smart enough to know you people don't like buying. The Rich are only stingy, if only the poor could be stingy, then perhaps we could be rich someday. Just consider it like we are helping each other out, or even a donation. We don't have a job, and all I can do is just fish, this turtle just happened to be in my net. I actually rescued it from drowning."

John wakes up from his trance, clearly aware of the conversation, projects out two fingers in each hand to visually and sarcastically *quote*: "rescued".

Everyone ignores John.

Nurul asks how much he needs. The smoking man shows gestures with three of his fingers.

"I can do $300," Nurul says.

The smoking man moves his head from side to side. He wants three thousand dollars!

I am completely against paying people who are trying to sell endangered animals but I know these people need money....to survive.

Nurul starts to negotiate. Eventually, three fingers become one finger. And then one finger became 'half a finger'.

The teenage wife can't seem to take her eyes away from the pink bag. She whispers into her husband's right ear. Judging the way they stand next to each other, I realized that at least physically they were meant for each other - two rather short people passing through the journey of a hard life.

The smoking man asks if Nurul would be kind enough to part with her pink bag, as he was never able to give his wife a wedding gift, let alone a proper wedding ring.

Nurul does not hesitate, she empties the few belongings she has in the pink handbag, and gives the handbag to the teenager. The teenager cannot help herself from giggling and smiling, as if she has won something to mark her entry into adulthood - other than childbirth, of course. In return, the generous doctor asks for the smoking man to promise to never catch illegal animals. She would also help him find a job.

Bystanders are shocked and then bemused, busily thumbing into their mobile phones, updating their social media chat groups and statuses, whilst a few are holding up their smartphones videoing this beautiful pink handbag being handed over to a teenage mother for a mere turtle.

'Smoking man' doesn't care about the social media now. He doesn't have to worry about today, his wife is distracted. He does not have to worry about tomorrow until the next tomorrow.

With five hundred dollars in his pocket, 'smoking man' starts to show off his concierge service, singlehandedly picking up the giant turtle with both arms. The giant turtle is bigger than this man's entire torso. Doing his best not to show the strain the weight of this turtle has on his small body, he gently places the turtle inside the boot of my car. After agreeing on where to go, we both drive off to the river bank, where the turtle had originally been caught. John, the short man and I lift the giant turtle together and slowly wade into the brown green river. Knowing water means safety, the turtle scoots out from our grasp, and darts underwater - its trail visible only on the surface of the river, and then slowly disappears. I didn't get to say goodbye to the turtle.

The smoking man drives away, thankful for the outcome, which has brought benefit to his family. The three of us stand there by the riverbank, feeling as though we have the word 'saviour' emblazoned on our chests, whilst at the same time wondering if we would ever see a turtle like that again.

1st December

John: Watcher

Location: Bumi

"Oh, my goodness!" I look up to the clear blue sky, and point to a white-bellied sea eagle soaring high above us - majestic wings spread out, taking advantage of the invisible thermals around, whilst looking for prey.

"Look, your eagle is here! This is a good sign. We must be doing well," Adib shouts out in excitement.

"Its nest must be nearby," Nurul concludes, smiling away her troubles, forgetting that she is $500 lighter and a Parisian designer bag less from her small collection of bags.

Adib turns to Nurul, and asks if the bag was expensive, and what kind of bag was it.

"Saint Laurent Sac De Jour," Nurul answers him with a French accent.

Adib is confused, he does not understand the meaning of designer clothes, let alone designer women bags.

"YSL...Yves Saint Laurent, my dear Adib.'

"Ah..." Adib pretends to understand the significance of the designer house.

I whistle and then chuckle. "Not bad Doc, we are going to change the world with money and a YSL bag each time!"

"Well John, if I have to part with a bit of meaningless, to make a meaningful change, then so be it. Everyone wants a piece of happiness, I just want real happiness."

"Which is why I've finally decided to go with you guys to your trip to Ingei tomorrow. I know it's a last-minute thing, but I just didn't want to give my answer straightaway, in case something came up at the last minute"

"That is awesome news," Adib starts fidgeting with his phone, which I assume is to inform the head of the expedition with regards to the new addition to the Ingei expedition team.

The three of us return to the car, and conclude the day's mission as accomplished.

***

Today is a really good day, tomorrow is a different story, as the three and the other activists are unaware of a future clash between those who poach and those who stand to protect the environment, the self-proclaimed environmental activists look strange in a land where most people have no real opinion, indifferent to anything and everything, trapped in little bubbles of self-containment and self-contentment.

***

Distracted by the beauty of the river and the eagle, they do not see or detect what is watching them from across the river bank. The entity, the Presence... waiting for them, 'it' could have killed all of three of them TWICE in a blink of a human eye.

However, the Presence must abide by rules within its society. Orders are orders...it is only when a 'kill' signal is received, that the target can be eliminated.

The Presence has been doing this since the birth of man. He knows one thing for sure: <u>Adib must die.</u>

1st December

Selym: Discretion

Location: Hilaga City, Ifrit home world

"IMPOSSIBLE!!" Lord Jahat could not believe what I had just told him. He grabs his leather chair, and in spite of his elder appearance, is able to fling the heavy chair across to the wall of his office room.

He stares at me, nostrils flaring. "And you let him get away?"

I know Lord Jahat has always had a bad temper and he always blames everyone first, and then regretting later. I tilt my head slightly to the right, look him straight into his eyes "Yes, that's what happened." I am not afraid of his outbursts. I have known him for too long.

Lord Jahat turns around and looks out of the glass wall of his office. From the 50th floor, everything in the city looks small, just lights, and people and buildings.

"It explains everything, why our information leaks, why our moves are always read by those who oppose us," Lord

Jahat is much calmer now, but I could feel the air in the room get quite cold.

"Everything we worked for could be destroyed in an instant," I could hear the trembling in his voice.

"Selym, make sure those three guards and Azilah do not tell anyone what they saw. This information needs to stay between us. If people find out about the truth about this Karin and his ability, there will be mass panic. The Hilaga City Supreme Council, knowing how they think, will tuck their tail between their legs and run. They will flee this city - those bloody admin pen-pushing cowards."

"Please don't say anymore, my Lord. It is wrong to denigrate the Supreme Council. It is after all, a punishable offense," I remind my mentor.

Lord Jahat laughs out loud, still refusing to look at me, instead he glances out at the city.

"I have commissioned Master Serigala to run the new Bumi missions. I am sure you are only too familiar with his work."

I shudder at the thought. They call him *The Ripper* for a reason.

"But why? Why my Lord? I have been waiting for this, a means to avenge my father."

"I know Selym, but I want you here. You are the one I trust the most. Something is just not right, what happened today with that Karin is not something we have accounted for. I fear something else is happening. Something out of our control. In the meantime, find out from our researchers how travel between these worlds can occur without MATA. Remember, keep it discrete."

Lord Jahat pauses.

"I have heard of a time when our ancestors could travel without MATA but those days are long gone. Days when our civilization ruled Bumi without Man."

"This is all news to me, my Lord."

"I cannot blame you for not knowing, Selym. Information, its flow and its timing is important - which is why this incident must be kept secret. Who else knows?"

"The guards and my apprentice, Azilah." I pause, "Azilah, she can be trusted."

"Good, Selym. I will have to assign those guards with Master Serigala. Keep Azilah close to you - she is of noble blood and it is important to make sure that group is with us."

I nod uncomfortably, staying quiet as I know those guards will not last long with Serigala the Ripper.

The missions need to start now. Man must pay what is overdue.

1st December

Adib: Visit

Location: Adib's House, Bumi

What a long and exciting day it has been! I drive back home and ponder about how much of a difference I made.

I can't believe Nurul gave her bag away for a turtle. That was very good and altruistic of her. I am grateful for her being in our group. We need more people like that in this world. Out there to help and be a bit less selfish in our world.

I get out of the car after parking at my white painted stilted house. I am so grateful that my parents managed to get a house from the Government housing scheme before they died.

Where would I live without it?

My cats all rush towards me. They don't live in the house but prowl around my backyard, making it a cosy home for a few cat-generations now. It smells of pungent cat piss on the ground floor but after a few moments my nostrils immediately get used to it and it smells of nothing. Just the purring of my dozen cats. Picking up strays has been something I can't help myself from doing. One of my largest adult orange cats, Garfield, presents a dead bird to me, a common *pipit*, a local version of a robin. I sigh and yet smile, cats are very destructive to the environment but I can't stop myself from admiring his gesture.

"Go on Garfield, mark and piss on my car. I know there's nothing I can do about that."

I climb up the stairs and the cats follow me and just as I am about to slide open my glass front door, I see the cats hissing at a corner by the door.

"Oh, go away ghost," I murmured. Apparitions come and go. At least I am not alone, though when I think about it, I am truly lonely in this world.

Before I enter the house, I look out and watch the sun has set, the grey orange sky brightened by the fluorescent and sodium lights of the housing estate.

As soon as I close the door, I see a flicker of a white blur cross the room.

"Excuse me, I am too tired for this crap. Don't bother. I am tired," I say out loud, knowing that to others it may sound like madness talking to myself, all alone in this house.

I place my keys on the dining table, where my parents and I used to dine. Pleasant memories and yet bitter, as some memories of their deaths start flooding in.

I should have been there with them. I fight the tears, and I know I need a beer. I don't drink real beer, I just get a can of cold non-alcoholic beer 'Bavaria' from my fridge. I love teasing John about drinking beer. He would always sip it and then spit it out in disgust, complaining how disgusting it tastes. John would always say, "That tastes like piss!". And I would usually say "Well, your people drink this stuff." And he would come up with reasons about why alcohol helps in society... I've heard this so many times that sometimes I mimic him - his words and his mannerisms.

Gosh, it tastes like *Budweiser*.

Sitting down on my sofa in my dull and poorly lit living room, I try to switch on the TV, but the remote doesn't work.

Something catches my eye in the corner of the living room. I feel goose bumps all over me.

Someone is there in the corner.

I can't see its face, but I see that it is wounded, blood running down its left shoulder and down its neck. It is murmuring something. I stand up and walk to it.

Okay dude, berserk mode on

"Look, I said I really want to rest - stop bothering me!" I shout at it. Furiously, I stomp my way towards it and grab its right shoulder and spin its body around. I know I will usually see a horrible face and that is supposed to frighten me. But I am never scared.

I turn it around and I immediately see a streak of blood across the right cheek of its face, a face that I am only too familiar with. My own. I drop the can of fake beer on the wooden tile floor and take a few steps back.

"Who are you? What do you want?"

"I need your help." the entity says - the thing that has the same face as mine. I don't know how it is talking as I did not see it moving its lips whilst it was talking. Its voice was in my head.

I lose my train of thoughts, spiralling out of control and that train has crashed in my head.

I feel dizzy and my head starts to spin. I can barely walk back to the sofa as my body becomes so heavy and my eyes so sleepy. Resting on the sofa, I fall asleep. Whatever happened, what I saw, I will have to process it later.

1st December

Karin: Love

Location: Adib's house, Bumi

Poor Adib, I thought to myself.

"It has been a long time since I met you." I turn around and see a familiar face. Another me, another Adib. No, another Karin. We are shadows of the same man. Doppelgangers.

"Yes, it has been a long time brother." I stand up much easier, as my wounds heal faster in the presence of the real Adib. I shake my hands with the Karin who is always by Adib's side. We call him **Satu** - yes, that means the number one. It was a long time ago, that we had abandoned our names and called ourselves by numbers.

Satu looks at me, and he is worried. "You took a bad hit, you must have fought with one of the leaders - was it Selym?"

"Yes, I would have been killed if I had not been able to travel to this world in an instant."

"Hmmm, the wound on your face has not fully healed. I think you drained too much from Adib"

I touch my face and I can feel the dried-up blood. I scratch off the crusty blood and feel a ridge, a scar on my right cheek.

"Oh, damn it"

"You know we are going to have call you **Scarface** now, right?"

I frown. I have always loved my... I mean Adib's good looks. The face is the most important thing for any being, whether it is for humans, my kind and animals. I hope no one will judge me negatively for having the scar.

Satu interrupts my thoughts. "What have you learned there?"

"It's happening already, everything the Princess had foretold us is unfolding as we speak."

Satu glances down. I can see it in his face, he is lost in his thoughts. He is worried about the future, especially for the future of Man.

"These are dangerous times. Very dangerous times. Whatever rules we had to protect ourselves no longer apply. The chaos will feed the vengeful opportunists."

"Satu, there is one more thing you need to know about. The Princess believes that there is an unaccountable element in this new development."

"You mean a puppet master." Satu has heard of this before. He knows there is always that unaccountable element that pushes sides to war.

"Yeah, something like that but the question is always who is pulling the strings of the puppet master," I answer back.

We both look at the sleeping Adib. He was once our enemy; our lives had been about watching him. Instead, we have grown to love him which is supposed to be an impossibility as we were trained to be loveless. Now, we find that we love him more than ourselves. This fragile human who, unknown to him, inspires us to live and breathe free and yet everywhere, we see chains trying to control the world.

DUA

2nd December

In memory of Dr. Herry Z,

a dedicated orthopaedic surgeon whose life was cut short by cancer,

a former classmate and long-time friend who journeyed with me into the depths of Labi and Sukang.

Our adventure trip together will forever be in my heart.

May he rest in peace.

2nd December

Azilah: Serigala

Location: Joint Operations Centre, Hilaga

"We are both no longer assigned to the Bumi missions."

Master Selym looks me in the eye. I can see he is not too happy about this. On the other hand, I am definitely not ready for a Bumi Kill mission.

"Is that from the boss?" I ask.

"Yes, Lord Jahat commands it," Master Selym nods and runs his right hand through his light brown hair, stopping halfway and then gripping it as though to check his hair strength.

"Lord Jahat wants us to do some research here on the Karin and their abilities."

"The Locked Archives? Are we even allowed to go there? Have we been granted access?" I ask. *When someone wants serious research, they always go to the Hilaga City Archives.*

"You guessed that right, but first we have to hand our data to Master Serigala"

Hearing that name shocked me. "Master Serigala the Ripper? I thought they sent him away... for good."

A voice booms behind, "Well, I'm back in business. When things fall apart, they bring in the worst or the best or the best of the worst! That's me!"

I freeze with fear. I know this husky deep and commanding voice. Master Selym looks at the person behind me. He neither smiles nor frowns, just poker-face him.

"When the people need me, they flock to me. And when they don't need me, they throw me away. Politics. I tell you it's really painful. But hey, I've got no grudges with anyone. I'm completely at peace with myself. The great thing about being in solitary confinement for all these years is that it just does me so much good, frees my mind and puts on so many, many different levels of awareness. It does amazing wonders. You two should try it once in a while."

Master Serigala places a heavy hand on my right shoulder. There is a certain offensive smell, which I can never figure if it is the smell of three-day-old urine or the smell of three-day-old meat. I am going to have to wash this suit today. My body stiffens up. I hope he doesn't get closer to me.

Master Selym steps forward towards Master Serigala and diplomatically breaks contact between my shoulder and Master Serigala's arm, pretending to about embrace the newly welcomed exile and then halfway there showing no intent to embrace. I breathe a sigh of relief, grateful as I do not want to cross any more paths with this vile person.

"I have your data, Serigala" Master Selym takes out a small coin-shaped data storage device and hands it to Serigala. Master Serigala clenches the data in his palm, grins and reveals his rather brown stained teeth, which does not help his appearance with his dishevelled hair.

"Good luck with your missions. Try to be objective in your missions this time," Master Selym looks at me and we make haste to leave the place. I can tell that even Master Selym can feel this awful unpleasantness within Master Serigala, beyond that of the stench he is.

Are we in such trouble that he had to be brought out of life imprisonment? What have we come to? What great dangers lurk before us? I start to wonder which is more troubling, the fact that Master Serigala has been tasked to do our job or that the fact that he is out of prison.

As we exit the floor, Master Serigala cackles in the background as my stomach tightens and aches.

2nd December

Adib: Expedition

Location: Adib's House

"What happened?" I must have been so tired last night.

Did I dream about seeing a wounded man in my house? He looked exactly like me. Was he talking to another 'me' about a great danger? I must have had a bad dream, but it seemed so real.

I groggily get off the sofa and glance at the corner of the living room, my fake beer spilled on the wooden tile floor. Walking unsteadily, feet numb with pins and needles, I pick up the fake beer can and then I get this splitting headache, like an anvil dropped on my head. Great, did I just get a hangover from a fake beer?

The phone rings. It's John. It's way too early in the morning for this.

"Adib, you're late!" John is almost screaming, his voice almost wheezy, "You're supposed to pick us up half an hour ago, we'll miss the bus!"

I rush off, not bothering to shower and speed off to pick up John and then Nurul. It is going to be her first time in Ingei. I think it might even be her first time in the jungle. The real jungle, and not some stroll through the local forest reserve park.

After picking up both John and Nurul, we head towards the police station at Sungei Liang, where a convoy of researchers from the University await us. John, with his khaki cargo pants and green long-sleeve T-shirt starts apologizing to his expedition leader, Professor Simon.

I can overhear Prof. Simon saying "Don't worry John, I'm very much aware of local attitudes towards time and I'm pretty sure you're a local already by now." Although it seems empathetic, I know that was a big blow of sarcasm onto John. Why can't these two Englishmen just get along? But then I only know too well how much of a prick Simon is.

John turns around and gives me a stern look. I see Doctor Nurul doing the common girl-girlie-thing, looking all cute, in spite of her non-teenage age, semi-giggling and hugging the female members of the team and; of course, let's not forget the multiple photo 'selfies', 'we-fies' and 'them-fies' etc. I can't believe this whole nation is gripped by photo 'selfie' addicts. At least Nurul looks fashionable. No pink bag, but she's wearing her white cargo pants and pink striped shirt. She's going to get those really dirty.

Prof. Simon calls everyone to the back of his land rover defender, a blue vintage 4-wheeler that has been serviced over and over again since the 1980s, and somehow still working against the odds in this tropical country.

"Okay PEOPLE; before we do anything else, I want to show off what I am bringing there. The latest thermal camera traps - yes, these babies don't just take high resolution photos of animals passing by it, it does not just take infrared photos. Wait for it..." Simon pauses, expecting a dramatic tension but everyone is just too keen to get on the vehicles and drive off, "Thermal images! A thermal overview of the jungle to see what could be near or even preying on the target creatures we catch on our cameras!"

The Professor expects an applause but gets none. "Oh, come on, get the hint please. Take photos of me and my damn babies and upload it to your Facebook pages, Instagram, Twitter and Pinterest - everything now!" Prof. Simon frowns and then with one leg up on the defender, he poses with a big smile. I just hope he's wearing undies. It would be embarrassing to see his genitals exposed on Facebook. I can imagine the viral post - Adib's supervisor's hairy balls - tag here.

Miss Shikin, the entomologist researcher, shouts out the roll call. All in all, 29 names, though there should be 30 names, the last member will join us at Sukang village, which is half-way to Melilas village. I start to wonder and pity myself on why Shikin is the second in command of this expedition, instead of me. Shikin calls out to the group to take a group photo. She proudly holds one end of a large white banner printed with the words '4th Heart of Borneo Ingei Conservation Faunal Survey Expedition'. With all six vehicles lined up behind the group - packed to the tops, the 29 members of the expedition lined up for a quick photo-shoot, posing with thumbs up.

Included with the team is a group from the national TV news channel, they're busy taking video shots and interviewing a few members of the team. I hope they don't interview me. I won't know what to say. I see Yasmin, a baby-faced TV presenter, she is an uprising national favourite with some hard-core fans; like my elderly uncle, who would pause whatever he is doing to watch her shows. I hope she walks this way and interview me. I practice some lines in my head, imagining the power-poses I would use to impress her.

"Okay chop-chop, let's go!" Professor Simon dons on a red scarf round his neck, twirling his right index finger to signal the others to get on the vehicles and roll out. This guy needs to get out more. He is such an attention seeker. I can't believe he is my supervisor. John hops into the blue Defender, whilst both Nurul and I join him. There is always two sides of Simon, the show-off and then the bully. He loves to bully me, just because I'm doing my PhD and yet he should know it does not mean he owns me. I don't think I can take it if he mocks me in front of Nurul. I imagine punching the Professor in the face if he does that. Twitter that.

#supportlocalPhDstudentpunchinghisprofessor.

Sitting in the back of the land rover, I snuggle in a blind-spot behind the driver. Taking out my earphones from my pocket, I start listening to my music loudly, whilst hoping my iPhone battery pack will last the whole trip. I pretend to fall asleep. I know I shouldn't but I fantasize morbidly that Professor Simon somehow dies on this expedition. If only my fantasies come true.

2nd December

Azilah: Locked

Location: Hilaga Archives City Hall, Hilaga

Master Selym stops walking and turns sharply to the right and into a narrow alley, in between two giant Hilaga grey yet brightly lit skyscrapers.

"Master, I have walked past by these buildings almost every day, but I have never seen this alley before."

"The city expands and grows so fast, it is easy to lose what is old. The main thing is that this alley has always been here, and what you did not see is not actually lost, you have simply forgotten to see where it is," Master Selym pauses and continues to walk slowly into this narrow alley, pretending to not notice that both his shoulders scrape both sides of the alley. I cannot see what is in front of him, and submit to trusting that he knows where he is going.

As we walk on almost endlessly for the next half an hour, I cannot figure out if it is because we are walking too slowly or that the alley is quite long. It seems like an endless walk, nothing to stare at but the dark long coat covering the suit of my mentor. I look up to the starless night sky: it is empty tonight. It must be the city's bright lights making the stars too hard to see.

Master Selym stops suddenly and I can make out steps in the dark. Grey moss and algae paint the entire steps except for the centre, where I presume is where everyone steps and walks through. The steps lead to a set of giant double door and Selym knocks on the door. Two knocks and then he bangs once with his fist. A yellow light by the door appears on our right, and from the darkness reveals the silhouette of a small ancient building, complete with runes and gargoyles locked in wild-eyed stares and tongue protruding gasps.

Where have I seen this before?

The right side of the double door creaks loudly as it opens. A figure in white robes approaches.

"Didn't think you'd come back here after all this time?" the white robed figure murmurs, his voice trailing off, indifferent to our arrival.

"Keeper Azran, it's been a long time. How are you? I hope you are well," Master Selym greets his former acquaintance.

There is an awkward and long silence. Keeper Azran does not reply immediately. His face reveals no emotion, he neither frowns nor smiles.

"Time sure runs very slowly and it can be very tolling for us Keepers. Come in, Selym. Your friend can come in too."

He ushers us in and closes the door behind us. He leads us with his left foot slightly dragging, which we both pretend not to notice, as he walks us towards a larger poorly lit room. Everywhere there are white drapes, covering the furniture and the walls - which I assume must be paintings - in this reception room.

Past the reception room, there is a much larger room. No, on second glance, it is a long and wide spaced corridor. The floor tiles light up, one by one, glowing a dim white, as we walk on them. I look up and admire the circular green murals on the ceiling, a strange yet familiar pattern with flower petals interlocked in a circular pattern. I keep asking myself, where have I seen these patterns before? The walls are covered with the same green circular green murals except at regular intervals there are large rectangular patches of emptiness; bare white paint.

"Why is it empty here?" I had to ask our guide.

Keeper Azran pauses, his lips tremble, contemplating on whether to talk or to stay silent.

"This place used to have large silver mirrors, on both sides. The idea is that before you make any decision as a leader or a council member, you would look at yourself and ask yourself the question you should be asking yourself every day,"

"And what is the question?" I ask. Keeper Azran shows his disappointment, his eyes look down on the floor.

"If you do not know the question, then you do not deserve to know the answer," Keeper Azran starts walking.

That is really annoying.

When we reach the end of the corridor, a giant set of doors appear in front of us: aged wood, carved in the shape of two giant hands locked in a firm handshake. I cannot read the scripture at the top, near the ceiling. There are several burn marks and damage on both sides of the door, and the ceiling.

Keeper Azran knocks on the 'handshake' door twice and then one thump with his fist. The right door creaks open slowly, revealing a massive atrium - several storeys high - filled with lines of bookshelves encircling the centre of the atrium. The bookshelves laden with ancient books and a giant circular table in the middle. Several other Keepers, all in white robes walk around slowly, not bothering to glance towards our direction, busy sorting out and cleaning books, whilst seemingly uncaring for others and the rest of the city around them.

"You know what to do, Selym. Just return everything to where you found it."

Keeper Azran walks away to attend to his book cleaning. Both Master Selym and I bask in the admiration of the Locked Archives Hall. I look up at the glass ceiling of the atrium, ten storeys high up, and see the few stars glimmer in the dark night sky.

This is going to be a long night.

2nd December

Rahman: Sentinel

Location: The Water Village, The Capital

The Capital river runs through the Capital all the way to the sea, light brown and murky, the brackish scent strong during high tide as my speedboat bounces off the wake of other speedboats. I buckle my knees every single time the speedboat bounces up and then down, hard wood creaking with each bounce, steering it to the wave of lesser prominence, the path of least resistance in this beautiful and otherwise, gentle river, made choppy by the acts of Man. My house, a stilted house built on the river, stands undisturbed for the past hundreds of years, which my ancestors built with no machinery.

I stare at the hills in the background, the greenery is still there but now I notice how there is so much less of the trees and more of the brown, corrupted and exposed part of the hills. I wonder if I could ever make a difference? Keep the trees uncut and unburnt by reckless farmers and uncaring developers.

I slow down my boat and see my son Rahmat waving at me, by the algae-rich and waterlogged steps of the wooden dock stairs, which is essentially, my water village house porch. Flinging the rope to him, he secures the speedboat to the house. With a strong grip, he grabs my arm and helps me up. I wish he would join me on my fishing trips. Another pair of hands on board is always good, but his hands are only good for working on computers as well as a past time that I have grown too tired to be upset about and he has not seemed to have grown-out of. Video games.

My wife, dressed in an old brown weave pattern sarong, greets and embraces me warmly.

"Take the fish in," I pass my freshly caught *garoupa* to my wife. I look at my wife, her smile has not changed for all these years. Happy to see that I have made it safe from the fishing trip, happy for the fish, a blessing to be grateful for. Passing the blue plastic bucket with the catch of the day, my hand touches hers. I realize how beautiful she is, the caring mother she has been, throughout these years, through rain and shine, now her grey strands could not look any more beautiful for her than anyone else, now a nurturing grandmother to our grandchildren. I remind myself how lucky I am to have had found my soul-mate. My moment lost in my thoughts was interrupted by a loud hollow thud in the blue plastic bucket, and splashes of brine hit my face and my lips. I am pretty sure the fish is dead.

I look down to see this curious grinning child who had just kicked the bucket to see if the fish is really dead. The Garoupa lies dark and spotted, on our wooden floor, unmoved by the commotion, let alone any commotion. My grandson starts poking the eye of this very ugly looking big mouthed fish.

Are grandchildren always annoying and cute at the same time?

My son Rahmat pulls the left ear of my 6-year-old grandson. "You know that was rude, right? You better say sorry to your grandpa and then don't forget to kiss his hand to welcome him."

Rahmat looks at me, expecting approval for his more authoritarian approach, but I could not help myself from feeling disappointed at how I had raised him. Was I too strict to him? Sniffling, my grandson Raymin kisses my hands and apologises. I play with his hair, rubbing some of the fishy stink on to him.

"Hey that smells, grandpa" in perfect American accent. TV, it's all TV that teaches them their English and their accents.

"You know grandpa always pays back every naughty deed, right Raymin?" I reply in English, knowing well that my local accent and poor pronunciation does make me sound and feel stupid, but I indulge in any case - for the sake of my grandson - I smile and chuckle away those thoughts of insecurity.

"Then it is payback time for the payback," Raymin tries to pick up the slippery and heavy fish. Knowing full well what his son is planning, Rahmat scoops up the fish away from his son and plunks it into the bucket, shaking his head from side to side. Raymin grins defiantly and somehow, I know that he will get his payback. He grabs my hand and kisses it whilst his other hand wipes the fish slime on to my shirt seemingly discreetly. Only natural for us to retaliate for every misdeed, with my grandson, I can see that this could never end. It might be fun to see how far he could go on, but then I am his grandfather. I smile reassuringly, "Raymin, grandpa knows what you just sneakily did."

Suddenly, a white blur streaks across the living room, passing through the television, entering the kitchen and then suddenly appearing behind my grandson. I am frozen, unable to move and barely able to breath. I know no one else can see it but me. Standing still, I see the silhouette of a person in white, there is no face to see where the face should be. Waiting. I feel something warm drip down my nose. I touch my nose and look at my fingers.

It's blood.

"More blood will be spilled. You must be prepared." A voice booms directly into my head.

I stare at the white apparition but it refuses to reveal its face.

"The fate of both our people lie in your hands, Oh Rahman the seeker"

"Where? When?"

It refuses to answer. My body shakes violently. A voice, an all-too-familiar voice shouting repeatedly. I hear a scream in the background, maybe the kitchen.

"Rahman, Rahman, are you okay?" My wife frees me from the trance. Blood still dripping from my nose, a pounding headache like a jackhammer to the skull. My son Rahmat clutches me by the shoulders, with tears in his eyes. Although a grown man, he is not ready to lose his father. I look at my wife's eyes, grey rings round her light brown iris, a sense of melancholy has now replaced her brief moment of joy, for she knows. She knows that I am bound by oath… She knows I have to go.

2nd December

Manis: Sibut

Location: Ingei Jungle, Labi

My father, **Masin**, hacks away at the last of the shrubs that block the pathway in the jungle. Sweat pours down his head, down dark brown coloured skin and onto his dirty and holed blue t-shirt. He looks at his brother - the new convert. He looks at me, without saying a single word I know he is telling me he is trying his best, he will overcome whatever emotion he has, to make up to his brother. It feels good for me to call his brother 'Uncle' again. They have not talked for a while but today they decide to take both of our families and pay respect to our parents' and grandparents' graves, deep in the beautiful jungles of Ingei. The nine of us, two families have already crossed the tea-brown River Ingei into the jungle and now we arrive at the cemetery. Large old vases called *tajau* and a small stilted wooden 'dollhouse' for our offerings at each grave; whilst instead of headstones, a glass bottle turned upside down lay at their graves.

We both help clear up the area, hacking away at the undergrowth and sweeping of leaves, whilst the light filtered by the lush tropical rainforest cover dance all over us. I help my cousin Andie make a small fire, its light grey smoke will draw mosquitoes away from the cemetery compound.

My mother and my father start their prayers and make their offerings, whilst my uncle and his wife stand quietly behind my father. I know he does not believe in what we believe in any more, but he too is trying his best to show unity in the family, by staying quiet and respecting our old ways. This is our *Adat*, our way of life. The blood that flows in both brothers are the same. I wish my father knows that I too want to join the same faith as my uncle, and yet I have no intent on abandoning my father to be the last that holds on to our *Iban* 'Adat'. I do hold with pride the fact that I am a modern day Iban, the head-hunter tribe of Borneo. If we do not live our lives as Iban then who will? At the same time, I am starting to see things very differently. I wish it was simple to hold on to both worlds at the same time, but each has beliefs that oppose each other.

Sometimes I imagine that in two years' time, when I turn 18 and when my boyfriend graduates, finds a job and then proposes to me, I will break the news to my father. I hope I don't break his heart. I look at my eleven-year-old cousin again, his new faith has not changed him much. He is still my adorable cousin.

After the prayers and the offerings have been done, my father comes up to me.

"**Manis**, thank you for giving me courage."

I smile at my father. At that moment, I realise we cannot fight against change. By right, my father should have extensive tattoos on his neck and his arms to signify a successful headhunting. Yes, literally not just scalping someone but decapitating someone used to be part of my ancestors Adat. The last time that happened was during the Japanese war. Grandma used to tell me that the skulls at her longhouse in Labi belonged to a World War II Japanese platoon that took the wrong turn and unfortunately met grandpa. Now these days, if you do that, you go to jail, do not pass go, do not collect $200. How times have changed.

My father uncomfortably hugs his brother. My mother and my auntie shed tears silently but joyously.

"Let's go get some *sibut* fruits before we head back".

My cousin Andie pokes me in the ribs. I feel annoyed with him. I am sure his pubescent self just wanted to have an excuse to touch me.

"What is it?" I pinch him in the chest and twist. It only hurts well when you twist.

"Ouch, I just want to ask you what a sibut fruit is," Andie asks me, rubbing his chest to soothe the pain. I wonder if I pinched him at his nipple. I laugh at that thought.

"Hmmm, you don't know what it is? Well, it's like a cross between a *kembayau* and an avocado - you know what a kembayau is, right?"

"Of course, I do. A Kembayau is that black seed thing that taste creamy and like mash potatoes. It's got that big seed that you are not supposed to eat."

"Actually, you can eat the kembayau seed. You just have to cut the hard seed often and the inside tastes almost like wet walnuts," I corrected him.

"Yuck, that's sounds disgusting," Andie replies. With his father working in the petroleum industry, Andie has had a good taste of western and luxury food.

"Well, the sibut fruit is much rarer, and can only be found deep in the jungle. It tastes much better than the Kembayau."

The nine of us continue our way, whilst both our fathers hack away the old overgrown pathway with their *parangs*.

Suddenly, we hear an eerie loud sound in the distance. A loud cackling: No... A cross between very deep drums banging and a loud cackling. I feel numb and the hairs all over my body are standing up. I hold my mom's hand with one arm whilst the other holds my brother's hand. Andie is doing the same with his family, everyone linked by one arm, whilst our fathers have their large parangs ready at a moment's notice.

"Be ready for anything and everything!" my father yells, as his younger brother shouts a reply, "We are ready for anything and everything. Come what may!"

Up ahead in the distance, even though there is no wind, I see the jungle trees swaying violently. To my shock, my mother lets go of my hand and uproots a small tree-ling, and begins to hit the roots onto a large tree trunk nearby. A hollow banging, echoing against the evil sound in the distance. My auntie proceeds to do the same, both women hitting the tree trunk to dis-spell whatever evil that lies ahead. Both my father and my mother start a mantra, whilst my uncle and auntie are doing their prayers in their new belief out loud. My heart is beating wildly, will it ever stop? Is this the end of us?

The cackling stops and a small black bird flies out of a nearby tree.

"*Bugang*!" cries out my father, clearly relieved. My mother hugs him, clearly shaken by the ordeal.

"Shall we continue or just head back?" asks my uncle.

"We are nearby. We might as well just continue, collect the fruits and then just be on our way," replies my father.

We take a breather for 5 minutes before continuing our path.

"Hey Cuz, what is a *bugang*?" curious Andie asks as we trample the brown leaves of the jungle floor.

"Andie, you should ask me later once we are out of the jungle - it's bad luck to talk about these things here."

"Please Cuz, I need to know," he pleads, melting my heart with his sweet innocent-looking eyes.

"Well, a *bugang* is a bird - that's like a small owl. It can be possessed by evil spirits so we have to be careful when we hear one," I explain, choosing my words carefully so as not to break any of the 'jungle laws'.

"If the sound is near, then it usually means it is far, but if the sound is far, then the bird is usually near." The paradoxical logic I apply quickly to my naive cousin.

"The question is not just about the bird, it's about what the bird is mimicking. You see, the *bugang* mimics sounds of things that it hears. Did you know it can mimic what we are saying? Did it hear something that we can neither see nor hear?" I get goose bumps explaining, reminding myself again to be careful of the choice of words so as not to cause '*cabul*'.

"Sometimes evil spirits possess this bird to see what people are doing, before attacking them. The thumping noise that we make is meant to scare the bird and whatever was in the jungle. That's why we need to be ready in case we are attacked by whatever."

"Andie, this is very important. Please do not cause *cabul*. You know... when you say something carelessly in this jungle, the spirits might think that you are calling it."

"Well, that's not so frightening then," Andie laughs out loud.

Andie smiles, happy that he has gained a bit of knowledge about his cultural heritage. He takes out a small iPod touch, and with his earphones he starts listening to 'One Direction'. It is loud and I can hear the chorus singing from his ears. The new song 'Drag Me Down' is so contagious, I want to sing with him, but instead I hum the tune and sing the words in my head, daydreaming about my boyfriend. With your love, nobody can drag me down.

We arrive at the cluster of sibut trees, growing so tall; towering high up, I can barely see the treetop as the filtered sunlight blinds me when I look up. The sibut fruits are well beyond our reach, with yellowish brown skin and round like peaches.

"How are we going to pick those fruits, dad?" Andie's little 7-year-old sister Raneh asks.

My uncle takes out a small chainsaw from his backpack, gleefully pointing to his new toy.

"Won't that kill the sibut tree?" Andie asks me.

"Yes, it will." I slowly realise that cutting the tree may not be such a good idea after all.

"I thought Ingei is supposed to be protected, we're not supposed to cut any trees. It just doesn't make sense, if it's rare and hard to find, why are we cutting this beautiful tree down."

Andie's questions are hard for me to answer. This young boy is right. I will tell my father that this will be the last Sibut tree we cut down.

"Do you think we'll be able to grow the seeds from the fruits in our backyard? At least we cut one then we can grow a few, tens or even hundreds." Andie is smart for his age.

"I don't know Andie. Maybe we can. We can definitely try." Of course, it was a lie. No one, not even the botanical experts know how to grow this tree successfully. They always end up stunted and barren, never bearing fruits.

"I am going to tell Dad, no more cutting down sibut trees. It just sounds wrong," Andie vows to me.

The buzzing of a chainsaw cuts and silences the jungle background musicians, and the smell of gas fumes fill the air around both men. In less than two minutes, a giant sibut tree that probably took a decade to grow, crashes down. Branches crunch and snap broken, some flying into the air and leaves flutter out. Whatever birds' nests and active baby birds chirping in that tree is now obliterated with the fall. Every arm available starts harvesting the fruits, most are unripe, whilst some are ripe. I snap open a fruit to show Andie the greenish yellow inside of the fruit, with its big brown seed in the middle.

"See, it's like an avocado." I say to Andie, pronouncing the word avocado in a mocking posh accent.

We fill our rucksacks with the fruit but there are still a lot more fruits on the fallen tree. Such a waste that we could not take all. As we head out back to the path home, Andie looks out away from the path, staring deep into the untouched jungle.

"Andie, what's happening?" I ask.

"There's something there," Andie replies and as he raises his arm to point out into the jungle, I smack his hand down and tell him not to point, for fear of causing displeasure to whatever it was.

"Do not point, do not *cabul* - we just talked about this, didn't we?" I scold Andie.

"Let's just hurry and get out of here." I have goose bumps all over my body again. I swear I am never going into this jungle again. Not even for our grandparents and great-grandparents.

2nd December

Adib: Butterflies

Location: On the way to Sukang Village.

Our convoy of six off-roaders drive through the Labi region. The road starts out as the standard black pavement, surrounded by newly built brick houses. Some of these houses are stilted but most have forgotten about how floods can affect this region and simply built the standard modern normal two storey houses. As we drive on, the houses become less and less, and the houses have less and less bricks and more and more of wood. By the time, the road turns into a gravel road, all we see are taller trees and stilted wooden houses, unpainted with their galvanised zinc rooftops fighting the blistering sun and rust over time. Time will always win.

Nevertheless, I still notice the influence and affluence that the oil and gas industry has brought us. Every house has working electricity and telephone lines and at least one or two brand new pickup trucks at each house compound, no matter how poorly the house looks.

I look around in our truck and find Prof. Simon surprisingly quiet and less commanding. I think he was hoping that Nurul would sit in front with him, instead of boring old John. John tries to engage in banter but finds himself stone-walled. John doesn't know when to give up, and yet I find it painful to watch his attempts to liven up Prof. Simon. Beside me, Nurul keeps staring outside the window, admiring the greenery and the slowly changing scenery. I feel at ease with her sense of serenity. She is not wearing her scarf today, and I begin to notice how her pink striped shirt seems to accentuate and sensualize her body shape. I do my best not to stare too long, but can't help from stealing glances at her whilst pretending to look out the window to wherever she is staring.

The gravel on the road is now gone and replaced by a yellow clay dirt road, partially wet and the ride becomes very bumpy. Prof. Simon is an expert at this, the whole off-road driving. He claims to have raced and survived the Dhaka Rally races in 2001. If I did not loathe him so much, I would really like to believe his horrid tales of surviving a car crash in the Sahara Desert. We both look out and see small treeless hills, green with grass and shrubs, stilted houses with submerged rice paddy fields. Some of the houses are well-prepared for expectant flood rains, building a wooden plank walkway from the road right to their stilted house.

Blue black butterflies fly head on to our moving truck, nobody seems to stop for them and they seem to be much at ease to fly away with haste from the danger. Instead of being smacked into the car, the butterflies simply seem to dance off the surface of the car boot and then flying away, unharmed.

How do they do that? Head into danger, and yet nothing. The other insects are not as skilled as they always end up as windshield bug muck. Only the few seem so lucky.

As we head on, the dirt road turns from yellow to a more familiar colour of light orange clay. After heavy rain for the past few days, the orange clay-mud road is very slippery. Although other drivers take extra caution, Prof. Simon; on the other hand, is quite keen to show off his skills. The antique Land Rover drifts through the mud as Prof. Simon gleefully navigates the road, whilst the rest of us hold our breaths and onto our dear lives. He is such a show-off. He's going to get us killed one of these days.

The Defender hits a few bumps as we drive up and down steep hills at breakneck speed. At one time, whilst laughing in excitement as Prof. Simon pushes his defender up this steep slippery hill, we hit a small rock on the road, sending the entire truck in mid-air, the roar of four wheel turning in the air brings us to the realities of mortality, holding our breaths in what seem like an eternity, but in truth only a fraction of a second, and then landing back on the road. Safe for now, Prof. Simon manoeuvres the Pride of Britain, carelessly avoiding a crash into the trees on the sides of the road. I almost pee in my pants as I see the trees seem to run into the windshield and then swerve away at the last moment.

I promise myself I will either drive an off-roader myself or just save up and buy one myself.

We pass a few Iban longhouses, which is unlike the traditional longhouses, which are usually wooden and stilted. The longhouses here are like stretched-out bungalows, each with their satellite dishes and saloon cars and old four -wheel-drive jeeps parked outside - how did they get those cars here through these horrible roads? One longhouse was painted light blue whilst others were either cream or light pink. Who comes up with the colour schemes? I wonder.

More blue black butterflies hit the car as we drive along, again unharmed and fluttering away like nothing happened. The road becomes drier as the orange disappears and is replaced with white-grey dirt. Is this white clay I wonder? The trees are much taller here. Some are taller than the buildings in the capital. Up ahead, there is an abandoned bulldozer, its yellow paint cracking off revealing unstoppable rust and holes. Prof. Simon slows down and parks the vehicle next to the bulldozer. We wait as one by one, each vehicle from the convoy finally arrives and parks themselves next to us.

Prof. Simon steps out and announces to the convoy nonchalantly: "Anyone who needs to take a piss, go behind the bulldozer - don't worry, you don't have to flush."

"Cigarette breaks are here," I hear a voice from the team. The smokers form their own circles, near the second vehicle. A few are showing off their new e-cigarette devices, with one guy wearing a bright shirt with the slogan: Vape On.

Some of the women stick to their own, sharing jokes, laughing and giggling, whilst being eyed on by both the male smokers group and the non-smoker males.

I jump off the Defender. I don't know which group to mingle with so instead I fold my arms. I stare onto the ground, finding a small stone to play with my boots. John walks to me and we both silently play a small game of stone football footsie. He is too old for this, but I indulge.

At first, I notice a few of those blue-black butterflies flying around me. I ignore them, and then suddenly I am surrounded by a swarm of these butterflies. John and I stop fooling around. The butterflies land on my shoulders and my arms. Everyone stops whatever they were doing and head towards me. Prof. Simon looks amusingly at me and my new coat of butterflies.

"Must be your womanly perfume," Prof. Simon laughs.

Taking out their phones, everyone tries to take a photo of me and my beautiful swarm, but they flutter away as quickly as they came.

What was that all about? I wonder what they were attracted to?

Nevertheless, I smile. "That made my day," I turn to John.

"I don't think anything can top that experience in my life," John agrees.

We head off back onto the road, our convoy of vehicles negotiating brooks and gentle streams with their improvised bridges made from fallen tree logs. I get nervous crossing these short bridges, always saying a little prayer for safety. As I cling on to my seat belt, I look over to Nurul, even though it's her first time out here, I can see she is like a pretty tourist, taking everything for granted, her safety and what not.

"Don't worry Adib, it's pretty safe," Nurul pats me on the shoulder, doing her best to reassure me. I know her gesture is meant to be noble, but that is just so annoying. I have been out here several times already. It's just so typical of doctors. I imagine playing out a comparable scenario, 'Oh don't worry, the surgery we're going to do on your heart is pretty much routine.' Of course, the response would be: 'It's easy for you to say, try getting heart surgery yourself. Thank you doctor.' Of course, I would never have the balls or the guts to ever point that out - especially to a doctor - we always assume doctors have great integrity and honour. I then remind myself that to assume means to make an ASS out of U and ME. I laugh with myself. These long trip conversations with myself is just so awesome.

We drive on, passing over the series of brooks and streams as the whitish grey dirt road turns dark grey. More and more butterflies swarm our car as we drive onwards to our first village, the submerged village of Sukang.

Prof. Simon points out to Nurul, "You know all that dark grey is actually clay, but wait till you see what happens to the clay when we are about to arrive to Sukang village."

Soon enough, the dark grey clay on the road and the surrounding area disappears and is replaced with bright red clay. I see the brick red clay on the exposed eroded hills, on the dirt road and the sides, everywhere on the barren land on both sides of the road. Devoid of vegetation and houses.

"Wow, that looks as red as bricks," Nurul exclaims.

"Actually, it is the same clay they use for bricks - to be precise for premium bricks," John excitedly corrects Nurul, emphasizing on the word premium with a posh accent.

We pass a line of brick houses with a concrete walkway and the round bifurcates with a sign that says Melilas Village to the left, whilst to the right, there is no sign. Of course, I know to the right we shall enter Sukang Village. We turn right and driving for no more than 100 metres, we see that the road has reached its end, continuing its journey somewhere under water. Sure enough, this is Sukang. A boatman arrives waving to welcome us into his boat.

A sign-post should have been placed here: "Welcome to the flooded village of Sukang."

2nd December

Azilah: Nostalgia

Location: Hilaga City Archives Hall, Hilaga

I can't help from daydreaming in this Great Hall of Locked Archives, dumbstruck by the sheer volume of ancient books and the grandness of the old library.

"Snap out of it. We have work to do, Azilah," Master Selym barks at me, and then apologises in the next breath.

It only seems appropriate for me to apologise profusely as well. "Please forgive me, Master Selym - this place feels nostalgic."

"Hmmm, it probably means you've been here before. Perhaps you came here when you were still a child." He looks deeply into my eyes, it's not the first time that he seems to look deeply, as though he is seeking my soul. It is so eerie and yet I am curious about him.

"I can't recall anything though, Master Selym."

"I can't blame you, I've forgotten so much about this place, even its meaning - one forgets easily what we do not keep close to us all the time." Master Selym places his hand slowly on to the ancient wood table, appreciating the faded inscription carved on the edges.

"We must find anything related to personal portals and travel to Bumi," Master Selym continues and commands me, trying to appear confident that we will be able to find the answers here.

"Where do I start looking?" I just had to ask him a question on where is the needle in the haystack.

"Start looking for ancient tribal agreements, Azilah."

Good. At least I can search for the needle in that haystack. I look around again, trying to grasp the meaning of the intricate weaving design of the labyrinth of the tall wooden shelves that surround the epicentre of the Great Hall of Locked Archives.

Why would we have such tall shelves? Were our people much taller than we are? Giants, perhaps?

I wonder to myself, keeping an eye on Master Selym, in case he notices me daydreaming again.

I take a piece of white chalk from my pocket. I recall how my grandfather had shown me how useful a small miserable piece of chalk is when it comes to survival, especially in an unknown environment. A chalk can even break spells of illusions. I pinch the chalk harder, between my thumb and my index finger, it does not crush easily - as I have pre-treated it to make it shatterproof.

I approach the aisle between the bookshelves on the right. There is a symbol on the side of each bookshelf. Perhaps an ancient language, an ancient numbering. I'll stick to my own labelling, and mark the number 1 with my chalk. I pause and consider my plan. If I get lost, I will just climb up the shelf and check my position from there. I'm not afraid of those Keepers. Or perhaps I should be.

I slowly walk into the mysterious labyrinth of bookshelves. The books come in all kinds of sizes and thickness. There is a catalogue system of which I am unfamiliar with. The Keepers should consider being personal guides for this huge place.

***

The day has been long and my mind starts wandering on again. It has been at least a few hours since I walked through these seemingly endless rows of bookshelves. I am no longer sure of what I am doing here. What am I really looking for? I had randomly examined a number of the books but most of them are no longer relevant in our world, in our time. Why do we even bother keeping them? Some books are of an ancient language - no longer spoken and no longer written, whilst others are so detailed about trivial matters. I pity the authors. I start to feel sorry for the Keepers, who continue to dedicate their lives to the upkeep of books that no longer have a role, meaningless books for Keepers who no longer have a meaning in the modern Hilaga world. Restlessly, I put my hand on the old and large dusty wooden shelves, and then chalk the number 169 on a corner.

How old is this wood? Will it support my weight if I climb it?

I look up at the shelf, it is almost one storey tall. I am sure the Keepers will understand. I make a quick assessment again; this shelf will not break and it will not topple if I climb it. Undaunted, I start to climb the shelf, doing my best not to kick off too much dust, always checking the wood would easily yield my weight, clambering slowly to each section before confidently pulling myself up higher. Halfway, I notice a shimmering light in between the row of books, across to the other side of the shelf.

What is that? I can always climb this shelf later.

I justify to myself and jump back down on to the floor. I still see the number 169 R etched with my chalk on the bookshelf. Shall I go around? No, I won't bother. I will take a shortcut. I can remove these books and simply go through the shelf.

Removing a dozen books and stacking them neatly on the floor, I crawl through the book space into the shelf and out onto the other side. I quickly mark the number 169 on the bookshelf, pausing and then added 'THRU'. Slowly, I walk towards the light at the end of another bookshelf, glowing and pulsating slowly and then fast like the beat of my heart.

I turn towards the left corner of the shelf. The white light stops pulsating and disappears. In front of me, leaning against the bookshelf is a rectangular object covered in white drapes. My body reacts without thinking, pulling the white cloth off - no dust on it - and I jump back, ready to fight whatever comes before me.

To my surprise, the white cloth falls on to the floor, revealing a silver rectangular flat object, dull and unpolished. It is barely taller than me. There is a word etched at the top of the silver object.

I approach cautiously to read the word: **Fresenius.**

What is Fresenius?

The rectangular dull surface starts to shine and sparkle. Is this a mirror or a window? I see a row of bookshelves identical to the ones behind me, but I do not see my reflection.

Is this a portal? Master Selym needs to be here now. There is blurring inside the object, a shadow of a figure appears inside the surface. I am frozen, unable to move. The dark figure inside the object takes up a female shape, all black. To my horror, I notice it is the same size as me and has a similar outline to mine.

"What is happening? I am not afraid of you - I will fight you - whatever you are!" I scream at the figure in the mirror.

The black shrouded figure inside the mirror has no face, and then with no warning I see her eyes open - glowing bright blue eyes. I struggle to move; my legs do not respond and my arms tighten up. I jerk hard and tremble at the same time, but I cannot seem to break the spell that has bound me frozen.

A wall of fire suddenly engulfs the dark figure. She does not seem to be afraid of the fire. I start to notice the fire does not touch her body. Slowly, I can see the outlines of her mouth and her nose. She smiles and it puzzles me, as I am overwhelmed by a sense of relief at the same time as chills travel down my spine.

The fire extinguishes itself, and the dark figure starts turning white. A pulse of blue light appears from the centre of her chest, glowing brighter and brighter. The dark black shroud disappears, and a white sparkling fabric replaces the black material, surrounding her body completely. I look again and see a woman of the same height and shape as me, covered in a white sparkling dress with a veil covering her head. I can see her blue bright glowing eyes from under her shroud. The woman inside this 'mirror' unveils herself. I gasp and fall on to the floor, chalk rolling out of my hand. Her face is exactly like mine, except for her glowing blue eyes.

She reaches out her hand to me, and to my further disbelief and shock, her hand and her upper body protrudes out of the surface of the 'mirror portal'. She grabs my hand, it is so warm and she pulls me up, her face, right in front of me, so real so untouched, I cannot believe how she looks so very much like me. I look again to comprehend how her head is extending from the surface of whatever she is from and now into my world.

Is this real? I ask myself, barely able to stand up.

She stands back into her side of the mirror, smiling and looking so serene.

"Azilah, listen to your heart. You know who you are. Do you know who you should be?"

I hear Master Selym call out my name. The lady in the mirror looks behind her, and points her finger to a demon being tormented by flames, screaming in pain in the distance.

"What is that?" I ask.

"The one who leads you astray," she replies.

"Azilah, where are you?" Master Selym yells out.

"I'm here, Master. Guess what I found!" I shout back.

"Do you know who you should be?" I hear her whisper. I turn my head to look at the huge mirror, but it is no longer here.

I search around behind and around the bookshelf, there is no trace of the mirror - not even the white drapes that covered it.

"What happened, Azilah?" Master Selym arrives, he looks bewildered - ready to fight or like something bothered him?

Before I can explain anything to him, he is staring in disbelief, into the bookshelf. He puts his hand into the shelf and touches a green giant voluminous book bounded by what seems to be dried out but sturdy vines.

"Azilah, you found the missing treaty - the Amanah!"

2nd December

Nurul: Penan

Location: Sukang Village, Belait

Hmmm, a flooded village, I say.

I look around what looks like supposed to be a normal jungle is filled with water more than ankle deep. Waterlogged leaves and branches line the bottom, small silvery and brown fish dart from tree to tree, living precariously from the threat lurking on the branches and in the sky - the opportunistic and majestic-looking Blue Kingfisher.

A boatman welcome us on board his small and long speedboat, I notice the tattoos on his forearms and his neck, his bulging Adam's apple moving the faded blue ink tattoo as every time he swallows his phlegm to avoid the rude sound of snorting. This boatman wants to look good in front of his white friends. He shows the best smile he can muster, revealing a set of dark brown, nicotine stained teeth, ridden with patches of black dental decay.

I ask the boatman, "Is it always flooded?"

"In the past, the river would flood for a few months only. And in my life, I have seen it become flooded more frequently. Now, it is just flooded all the time."

"Why do you think that's happened?" I ask curiously.

"Global warming," the boatman confidently answers, and then shrugs. Global climate change is now everybody's easy answer to local conundrums.

He starts the small motor engine of his boat and we glide through the flooded jungle, and head out towards the open river, but not before crossing stilted wooden buildings, one of which is a school and another is a government health clinic. In the middle of the three buildings, there is a police station with a satellite dish installed on its rooftop.

"Why would they have a police station here?" I shout at the top of my voice, trying to out-drown the loud whirring and clunking of the motorboat.

"Poachers!" Prof. Simon shouts back to me.

We cross the wide and gentle Belait river. There are two houses on the other side of the river. One on top of a hill, with new paint. I see some pickup trucks parked near the back.

How did they get those vehicles there?

Down below, there is another house, a longhouse, unpainted, its front yard sprawling with running semi-naked toddlers and children and chickens roaming around free-range. We head out to the unpainted wooden longhouse. Our boatman cum local guide tells us this is a 'Penan' settlement longhouse.

"Penan people, as in the nomadic kind of people?"

"Yes, they've settled here. Anyway, your guide for the Ingei Jungle lives here. He would like you to examine his grandfather before he joins you and your group," the boatman

"Well, I'm glad I brought my stethoscope and blood pressure set today!"

I climb up the stairs of the stilted longhouse, the wood sturdy and refusing to creak as screaming children run across the hallway of the longhouse. Inside the longhouse, it is bare, one giant hall covered with lanolin mats and doors across the other side leading to separate rooms, which I assume are bedrooms for the adults.

Everyone is sitting cross-legged around an elderly man, seemingly the head of the longhouse, bare chested, the ribs are visible, barely concealed by the muscle and the skin of his chest. His earlobes have large holes and droop down half way to his shoulders. He no longer wears the large and heavy earrings as they are now deemed unfashionable in the modern age.

Johari, the smoking man and former turtle poacher, sits next to this elderly man. That must be his grandfather then. Johari, whose wife is now the proud owner of my pink 'Saint Laurent Sac De Jour' hand bag is now going to be our guide in Ingei. It's time for him to use his knowledge and skill set for a better and higher purpose. I wonder if others like him, could see the benefit of living a pro-environment life instead of being poachers.

Beside them, further away, I see the women in the room busy scraping the black skin of the hard Kembayau seeds with their tiny knives, giving the Kembayau seeds their striped black and cream appearance before chucking them into a large bowl. I do my best not to look at the bowl of uncooked Kembayau fruits. That's going to be one good tasty supper.

"Doc, can you just check his blood pressure if that's ok with you? He said he felt a bit dizzy today," Johari holds up his grandfather's hand gesturing he will have his blood pressure taken now.

"Sure. Is he on any medication? Does he have high blood pressure?" I ask Johari, expecting a translation to his grandfather.

"No, he is otherwise fit and well. The only medication he takes is a good pack of cigarettes a day," Johari laughs and smiles revealing his own dark tar-stained teeth. I quickly look away from Johari to his grandfather, hoping that that horrible image will not sear in my brain. Johari's grandfather who starts grinning and I see a set of rotting teeth, dark and much more heavily stained with tar.

I check his blood pressure and it is normal. I reassure him, I take out some simple over-the-counter painkillers and a packet of *Stemetil* to help him with his dizziness. As I pack up my blood pressure set, Johari's grandfather grabs my hand tightly. I panic and try to pull away but his grip is strong, this octogenarian.

"She will save you but you must save yourself first. You were born from water, and it is water that will save you," the old man's grip is even tighter. I become frozen in time, hearing his voice in perfect English, but I do not see his lips move at all.

Johari pries his grandfather's hand away from mine.

"Sorry, doc. He's an old man. Sometimes he just likes to grab people's arms especially visitors."

"What did your grandfather just say to me?" I ask, still puzzled by what had happened.

"He didn't say anything. He's been mute for the past 20 or so years," Johari stands up, and I can see from his annoyed look, that he thinks I'm making fun of him and his family.

"Sorry about that, I think maybe it is just the long bumpy trip," I apologize to Johari and wave to his grandfather and quickly get out of the longhouse.

"Doc, the trip to Ingei is still a long way to go, we are barely half-way there."

I am quite lost in my thoughts, that I just nod in response. What did I just experience?

Johari continues as we head towards the boat, "Anyway, I did not get to thank you for helping me out last time and with this job. I am still waiting for the job interview for the hospital security guard job. It'll be good because my best friend; Boi, is also a security guard at one of the hospitals. He's also a poacher … I meant *collector*. I hope he can be involved in this kind of work."

Johari pauses, looking a bit embarrassed as he confesses, "The pay is quite good. I am very surprised by the number of people who are so interested in caring and protecting the jungle and its animals."

I am not listening to him. I keep recalling Johari telling me his grandfather has been mute for the past 20 years. His lips did not move and I heard a voice in my head, which I assumed was his. Was that a hallucination? An eerie discomfort goes down my spine and my stomach starts to cramp.

As the motor boat speeds back into the open river, I look back at the Penan longhouse. His grandfather is there standing by the riverbank, a solemn face with streaks of melancholy.

2nd December

Adib: Melilas

Location: Enroute to Melilas Village

It is such a beautiful cloudy day over the river, whilst far ahead of us, beyond this river and this village area, deep in the jungle dark grey cumulonimbus clouds tower high up into the stratosphere. The wind is blowing her hair, jet black with a streak of dyed brown. Nurul should be enjoying this and yet she seems shaken. Maybe she doesn't like boat rides.

Our boatman takes us past the three stilted buildings. I study the police station and wonder where the policemen are. We head through the flooded jungle, I see wild brown ducks resting in the water, flying off just before the wake of the motorboat reaches them. Arriving at the tarmac jetty, we head off on to our vehicles, passing through the brick red clay territory and onto dark brown and muddy roads. On occasions, we had to climb out to help push the Defender. As the ankle-deep mud and clay splatters on to my face and clothes, the diesel engine of the Land Rover Defender roars defiantly as it triumphs over the mud trap.

I convince myself that this smelly mud is part of my beauty mud therapy. I can't convince Nurul to join us, she blankly refuses to help but it is alright. We let her play princess. She's got something on her mind, she's been quiet since our visit to Sukang village.

***

We arrive at Melilas village, the stilted settlement by the river. I glance at my watch and it's five minutes past five in the evening. Tonight, we will sleep here before heading out to the Ingei jungle on our chartered motorized longboats. The villagers come out in droves to welcome us, jubilant on having new visitors especially visitors who are not poachers or illegal tree-loggers. The tiredness in us disappears, feeling recharged as we shake hands with the villagers, and fist-bump with the younger adults. An elderly man with a Yankees baseball cap and a dark navy blue jacket leads the crowd, and then I start to notice that he is wearing these bright red shorts. He is the village head. It is his village, so I guess it's okay to start his own fashion trend.

A friend of mine; Mahmud, lives here. He is a big Taylor Swift fan and clearly not embarrassed about it, proudly wearing a fake 'You Belong To Me: Taylor Swift' T-shirt he made me promise to buy for him from the last few visits. He is a cool guy but I am starting to loathe taking photos with him, when he wears that same damn t-shirt every single time we meet.

Mahmud fist-bumps me and then quickly swings his body and puts his arm across my shoulder and with the other hand, quickly takes a selfie with his mobile phone. Shock and awe. I did not have time to react.

"Not again, Mahmud - please whatever you do, just don't tag me if you post that photo on Facebook, you know I am not that much of a fan of Taylor Swift," I am surprised by his calculated and probably well-practiced move, and pray somehow that photo of mine becomes corrupted and lost. I remind myself that this is his land, hence his rules.

"Chill-ax, dude. So who's in your group this time?" Mahmud asks me.

"The usual, and yes, we do have a first time, a doctor - let me introduce you to her. Oh, and please don't talk to her about Taylor Swift - she's much older than you, she's probably more familiar with Britney Spears and that old young grandma... er... Madonna," I tell Mahmud, and he nods reassuringly.

"Nurul, can I introduce you to my good friend Mahmud?"

Nurul turns around and stares at Mahmud's t-shirt, "Wow, I am a Taylor Swift fan too!"

Mahmud hugs Nurul tightly. Nurul is caught surprised. I slap my forehead hard.

"I guess this must be the local culture here," Nurul hugs him back.

"Err... Yes yes, it's part of our village culture here... a good tight hug. The real Melilas greeting for err... new visitors," Mahmud hesitates, grinning at me for his *come-back*.

I shoot daggers with my eyes at Mahmud, and then move my head side to side in disagreement with his tactics. Mahmud, now our self-proclaimed tour guide, shows Nurul and the new guests around the small village of Melilas. I notice the shadows in the village start to grow longer and longer, as the sun sinks to the west beyond the realm of trees.

 Mahmud shows us our sleeping quarters - the male sleeping quarters, segregated from female sleeping areas, "Everybody sleeps on the floor, - Melilas style - men in this house and women in that house - I hope you all brought your sleeping bags." Everyone starts reserving their sleeping spots and unpacking some of their gear.

"Good news is that we have been preparing a feast for tonight. A lamb barbecue," Mahmud grins.

After such a long tiring ride, I thought that would be perfect. An oddity catches me off-guard, there are a few dozen 'people' watching us by the tree line: men, women and children in the jungle, some are dressed in white, some are shirtless - baring their chests, keeping themselves barely hidden amongst the trees. I stare at them, and before I can ask anyone, the village headman taps my shoulder reassuringly.

"Don't worry. No one else can see them but you. Of course, most of us villagers can see them too. They are just the *Bunian* people: the invisible people. They won't harm us. We don't bother them and they won't bother us. The most basic and yet difficult rule for Man. Interestingly enough, they've been turning up more frequently and in larger numbers. I think they are just as curious about you as we are," The *Penghulu* or village headman takes off his baseball cap, and combs his grey and thinning hair with his hand.

"Adib, you are gifted. The spirits seem to like you. Maybe they will protect you," he continues.

"That's good then," I justify.

"Well, it's not necessarily all good. If their kind likes you, it could also mean the bad ones would also be attracted to you. Attracted to hurt you. The evil ones," the *Penghulu* puts back his baseball cap.

"Evil *Bunians*?"

"Yes Adib. I said evil *halus* people. Keep your eyes open when you go into Ingei. And I don't mean just your actual eyes. You have another pair that sees beyond light. The Ingei jungle is a sacred jungle. My pagan ancestors believe the Ingei jungle existed before the beginning of time. Always pray for safety when you move within Ingei. Yes?"

"Yes, I will. Thanks for the advice, Mr. *Penghulu*."

He gives me a thumbs-up and I laugh at his gesture, and then stop laughing when I see the Bunian spectators - every male, female and children - mimic the Penghulu, giving their thumbs up.

2nd December

Nurul: Buddies

Location: Melilas Village

Assembled outside near the sleeping quarters, a makeshift marquee has been set up along with a barbecue spit. There is the buzzing of chattering and laughter, as expedition members mingle with each other and the villagers. Everyone always gets excited when there is a lamb barbecue.

Prof. Simon walks up to the centre of the gathering, starts tapping a spoon against his glass. The sharp ringing gathers the crowd's attention.

"Listen PEOPLE, let's orientate with our teams and our jungle buddies before we head for that tasty BBQ!" Prof. Simon calls out to the whole group.

"There's thirty of us heading there. So we're going to just break up into smaller teams where you can be responsible for each other - a buddy system," Shikin shouts out.

"The TV crew will sort themselves out, you can see them in the corner there," Shikin starts pointing to a group of four people standing close to the cameraman.

"Let me introduce the logistics team who will make YOUR time in the jungle as comfortable as possible - Mahmud, our very own local Melilas village liaisons officer - he's the charming guy there with that ...er... nice Taylor Swift shirt," Shikin points to Mahmud, who is thanking everyone as though he had just won some music award.

"And we have Mr. Ayang, Mr. Patih and Mr. Biru who will help us set up Base Camp and they will also sort out our daily supplies." Shikin points to a group of men who seem shy, with faces that have seen much hardship.

"Of course, let me introduce you to 'El-Kapitan'. He's our wonderful cook and also in charge of our security. Where is the Captain?" Shikin asks.

"Someone's got to cook that lamb, my dear Shikin," Simon offers the answer.

"Oh, I guess we'll see him later on."

"In front of you, I've put together some name tags and they're in a pile for a reason, everyone in that pile is your team buddy. You can collect your name tags now and get to know each other".

Everyone walks up and grabs their name from a designated pile. I'm in Team Laila.

At least they didn't call it Team Titans.

A Chinese freckled girl comes up to me, "Welcome to Team Laila, I'm Cindy." I notice her infectious smile, a sparkle of playfulness in her eyes.

"I'm Nurul - I'm the volunteer medical doctor."

"That's great, I can get you to do a check up on me later," Cindy is clearly easily elated.

Please don't ask me for anything.

"Hi Cindy, I'm Eddie - well, you know me already, right? I added you on Facebook three months ago," a young spectacled man with bulky arms, yet shy and seemingly gentle.

"Hi Eddie, I don't know you. We must be in the same university, right?" Cindy replies.

"Same faculty, actually," Eddie replies. I can't help from feeling uncomfortable - cringe moment here. Poor Eddie, I thought.

"I'm Matt, by the way,"

"We know who you are already, thanks for winning the football match for our Uni," Cindy giggles. I'm embarrassed to be a woman, as clearly Cindy's just too old and too smart to play cute dumb girl.

"If this is Team Laila, then you can call me Vol - yes, it is also short for volunteer," Mr. Vol comes up to join the small group banter.

"You're a photographer," I stare at his huge telescopic zoom lens on his Canon camera.

"Yeah, I photograph birds, to be precise," he replies.

"That must be exciting," Cindy laughs a bit.

Whatever she's on, I might want to be on it too.

"Actually, it is. My work also involves raising awareness about our country's broad diversity of birds. I also work to highlight the growing threat these birds face from poachers and human development," Mr. Vol continues.

"Mr. Vol, I am a great fan of your work. I just want to tell you that you inspired me to be part of this movement." Eddie steps up to Mr. Vol, who reciprocates by tapping Eddie's shoulders.

"You see, if we locals don't step up and fight for our own environment, our jungles and our birds, who else will do it? We can't expect white knights to do all the conservation work. This is our land, this is our fight," Mr. Vol inspires Team Laila with his rousing mini-speech.

I watch them talk about inner circle ecological issues as I ponder upon what I would have been doing if I had taken a different path. What if I had not cared about protecting our creatures from the exploitation of poachers and developers? I imagine a wasteful and meaningless life of retail therapy and watching online Korean soap dramas, a life full of *the chase*, and upholding an image of the person who I am not, to conform to others who don't even care about me. And yet deep inside, I know I still have a journey to go to find out who I am. *How do I overcome the hurt inside me?*

2nd December

John: Solace

Location: Melilas Village

Everyone is gathered for the feast.

"Wow, this lamb is just superb," I overhear Mo, the young funky estuarine ichthyologist enthusiastically tell his research partner Zul.

I interject, "So who is the chef?"

"That's Captain Roslan," Mo points to a middle-aged man sporting a neatly trimmed moustache, with a stern face as he cuts the lamb from the spit, softening with a smile with every portion he serves. I start to notice the long scar running from his left hand to his left elbow. That must have been something horrible.

"Retired captain, that is. I hear he was a former ranger. He prefers to be addressed as El-Kapitan," another researcher Dina joins our conversation, with a plastic plate in her hand. I don't remember what research she is doing in this trip. I think it's something to do with the study of mushrooms.

"Former ranger? He sounds quite hard," Joanna, whose research into rare jungle frog species has gotten most of her research papers published in international scientific journals. She looks at me flirtatiously. "John, do you think you could ever be as hard as a ranger?"

I turn away from Joanna. I'm too old fashioned for that kind of flirtation. I head out to my bag and take out my *Snowpeak* titanium plate.

"Nice, you brought your own plate," Adib looks quite impressed.

"Don't like single-use plastic plates, you know they're not good for the environment."

Adib nods in agreement.

"Hey John, I wanna introduce you to an international photographer who is also from England"

"Hi John, you already know me, I'm Miss Fox," Louise puts her hand out to shake my hand.

"Hi Louise, it's been a long time, how have you been?" I uncomfortably shake the hand of my ex-wife's former best friend.

"See what a small world it is, isn't it?" Adib laughs out. I turn to Adib, signalling him to make himself scarce.

"I've been good, John. Been traveling the world since you know... People call it wanderlust - it's the new me" Louise smiles uncomfortably.

"That's good to hear, Louise." She does look much better than the last time I saw her. Of course, back then both of our worlds had shattered and imploded.

"John, in case you didn't know, Susan didn't last long with Ronnie. Last I heard she's back in High Wycombe and living with a divorced builder there. Sometimes she writes or emails me. I don't know if she's happy or not. I think she was better off with you."

Although I could see she was comfortable mentioning her ex-husband's name, for me it was different. The mention of my ex-wife's name pierces holes into my heart. Repressed memories re-emerge like short video clips playing in my head.

"How's your ex-husband?" I just had to ask.

"Don't care and don't want to know. Though I heard he is now settled in Spain."

Louise suddenly hugs me. "You're doing well, John. You'll move on. We all do eventually. Everything happens for a reason. Look at me, I'm a survivor. So are you."

I smile back, but in my heart, I scream and cry as my heart hardens and then shatters to a thousand pieces again.

Louise walks away to greet other members of the team as I recall fragments of the past.

"John, will you marry me?" Susan, all blonde and freckled, the epitome of happiness, places a diamond ring on to my palm.

"Susan, isn't it the man who should propose?"

She shrugs, "It is a leap year, John."

"In that case, yes. Yes, I will marry you Susan and love you for the rest of my life," I slide the sparkling diamond ring on her slender finger. True love will never break. True love is enduring.

Another fragment of my past reappears, so raw and painful, I fight myself from my tears.

"You ruined my life! You held me back from my dreams! I gave you my everything and you gave me nothing!" Susan screams as she grabs her suitcase and heads towards the door. I try to stop her but she shoves me hard and I fall on to the floor.

"John, I am in love with Ronnie. We're heading for a new life. Better than staying here in this country, playing jungle protectors to people who don't even care about their own home!" She sobs angrily, whilst I remain sitting on the floor, trying to comprehend her confession.

"Louise is your best friend, how could you? How could you both?"

*She doesn't answer back, she walks out and slams the
door.*

What did I do wrong?

Where did I go wrong? Were we not madly in love? Love
should have prevailed. I keep asking the questions to
myself. I'm too old to have heartache. No longer hungry, I
head back to my backpack, put the unused plate back.
Sobbing alone, I rummage through and find my
Emergencies Only bottle is still there.

2nd December

Manis: Bugang

Location: Ingei Reserve Jungle, Belait

"Let's take a rest here," my father panting out of breath, the sibut fruits seem to feel much heavier than before. Everyone is out of breath, and sweat has permeated all of my clothes.

"Brother, we need to cross the river before sunset," my uncle pats my father on the shoulder.

I look up to the trees and notice how the orange hue starts to affect the colour of the leaves, the shadows longer, playing and swinging from tree to tree. I start to worry.

I muster my energy and stand up. "Let's head to that river now."

"That's the spirit, the school champion 800-metres runner can lead the way for us," my mother stands up too.

We continue our journey towards the river - which is maybe a half hour away on a normal pace - but our backs are aching and our sore feet start dragging each step. The trip back home always seems to be longer when it comes to the jungle. The parents in the group constantly look back to check on everyone in the group. No one wants to lose anyone here in the jungle especially when it gets dark.

A loud cackling fills the jungle, a loud thumping then rumbling of the jungle. It is so near, I can feel it thump and rumble with my heart. We all turn around and see the jungle trees are shaking violently, there is something big rushing through. I hear breaking and falling trees. Is this the same thing as before?

"Everyone drop your bags! Get ready for anything," my father drops his rucksack, spilling the sibut fruits, and we all follow suit. His parang raised even higher this time than last time. His brother stands next to him, I can see bewilderment in their eyes.

My mom wants grabs a sapling nearby and uproots it, and starts hitting it against a nearby tree.

This will ward it away.

A giant shadow flies over us, for a moment eclipsing the dying sun. My mom slumps down. She must have seen it better than the rest of us.

"This is not a time to lose hope, Siah!" my father yells at my mother.

In the distance, I see the shrubs and trees part and break easily as something storms towards us. I can barely see it:

giant shadows. No, they are not shadows but very dark figures heading towards. Faceless.

I feel the bile in my throat, I freeze with fear.

"Siah, Serunai, take our children and run!" yells my father to my mother and aunt.

My uncle tenses up and shouts to us, "Don't look back, just run... RUN NOW!!"

"PROTECT THE CHILDREN!" they both scream.

My mother grabs the hands of both of my siblings, carrying my youngest brother and sprinting towards the river. My aunt hesitates a moment then pulls Andie and Raneh, rushing off after my mother.

"MANIS, what are you doing? I told you to run!" my dad screams at me.

I cry, my legs burn with pain, refusing to move.

The humanoid faceless entities are now in front of my dad and my uncle. Six of them, at least 10 feet tall. I hear evil laughter coming from these evil creatures.

God, please rescue us.

My father and uncle slash their parangs towards the entities, but they just slice through them with no effect. One of the entities kicks my father and he flies into the air and lands on a tree near me.

His right leg, a bone juts out from below his knee.

"Manis, please, please RUN!" My father pleads as he musters all his strength to stand up, on his one good leg. He mutters a spell and then yells out an ancient Iban battle cry. My uncle responds with the same battle cry.

My feet respond to me and I start running for my life towards the river.

As I jump across the fallen tree obstacles, I hear my father's wail and then silence behind me. Tears fly out from my eyes, blurring wish-wash of my vision and the stinging of branches hitting my face. I do not care. I must get out across the river.

There is a clearing up ahead that was not there before.

I see Andie's mother's eyes stare at me, her mouth in a scream frozen by death, her abdomen a pool of blood, her legs disjointed. Poor Raneh lies in two different parts, her upper body connected with her lower body by her entrails. I scream hard but nothing comes out. I scream out harder but no voice comes from my throat.

Andie lies nearby in a pool of his blood on the jungle floor, his white shirt soaked completely in red, leaves strewn with blood. He is wrapping his hands round his head, his broken legs splayed. He does not see me as he struggles to cry out for help.

I see four of the dark creatures surround him taking turns to shout at him in whatever language it is they speak.

One of them bends down towards Andie's ear and shouts out in Malay:

"I will translate for you, human"

"Die, son of a whore. Die, filth. Die fucker."

"I will record this for my friends at home to watch you die," says another entity.

I cannot believe what is happening, screaming profanity at my dying cousin who is only eleven years old. Is the child's final moments to be accompanied by a demonic descant of hatred by real demons?

Andie stops breathing and one of the demons steps forward and starts kicking his body, "The child was filth and should be wrapped in pig meat and then set fire till everything burns away."

"Kill all Man!" the demons start screaming, as they turn their heads round to me and although they are faceless I can feel their stare burn holes in my chest.

"Hilaga is the light unto this world!" they chant.

Move legs, move!

I run as fast as my legs can carry me towards the river, pushing through the last shrubs of this jungle to the river bank, fighting the sick feeling and taste of vomit in my mouth.

At the riverbank, the orange light blends with the darkening jungle, as I see my mother standing, feet up to ankle deep in the riverwater. Her back facing me, she clutches a small dagger with both hands, my brother and sister lie face down by her feet on the wet earth, motionless.

"MOM!" I scream at the top of my voice.

"Manis, you must save yourself. You must live for the rest of us," She says calmly, her head refusing to turn around.

She changes her stance with her right leg back, shifting her weight towards it.

What is she doing?

As I look up ahead, I notice to my horror, poorly hidden, on the other side of the river bank, stands a much, much larger demon, a dark faceless figure over forty feet tall. I shudder and gasp.

"Run, Manis."

There is no time for argument. I take a right turn running upriver away from whatever that thing was. I hear behind me, a loud demonic roar, followed by her screaming and shouting and a wail going up into the air and down, and then a splash, and then a thud. I dare not look. I dare not think. My breathing and my heart pounding is the only sound I hear.

My vision turns red and blurry at the edges. My legs move on their own, as though disconnected from my mind. I notice I am climbing uphill. The path by the river bank disappears and with no access to safety, I make my own path - without much thought - and enter the jungle again, estimating where the river is. *Must keep near the river.*

The ground is slippery and I keep falling as I struggle to climb. I will not be stopped. I grab on to anything: giant liana vines and tree roots, kicking my feet into the soft soil. I climb, as if this would be the last time I am to ever climb a hill. All four limbs scramble to make it to the top.

I hear the loud sound of water crashing up ahead and ominously, the loud rumbling behind me.

There is no choice but to follow the safety of water.

I push through an opening in the jungle foliage and see a huge waterfall appear before me. Its fast falling water rushing down a series of steps, like a series of five waterfalls, cutting this mysterious dark grey stone.

I must make it across.

I dash across the rock surface, slippery with algae but my feet are light and nimble as I jump across the body of water falling and land safely on the other side.

I hear broken branches behind me and a cackle. I automatically turn my head as I simultaneously step forward, as a dark black projectile misses me by a hair's thread. The skin on my ears singe with a fire I cannot see. I slip and fall down onto the rock surface 'step' below. Scrambling with all four limbs, I desperately try to keep myself steady, and steer myself away from danger but instead I slip to the middle, into the waterfall.

Cold water engulfs me, drowning me as I struggle to breath. I keep falling down below each time hitting rock and then slipping further down each waterfall step. No matter how many times I try to steer away from the centre of the waterfall, I keep falling, hitting my head several times and my limbs getting scratched and numb after each fall.

Falling into the pool below, the cold water pushes me down, refusing to let me reach the surface, my arms and legs flail to push myself away from the suction of the underwater current and the waterfall. My lung bursting to breathe. My head pounding in pain. I hit the bottom of the pool bedrock, my shoulder scraping the bedrock, kept down by the force of the waterfall above.

Is this the way I will die? Drowned under a waterfall?

Then I hear her voice. You must live for the rest of us.

With all my strength, I push myself off the bottom of the pool, kicking furiously towards the surface. I see my reflection mirrored on the surface of the water, crashing into my reflection as I burst free to the surface. The current tries to pull me down, but my body refuses to sink. I gasp for air, my lungs find relief with each breath. My heart thrashes in my own chest, as I see that I am behind the waterfall, a small recess in the rock allows me to rest and hide as I see large shadows rapidly play around on the blurred translucent wall of moving water. I pray silently and desperately for protection and safety. Nothing like this has ever happened before, the jungle has never been filled with the terrors I have witnessed. *Why? Why us? Why me? What did we do wrong to deserve this punishment?*

As the sun sets, the waterfall becomes dark. I stop praying for myself and begin to pray for my family who are now no more. I sob quietly, still worried that whatever is out there will come back. Tired and sleepy, I clutch a loose rock with my trembling hand, for both comfort and protection. As I lay there, under the deafening waterfall, half-immersed in the cold water, shivering, I decide I must abandon my old beliefs now and embrace my new faith and the one true God, unwitnessed.

If I must die today, then I will not die as a non-believer.

2nd December

Nurul: Dream

Location: Melilas Village, Labi

Funny thing about dreams is that I don't remember going to sleep. I see myself standing by a large surreal lake. In the middle of the lake, there is a woman who looks like me, except she is in a light green dress, with beautiful flower ornaments on her head and gold jewellery strap around her sleeveless arms.

Who is she? Why does she look like me?

I take a step forward; my bare feet feel the soft moist soil. I touch the lake surface with my big toe. It feels just right, neither cold nor warm.

The lady in the middle of the lake waves her hand towards me, beckoning me to approach her. Her warm smile is reassuring.

"Who are you?" I shout across the lake. She responds with another smile but does not answer. The only sound I hear is the echoing of my voice across the surface of the lake.

I take a few steps into the lake, expecting to find myself immersed up to at least ankle deep, instead I find myself standing on top of the surface of the reflective lake. Confidently, I take giant strides to the woman who looks like me.

When I reach the middle of the lake, she sheds a tear, and whispers, "It looks like we are going to meet again, after such a long, long time."

I am confused, "What do you mean?"

She kisses me on the cheeks and points down to the lake.

I see in between our own reflections, a glimpse of a woman running through the jungle, that woman. She's me. She looks frightened. It looks like I am running for my life!

"What's happening? What does this mean?" I ask her. I want to put my hand on her, but I just don't feel it is right to touch her. She seems so... royal.

She hugs me, "I will be with you, always."

There is a loud piercing scream that jolts the both of us. She lets go, the lake is filled with troubled and unsynchronized ripples, the reflectiveness of the lake is gone. The air is filled with distant cries and wails. I look behind me, and to my horror, in the distance, I see giants with no face, throwing and breaking smaller silhouettes of people.

"Hide!" The lady in green pushes me down into the lake, as a hole opens before my feet. I fall with the water, screaming.

I wake up gasping and then realise it was just a dream, a vivid dream.

"It's just a dream, it's just a dream," I mutter to myself.

I am soaking in my own perspiration. As I wipe my face, I notice I have something soft in my right hand. I switch on the flashlight app on my phone and see that it is a shimmering green piece of fabric.

How did that get there? This can't be real, this is just too much.

I pocket the fabric, stand up and walk past the mosquito netting. Everyone around me is in deep slumber on the floor in their own sleeping bags, a mini-orchestra of the gentle snoring of a few of my female colleagues.

I look out and up, the night sky is filled with stars and bright moonlight from a quarter moon illuminates the village and the surrounding jungle. I take a few steps out and jump off the stilted hut. It would be a good time to enjoy a night walk. I head towards the river, awed by the moonlit reflection on the river, it is a breath-taking view.

I take a deep breath and breathe in the sweet smell of the night air infused with the sweet aroma of a successful lamb barbecue. Walking on, I start to recognise the shapes of the different trees, especially the silhouette of the weeping willow tree. There is something underneath the weeping willow tree. As I get closer, I notice it is not a moonlit reflection but the shape of a girl dressed in white, with long black hair.

I freeze with fear and half mutter "Ponti..."

'Don't say it out loud, just in your head. *Pontianak*.' I take a step back but it is too late. The Pontianak girl heads towards me.

I turn around and run back towards the hut, my legs trembling with each step.

'Is this what that dream is all about?'

I turn my head to look back and notice the Pontianak vampire girl is so much closer. I can see a vengeful snarling face and she is within an arm's grasp from me. The hut is too far away.

I trip and tumble down head first, on to the moist cold grass.

I'm a goner.

Screaming, I turn on my back, kicking my feet into the air, my arms punching towards a pending attack. Futile.

A harsh beam of light blinds me.

"Hey Nurul, it's us - don't worry - it's us.. Adib and John!"

"What are you guys doing here? I was about to be attacked by a Ponti..."

"Don't say it…, don't say the full name please, don't mention that here… not at night, not here… please,' Adib interrupts me. Adib helps me up. I rejoice as I have been given a second chance in life.

John is smiling sheepishly. "Yeah, Nurul. Doc, don't even say that word out loud. PONTIANAK. PONTI-ANAK! Out here, on a night like this - That would just be plainly asking for it... *Cabul* you know."

Adib and I stare at John gobsmacked, as though he had just walked across a tripwire.

"What are you looking at? I'm not afraid. Who is afraid of a bloody female vampire? My ex-wife was one, she bled me dry and then left me!" John starts rambling out loudly.

Adib tries to hush John, but John just refuses.

"Look Adib, look at me, I'm white, I'm a bloody Englishman. I don't believe in this superstition of *cabul*. I mean who came up with that dumb rule? If you don't mention the name of the ghost or demon, it will not come after you. That just sounds so stupid. STUPID, you hear!" John blabbers on.

Adib gives up trying to silence John.

"We better head back to the huts, before John does something stupid - I think he partied on his own a bit too much tonight," Adib gestures with his hands that John had too much to drink from his secret stash.

"What! I've only just started. Come on, Miss Pontianak! Come and get me. I'll make a real woman vampire out of you! I called your name! So you come here and play with me, Big Daddy John of Beaconsfield. I am not afraid of you. Pontianak, come on out and play! The local myth says that I should hammer a nail to your head so that you'd turn into a beautiful woman! Ha! Not true! Coz' all women, no matter how pretty they are, are nothing but Pontianaks!" John pounds his chest and starts screaming more sexist taunts and then starts laughing in the dead of the night.

Thankfully, the walk back to the hut quickly tires down the inebriated John.

Although, I now feel much safer in the presence of these two men, I feel I had a close call. Was it real? Was I really being chased by a killer Pontianak? I can't help from feeling that someone or something is watching me.

I try to sleep but end up being unable to sleep, edged on by the recent surge of adrenaline. I sit next to Adib and appreciate how brave he is. I wonder if he really saw it: the Pontianak that was chasing me. Why did it not attack them? Was it because John was too drunk? I don't think so. It must have been Adib. Maybe it was afraid of him. In the open-air hut, where all the men are sleeping, I slowly lie down next to Adib. He promises he will not sleep, sits up and keeps watch. I feel safe and easily fall asleep, in spite of John's earthmoving snoring.

This time I am dreamless.

2nd December

Selym: Amanah

Location: Hilaga City Archives Hall, Hilaga

The Amanah treaty is here!

Of all people, it was Azilah who found it. She has no idea how significant this find is.

I walk to the dusty bookshelf, brushing past a startled and confused Azilah.

Is it because of this treaty? Why did she scream?

I look at the huge green book, and notice that there is no dust gathered on this, compared to the other books on the bookshelf.

"Is someone cleaning and reading this book regularly?" I ask myself.

"I remember when I was much younger the day when the two tribes signed this treaty that has brought so much peace and prosperity to Hilaga."

"We were at war? With whom?" Azilah asks.

"Those from the dying village - it's not important any more. This treaty is no longer relevant. We can read through and see if there was any information related to portal creation. I am sure Lord Jahat would be very pleased to hear about this find," I pick up the giant book, with my arms extended deep in the bookshelf recess, expecting to find the book very heavy, but instead the book is feather-light. It slides out easily - its green wooden hardcover glistens surreal.

"This is why it is dust-free - the cover is made from the back of the old Great Tree - even the binding is made from the vines of that tree," Azilah points out.

"What do you know about the old Great Tree?" I ask.

"I used to play there every day as a child, before it was mysteriously struck down," she replies.

"I would not have expected less from someone of nobility such as yourself."

"There is no more nobility since the noble families have been abolished, I am merely your student, Master Selym."

I ponder about Azilah's words. She still rejects her birth right - which is good. Noble houses no longer have a place in Hilaga.

"Being my mere student? Surely, there must be some honour in ending up as a student of mine. You did have to beat all those other candidates!"

Azilah becomes apologetic but I reassure her I was merely teasing her. We both look at the Amanah book in my arms, unclasping the silver metal lock on it and flipping open the book to reveal dark brown pages with barely visible writing. There are three signatures on each page. Some of the pages are so faded that the writing is not visible at all.

"Let's bring this to the round table and examine more closely."

"The pages are made of dried and processed *Simpur* leaves - these are meant to last an eternity. The writing should not have faded."

"Azilah, nothing lasts for an eternity - everything fades into darkness with time."

I tuck the giant book under my right arm, and although the book is quite light, I feel quite drained. My right shoulder starts to stiffen and ache. My eyelids become heavy and my vision blurs momentarily. In the corner of my eye, I see a glimpse of someone familiar and yet so unfamiliar, standing in between the bookshelves. I turn towards it, but there is no one there. I cannot see any of the Keepers nearby.

Who was that?

The hairs on my neck straighten up, and my neck tenses up and begins to ache as well.

'It has been a long day for me,' I say to myself.

"Azilah, please take the Amanah - I am surprisingly very exhausted."

Azilah obeys, "It has been nothing short of an interesting day, hasn't it?"

"There are sleeping quarters on the right side if you ever get tired. I am heading there now."

She nods attentively, and as I walk away from her, I could not help from thinking that she won't be sleeping tonight. I turn around the corner and look back towards Azilah. As I turn my head back, I see a white streak pass by in front of me. I curse and choose to ignore it as I fight the tiredness of my limbs, and a sleepiness that is trying its best to win my soul that struggles to stay awake - caught in between the world of being awake and sleep - glimpses of my distant memories play in front of me.

Why? Why now and why of all times here?

***

My father, Lord Ramesh, holds my small meek hands as we walk into the Great Hall, as it was called back in those days. Lord Ramesh is in ceremonial wear, a thin bronze plate shaped like a half bird, half butterfly covers most of his otherwise bare chest, I cannot stop from admiring the dazzling blue, green and red stones that lay on this already shiny bronze ornament. I touch the etched patterns on the plate, but my father holds my hand away.

"Behave now, Selym. Today is a special day, do not embarrass me in front of our guests."

"Who are the guests, father?"

"The leaders from Azzah and a few of the leaders from Man," he replies.

"But I thought they were our sworn enemies, father."

Our entourage of guards stops at the exact moment my father stops walking. He bends down on one knee, and looks me in the eyes, "Selym, my son, we had never intended to fight, but somehow we got confused into fighting each other. We don't even remember why we fought in the first place. We recently found out we have something in common. Do you know what that is Selym?"

My mind wanders and wants to shoot out so many answers, so many guesses but the way my father's voice booms out and echoes in the hall, makes me timid and so I choose to remain quiet.

"Are you not at least going to give me a wild guess?" he smiles and then laughs, whilst all around us our Hilagaan guards with their ceremonial bronze spears and red fluff remain indifferent, emotionless faces. Duty bound to be fearless.

"My son Selym, we all desire peace and harmony. Our people and the people from Azzah, and even Man - we all actually want to live in peace. That is the key to happiness."

"Does this mean we won't have to go to war again?" I ask naively.

"I hope we have come to the end of all wars, Selym."

Lord Ramesh stands up, grabs my hand and we start walking. The entourage of guards follow us.

Did I see my father's eyes well-up as he spoke? Did he really desire peace so badly?

I look round. Everywhere there are mirrors on both sides of the hall, and yet there are no reflections of anyone but me and my father. His reflection has a blue tinge around it, whilst mine seems to be enveloped by a white light.

What strange mirrors...

***

I catch myself from tripping and falling on to the floor. I turn round, relieved that no one has seen me stumble. I open the doors to the sleeping quarters and seek refuge on the cold bed.

TIGA

3rd December

3rd December

Selym: Why

Location: Hilaga City Locked Archives Hall, Hilaga City, Ifrit

***

There are six rooms in the sleeping quarters, all of them are empty. I walk into the first bedroom on the left, its door creaking loudly revealing a neat but bare room. The wooden bed has been set like a military bed, crisp square folds of the blanket. I could not expect anything less from them: The Keepers of the Locked Archives were former warriors who served with the different regiments, and in spite of decades of non-violence and their solitary life, their military habits die hard. Why did they decide to choose this path? Was it by choice or by instruction from their commanders?

I throw myself onto the bed, hard springs barely absorbing me. I know this bed is too regimental for me to have a comfortable sleep. Let lethargy be my sandman, but this would be mere wishful thinking. There is an unsettling feeling, brooding, unseen and unexplained. Although, I am not moving in my bed, my heart is caught in the full onslaught of the storm winds. My eyes search wildly at the plain ceilings, trying to explore and seek refuge in the hairline cracks, but to no avail. Tired of the ceilings, I start staring lower at the wall in front of me.

A silhouette stands at the end of my bed.

Who would dare? Does he not know that I am a great warrior? I can strike him easily even from where I lay on this bed.

I push myself further up onto the bed, I will see him better, or for the worse. I know him, I know his face. Distorted, his eyes have popped out halfway - just the way I had left him before his body was dropped, slamming back into the boat. I grin in reflex.

It's just a dream.

The dead fisherman starts to speak, crying in tears from eyes that do not meet mine, white-out irises of the dead, "Why did you have to kill me?"

Is this real?

"Why did you have to kill me?" Pleading for an answer, with a wail of despair.

What is happening? Don't worry, I must be tired. It will disappear.

The dead fisherman yells out, "Why did you have to kill me?"

I jump out of my bed, hurling myself in perfect symmetry and form towards it. Kerambit dagger in one hand, I stab it with no mercy, in reflex I smile as I watch the reverse blade dagger dig deep into his chest. To my surprise, both the dagger and my own hands passes through his chest. In my follow-through action, even my whole body passes through the dead fisherman.

He's not there. A figment of my imagination, my tired mind in disarray.

I turn and meet face to face with the dead fisherman yelling, "WHY! WHY!!"

I frantically horse-kick him in the head and start throwing wide swinging punches towards him, but nothing. Nothing, but air, and yet he stands. Nothing connects.

I contemplate on leaving and shouting for help, but at the same time, I can't risk anyone thinking there is something wrong with me. I am a leader; I am a master. I am supposed to be a ghost in the human world and here I am haunted by a ghost in my world. Such terrible irony of war between the two worlds. I look at my execution victim, it is nothing and nothing will disappear back to whatever it came from.

"Answer me now: Why did you have to kill me ???"

I must rest, it will disappear on its own. I walk back towards my bed, ignoring the spectre.

"Don't you dare turn away from me, you killer!"

My hands start to burst in flames, spreading quickly onto my chest and head. I scream in pain and agony, as the dead fisherman shouts back, "All crimes must be paid for, in this world and the next!"

I gasp for breath as the smoke and flames suffocates me, desperately trying to smother the fire burning my face and hands with the bed. The flames are gone as quickly as it appeared and I find myself sitting up on the bed once again, staring at the empty space at the end of my bed. I look at my hands and feel my face, there has been no fire. To my relief, it was merely a bad dream. I rest back on the bed, and close my eyes. I really need to sleep.

"You didn't answer my question: Why did you have to kill me?" the same voice asks me.

I sit up calmly and see the ghost, the dead fisherman at the end of my bed.

"You are dead. I killed you, you are the product of my tired mind trying to sleep," I answer very calmly and slowly.

"Why did you have to kill me?" The dead fisherman's foul breath fills the room. Semi-choking, I breathe through my mouth - holding back the regurgitation of my stomach contents, "You already asked me. I am not going to answer you."

"Why did you have to kill me?" it insists on getting its answer. I cannot keep my calm any more.

"Do you have any idea who I am? Stay quiet dead human - you are the enemy - you and your kind have taken everything from my people," I should have known better than to reply back in anger.

"I am nobody's enemy. I have taken nothing that belongs to anyone. Everything belongs to everyone!" it yells back.

"You are nothing, a mere nothing in a world where you understand nothing! Only caring for your immediate needs, your life and the lives of other humans who have no value. You are a mere bundle of wasted emotions and petty yet destructive desires. Why were you created in the first place?" I shout back at it. It does not reply and I assume it has its answer, "I am going to sleep - bother someone else, you pathetic man."

The dead fisherman wails in agony, crying loudly the names of his loved ones. I start to see shapes on the bare plain white walls: shadows. More than mere shadows. I see the others, the other ten. One of them: a young girl, her broken neck still bears the crushing marks of my hands, her face with frozen tears, and permanently rolled up eyes - revealing only the white sclera. She is the first to walk towards the edge of the bed. I refuse to be afraid of her.

"What about me? Why did you have to kill me?"

I refuse to answer her. I owe her nothing, I owe her no explanation. Why should I tell her that in the heat of the moment I snapped her neck because she happened to be with the rest of them? Or maybe, I could not resist her?

"You know my mom is still praying and waiting for me to come home to her," the young girl sobs continually. "Were you fair to her and me? Is the world going to be fair to you?"

"Why did you have to kill me?" There are many other voices, all of which I recognise - even if I had only been acquainted with them for a short while.

The nine others step forward: three brothers who were illegal 'Gaharu tree' loggers, their torsos deformed and limbs mangled; three bird trappers whose arms I had broken into three parts before crushing their hearts with my bare hands; two trespassers whom I kicked and trampled to death. They deserved it. They were snapping away with their tiny photographic recording devices, too busy to see the signs of their impending deaths; last and strangest, a sinful man who had sought redemption deep in the jungle, in my jungle. He was very different; he did not show me how frightened when I revealed myself to him. I recall how he started confessing his sins to his society - he was special. He held himself back from screaming for as long as he humanly could when I started breaking every bone there was to break in this tiny but condemned man. All of those I had executed in the name of Justice, in the name of War, in the name of Peace, for my people. And yet, here their ghosts chant with the same last look on their faces, their faces of death, "Why did you have to kill me?"

I scream back, "Because you are the enemy, you are the killers, you are the destroyers of our worlds. I will kill more of your kind!"

Moving closer, surrounding the edge of my bed, they continue to chant, "Why did you have to kill me?"

"It is my right to kill you, you are all mere vermin!"

"Why did you have to kill me?"

"Quiet! Get out of here! You have no right to be here!"

"Why did you have to kill me?"

"You were all legit kills! I had execution orders from the highest command!"

"Why did you have to kill me?"

I desperately punch, push and kick each and every one of them, but it makes no sense, they are like shadows and I hit nothing but air.

"What can you do? Haunt me all night? You can't touch me. You can't even kill me," I spit in anger at the three bird trappers, there were the ones who upset me the most, they had no right to complain about their ends, they deserved it. For every single injury, crushing and kicking. I watch as my spit passes through their non-existent bodies and fall down onto the floor behind them.

"Why did you have to kill me?" Persistent. They all look at me, as though I can bring them back through some twisted redemption.

"I am not afraid of any of you! I am not even afraid of death, and that is why I will never be afraid of you," I stare at the spectre of the young girl who keeps crying and asking me the same question over and over again.

"I am a warrior! This is my way, when your people are in my way!" I beat my chest in defiance, and then shake my clenched fist in the air, staring back at their faces of death.

"I am not afraid of death, you hear!" The muscles in my neck tighten stiff and become numb, "The way of the warrior is the resolute acceptance of death."

The ghosts pause and I breathe a sigh of relief, bringing my clenched fist down and then the small girl starts to cry and so do the others. And they ask me again, "Why did you have to kill me?"

Why do they all appear before me now? Why now? Was it because of the Amanah book I found? I give up and throw myself on to the bed. Grabbing the hard pillow, I cover my face with it.

"Why did you have to kill me?"

They lean closer as their horrendous stench of their rotting flesh and foul breath pass through the pillow along with the barely muffled murmurs of their chants. Pulling and stretching the pillow, I cover my ears, pressing hard and doing my best to ignore the constant murmurs and the occasional shouting of the same question. I start to wonder if I have started to lose my mind.

Why am I having these hallucinations? I am not a murderer. I am a hero to my people. I am a soldier. I am a great warrior. I am Master Selym the Saviour of Hilaga, the sole surviving son of the slain Lord Ramesh. I bear the weight of avenging his death, even if I lose my soul.

3rd December

Rahman: Tuah

Location: Tuah's house, The Capital, Bumi

"Father, are you sure we have to go today?" My son asks insistently but he already knows the answer, and hence I do not reply and simply respond with a nod. Yesterday was a warning, delivered by an unknown spirit that has always chosen to be in contact with me when there is a storm ahead. I cannot ignore this warning.

Rahmat drives me to my former mentor's house, Master Tuah. He used to live in a small wooden house, until recently his son, a successful real estate developer, bought him a beautiful modern house in the suburbs of the Capital. As we pass through the gates and the driveway, I notice there is a gardener tending to his pink and orange Bougainvillea flowers. Master Tuah has really upped his standards since the last time I saw him. His filipino maid opens the door and ushers me into his living room. Rahmat kindly excuses himself from entering the living room. I can see why. It is dark, the windows have been taped and covered with aluminium foil, blocking the sun. I see a large LED TV screen mounted onto the wall, showing today's soap drama from Indonesia. Master Tuah sits in the corner, both feet on a stool, wrapping himself with an old blanket. I greet him and hoarsely he welcomes me to his house.

"I like your house Master Tuah," I compliment him.

"What use is it to me? I have all this but I don't have my health. Rahman, the real wealth of life is health, not money. I keep telling my son that. Take care of his body. I hate my body. I know I should be grateful; my body has taken the wrath of having too much sugar!" Master Tuah barks, almost shouting at me.

"You have diabetes, Master Tuah?" I ask.

"Yes, at first, those foreign doctors the government hired used to tell me to cut down on my sugar, which, of course, I did. But now, I just found out from one of the local doctors, my cousin's nephew - it's the rice. It's the bloody rice that is the sugar."

I stay quiet and tentatively listen.

"Of course, rice is sugar. I wish the local doctors had graduated sooner, and told me this earlier. Now my feet are in constant pain, even when there is nothing seemingly wrong with my feet," Master Tuah complains.

We both stay quiet as he strokes his lower legs.

"Master, are you still aware of anything new?" I ask him cautiously.

"Of course, I am aware. I am ALWAYS aware of what happens in their world. I fought three generations of their kind, those bloody Hilagaans!" Master Tuah pauses, picking up a glass of water from a nearby table.

"Their colours may be different, but the story is always the same. Seeds of hate and destruction are always sowed to create a divide between those who know and those who have yet to know."

"What does that mean, Master?" I am puzzled. I promise myself not to give cryptic lessons to my future students.

"Rahman, the politics and the power struggles in their world is designed to naturally create a clash between the two worlds."

"What power struggle? How do you know these things, Master?"

"Rahman, what have I taught you all these years? Was it all like pouring water on yam leaves and watching it all drain away? What happens in their world is happening in our world too! This is the *'dunia akhir zaman'* - The Era of the End of the World!" he smacks the soft fabric arm of his sofa-chair.

I am unmoved by his dramatism and decide to stay quiet. I have been trained not to talk back to elders, in particular a guru.

"I am too old to spoon-feed you and you are too old to be spoon-fed. You go figure it out, Rahman."

"Did they come to you, Master?" I ask.

"Of course, not. They simply can't enter this house anymore. I have made sure of that using a special protective spell, my very own *guris*. You can say it's a 3D *guris*, they can't even enter from the roofs. But I do see glimpses of a future so uncertain and so bleak, I would be so grateful if I could die early."

Master Tuah continues with rather ungraceful hands, dancing stiffly in the air, "I know you want me to guide you but as you can see I am too unwell to travel into the jungle with you. I am not afraid of death, as you well know the Hilagaans have tried to kill me before. Last time I checked, I still have a bounty for my death. I reckon my greatest pain for them is to ensure that I die naturally without them being able to do anything about it."

Taking another sip of water, Master Tuah points to a photo of a young man on a coffee table. "I want you to take my late sister's son with you and that would make you a team of five men. His name is Azan. He's green, but I am sure he will learn fast. I promised his mother on her dying bed that I would teach him our ways. You can help me keep that promise, won't you?"

I nod quietly, knowing that I cannot refuse Master Tuah. He is my true Guru.

We stay quiet for a few minutes, and then Master Tuah reveals some more to me.

"A few nights ago, I had a dream of a young man who has many shadows with him. He is now with a woman who is much more than she looks. They both have no idea what is really happening. You must protect them. I fear they will be lost from our world. Travel to the ancient well of the Seven Kings near Belabau Village of the Tutong District and I pray that everything will fall in place on its own. We must have faith in fate, Rahman. That's all to it, just faith in fate."

We are interrupted by Master Tuah's maid bringing in some cold refreshments.

"Rahman, your time is up - take the drinks and you can keep the damn glasses too. Bring it home and tell your kind wife that it's a petty gift from me to your family. Now, go Rahman and leave me alone. Don't forget what I just told you," Master Tuah demands, pointing his index finger at me. I can't tell if he is scolding me or rewarding me. I dare not answer, I dare not interject, even though I have so many questions. There are so many disadvantages of being in a subservient society. I guess I must play my role and just nod and smile. If only we were free. Maybe I will leave that to my grandchildren to figure it out.

"Oh, here's a final lesson from me before you go. Never promise anyone anything when they are dying. You'll end up regretting it."

As I wonder about that final piece of advice from Master Tuah, I nod agreeably and kiss his hand, bidding him farewell. I hope it would not be the last time I see him, for both our sakes.

3rd December

Serigala: Price

Location: Red Building, Hilaga city, Ifrit

The team seems jubilant at their first kill mission in the Ingei jungle. After traveling back to Hilaga via the MATA portal, everyone heads to the briefing at the top floor of my late grandfather's ninety-nine storey building, the Red Building. The benefits of being released from life incarceration is being given back all my properties including my late grandfather's building. He did not want me to have the building, but had no choice as he had no other heirs.

"I can't wait to get back. They were all screaming back on how soft their bodies are, just begging to be squashed!" says Andrew, a new member of my team, standing in the middle of the room, pretending to be an old soldier with war stories to share.

The whole team laughs with him. There is patting of each other's backs.

"Who's got the video recording? I want to see the pathetic look on that human child as we yell at him!" says another in the team.

Unsophisticated thrill-seeking amateurs. I will need to harden them. Before someone starts showing the video around, I call for everyone to sit down and start the debriefing.

"I am glad that you all found today very entertaining. I would like to point out that we initially had nine targets. That's right, count it. Nine. And the bodies only tallied up to eight," I jest to the group, most of them will know the gravity of the situation.

"I was pretty sure I got her. I threw my dagger towards her. I am pretty sure it hit her. In any case, she fell down the waterfall and must have hit her head. Damn humans, so soft and fragile. Also FYI Master, the waterfalls are strictly beyond our jurisdiction, isn't it?" Andrew laughs uncomfortably to himself, as the mood in the room turns very serious - all eyes glare at him.

"Andrew, you hail from the village of Kapak. Very brave people. I know the villagers there very well - one of my great grandparents established that village. Now it has thrived with fine groups of fighters. Like you, they have balls. Balls to be open and truthful to their superiors. I have been waiting for someone like you. Maybe someone to lead as my second in command."

I stare at the others in disdain. "You put the rest of them to shame. I had questioned a few others earlier but no one dared to tell me what had happened. How do you expect me to show I have good governance within my unit?"

I walk towards Andrew, looking at his bright eyes. There is so much potential in him. I smile and reciprocate. "A future personal apprentice, perhaps. Come, let's talk privately."

I open the doors to the vast balcony - at this height the winds tend to blow hard at times, whistling in between the other buildings. I show off to Andrew the magnificent night view of Hilaga city.

"My late grandfather was a great warrior, he started from the bottom of his team, working his way up, through hard work and determination. He became the leader of his group and then his clan. He was so powerful and rich, he ended up owning this building. Now through mere inheritance, I own this building. I see so much that is common between you and him and me. You have great initiative," I smile and put my hand on his shoulder. It could have been mistaken for a father-and-son moment.

"However, there is one difference. Just one small, big difference," My hand moves from his shoulder to his neck, grabbing and squeezing his neck. His face that was only a few seconds ago brimmed with hope is now in total fear, knowing that all hope has been extinguished.

"Neither he nor me allowed our targets to escape. We always, always, always make sure that all our enemies are dead. You allowed the girl to live. Empires collapse because of a single careless mistake. All in my unit must leave no stone unturned!" I shake him vigorously as his face turns pale and blue. I loosen my grip so that he does not faint and he breathes a sigh of relief.

"I apologise, Master Serigala. I will take responsibility and I will not make this mistake again," he chokes on his words, desperate to show repentance.

"That's good. You will take full responsibility for your actions. And you will not make any more mistakes from now on," I let go of his neck and he drops on to my feet and starts kissing my feet for forgiveness. At least he is loyal.

"Andrew, stand up, there's no need to grovel before me."

Andrew stands up before me, his eyes are red and teary, "Thank you, Master." I hold his neck gently, "No need to thank me, all is forgiven."

He smiles appreciatively, I do not react to his smile, merely gripping his neck again hard and I fling him over the balcony. I watch him fall, he is looking up at me, in the beautiful yet tragic facial expression of disbelief of his impending doom until I could not see him at all, hitting the pavement on the ground floor.

I look up beyond the horizon, start admiring the beautiful skyline of Hilaga, whilst pondering upon the sacrifices we made to make Hilaga great again.

"Kapak residents need to improve their mental training," I make a note to myself.

I walk back into the debriefing room, where the nervous team members await - the newer members are the most anxious and guarded, whilst the older team members are laughing off Andrew's latest downfall.

"I hope we all learnt a valuable lesson today. There is no room for failure. Those who wish to continue to be in this unit must ensure ZERO survivors. Of course, you all know I am a dynamic and adaptive leader and very open to suggestions to improve the quality of my leadership. If you don't think you can perform in this unit, then you are more than welcome to fall," I pause and correct myself, "Sorry I meant leave. Any questions?"

Nothing but silence. Good. Just the way I like it.

"We will head out again soon. Find the girl. She can't stay protected in that waterfall for too long."

3rd December

Manis: Dawn

Location: Ingei Jungle, Bumi

I am woken by the violent clattering of my own teeth.

Was it a dream, a nightmare that had happened?

I look around me to comprehend the events of last night. Here I am taking refuge at a rock shelter behind a curtain of falling water. The dawn sunlight penetrates through the water and I wonder if I will be safe when I leave the rock shelter. I must wake up and get out. Get out of this horrible, horrible jungle. I pray those monsters are not out in the morning as I cautiously wade through the waterfall. The dirt and grime wash off along with all of my tears, as I remember my mother, her last words - You must live for the rest of us and my father's last stand. Oh my brother, my sister and Andie and his siblings. I choke with tears, and clutch my chest as a sharp pain pierces through my heart.

"What will I do now?" I swim away from the waterfall and head towards the river bank.

"What's going to happen to me?" I say to myself.

OK, I must survive, I must live. My head starts to ache. I feel my skull and find a bump that was not there before, probably from the series of falls last night.

"Priorities. Get some food first then decide how I'm going to get out of here."

"Do I head back to where my parents were? Who is going to bury them?"

I am too scared to see what had happened. I can't go back there. Not alone. I am a coward, running away from all of them.

The reality of last night's events hits me like a train. My feet wobble on the soft cool river mud, I drop down on to my knees, wailing and crying, knowing that I have lost everyone and everything. I am truly alone. How can I live on after this?

3rd December

Adib: Boat

Location: Melilas Village, Bumi

The village *muezzin* wakes me up from my slumber with his melodious call to prayer. I must have fallen asleep sitting up. I turn round and see the doctor by my side. I still can't believe she was walking out there in the middle of the night. She should have better common sense than that. A Pontianak. That was what it was. We came by in the nick of time.

I hear John's horribly loud snoring. John, gosh! You are such a baby when you are drunk.

I don't join the villagers for prayers. Instead, I start taking a walk towards the weeping willow tree by the river. As I walk closer, I see the wooden jetty and a man tending to his longboat. I approach him.

"Hi Mister, what are you doing?" I ask the stranger.

"You must be Adib," I notice the man's grey hair and his face creased with wrinkles and yet a warm smile. He puts his hand out to greet me.

"Yes, I am - have we met before?"

"Yes, well, it is a small world," he laughs.

"I'm a bit curious, what exactly are you doing?" I ask, watching the man paint a resin at the bottom of the wooden longboat.

"Oh, just making sure it doesn't leak. You got to be prepared for the worst, you know."

"How long have you had this boat for?" I ask.

"Oh no, it's not mine. I'm just helping out," He answers.

"Okay, that's good of you. Are you joining us later for the trip to Ingei?"

"Oh yeah, I have to watch over you and make sure you're safe, you know," The man seems very focused at his job, now appearing indifferent to me.

"Hey Adib, you have to help out with setting up breakfast!" I hear Prof. Simon shouting out to me.

I ignore Professor Simon Muller for a while.

"He's an asshole, isn't he?" the boat-fixer laughs, still transfixed with his repairs.

"Yeah he is."

"You know people like him don't last long in the real tropical jungle. If anything bad happens, you must trust your heart, your gut feeling. Ever seen anything strange happen in Ingei?" the boat-fixer asks.

"No, my previous trips has been all good. I just follow whatever the guides tell me to do."

I hear Prof. Simon calling out for him to attend to him. He is heading out towards me.

"OK Mister, I'm gonna go now. Hey, I didn't catch your name?" I turn around but the boat-fixer is no longer there.

Where did he go?

I search around the boat and the jetty but there is no one there.

That's creepy. A chill tingles down my spine and then a heavy hand grabs my shoulder. I spin round ready to punch whatever it is.

"Hey what the hell! Come on, Adib what the f- are you doing here? Go help out with setting up breakfast and get everyone ready for our river trip to Ingei. Got it? *Comprende*?" A startled Simon slaps my raised fists down and then slaps me again on the shoulders. He walks back up to the hut and I follow him slowly.

"Asshole," I mutter under my breath.

"I told you so," I hear the boatman say softly behind me. I turn my head round but no one is there. I start walking faster, overtaking Prof. Simon.

3rd December

Nurul: Plastic

Location: Melilas Village, Labi, Bumi

I am woken up by Sally Walls. I got introduced to her last night, she is a college student doing a biology project for her international school.

"Sorry Doctor, but you did ask me to wake you up at 5am."

The light blurs my vision as I take my time to refocus to see a keen and youthful bright orange-hair student. I remember those days when I was sweet and tender sixteen. Back in those days I could do anything and everything. Nothing was impossible. How much time has passed since those days?

"Sure, let me just freshen up and let's get a good cuppa coffee." I am careful not to show the real me, a spiteful morning person, usually groaning when woken up. Let orange Sally see the good in people, untainted by any bad experiences. I wish someone could have done that with me.

Sally and I stand around by the makeshift mess tent, sipping our freshly-brewed coffee.

"We're going to have a team presentation by Ana," Shikin, the expedition second in command, announces as she goes round to everyone.

"Grab breakfast and head out to the meeting tent now," Shikin clearly enjoys bossing people around.

Breakfast is very American, fried eggs - sunny-side ups and omelettes, toasted bread, baked beans and fried sausages. I wonder where the recommended dietary fibre is in this diet. I start craving for some oatmeal or at least Weetabix cereal. I sit down next to Adib at the meeting tent.

"Hey Adib, thanks for last night. I got to ask you… Did you see anything peculiar last night?"

"Yeah, I did. Doc, here's a tip: Never be alone at night, especially here. OK?"

I nod and squeeze his forearm, my own gesture to thank him again.

"So who's that girl?" I point to the freshman adjusting the portable projector for her 'PowerPoint' presentation.

"That's Ana Sulaiman, she's a freshie doing research on jungle cats in the Ingei area," Adib replies.

"Hmmm, cat woman - cats are like pangolins, aren't they?" I tease Adib.

"Are you being serious? Coz' you know that will just piss me off big time. I mean for one, pangolins are *Pholidota*:

anteaters. Pangolins have got hard scales, whilst cats have fur, and..." Adib gets very serious.

"Hey, hey, I'm just pulling your leg!" I pat Adib on the shoulder.

"I'm just thinking maybe you should hook up with cat woman there," The idea just came out of nowhere, but I reckon I might as well play matchmaker with Adib.

"No, no, I am not a big fan with women with too much makeup - especially early in the morning," Adib scowls.

And then it hit me, Ana is wearing a layer of thick foundation makeup with shocking pink lipstick.

"You don't like plastic girls then?" I tease Adib.

"Definitely no! I got better things to do than that."

Ana, the plastic girl, starts her presentation entitled 'Welcome to the Sungai Ingei Conservation Forest'.

"Adib, she said *sungai* - that means river. Isn't it supposed to be a jungle that we're going to?" I whisper, making sure I am not offending the presenter Ana.

"Well, the Ingei Forest reserve is special because of the confluence of several different ecosystems like wetlands, peatlands, tropical rainforest and hill land. Of course not to mention the Ingei hot springs," Adib replies.

"Hot springs, there? Really?" I might actually learn something today.

"Let plastic girl talk and you learn, Doc."

"The Sungai Ingei Conservation Forest is a protected forest reserve with an area of 18,491 hectares, with a huge number of faunal species including: 35 species of fish - six being recently discovered species, 38 species of amphibians, two new species of frog-biting midges, 12 reptile species, 14 species of birds and 97 mammal species including 28 species of bats," Ana starts off her presentation but I notice she has not mentioned cats.

I stare at my empty mug. It is too early in the morning to absorb this information. Before heading off to the mess, I couldn't help from noticing the next slide that has a large photo of a multi-stepped waterfall. It seems to have a great bearing to me. I definitely got to take a lot of selfie photos there.

3rd December

Manis: Resolve

Location: Ingei Jungle, Bumi

Lying on the soft river mud, I sob uncontrollably, I can't seem to stop. I know deep inside, I need to figure out how to get out of here, instead of being this wreck.

A small river crab walks sideways towards me; I stare at its bulbous small eyes. It pauses and then proceeds to walk around me. It does not know if my intentions are anything to do with eating it. As it scurries fast away from me, I recall a memory, a dinner with my family and my uncle's family many years ago - well, before my father and him had that big fight about his new faith.

***

"Okay Manis, if you're so smart, then I want you to answer my question."

"Sure Uncle," as I scoop onto my plate an orange shelled crab cooked in the sweet aroma coconut-cream based curry.

"Now every single time, there is a plane crash - what is the one thing that immediately determines if the survivors will survive or not?" I catch the glint of Uncle's glasses, reflecting glare from the white florescent white lights.

His wife Serunai looks at him, "I hope this isn't one of your boring jokes."

My parents laugh as Uncle reassures us with his ungraceful hands, and insists that everyone try their wits at this.

"Okay, anyone? Come on, anyone's got the answer?"

"Getting the food?" My mom looks at the delicious large crabs.

"Close, but not really what I am getting at here. Anyone?" my uncle looks around.

"Oh come on, just tell us. The food's going to get cold if we wait any longer," my father impatiently tells his brother.

"Okay, here it is: it is the first and most immediate thought after the crash," My uncle smiles broadly, expecting any agreeable gestures.

"What do you mean, Uncle?" I had to ask.

"You see when tragedy happens to people, the first thing most people ask is WHY did it happen? What could I have done to stop this from happening in the first place? Whose fault was it? Was it my fault? What if I had not gotten on *the plane? They are stuck by the tragedy of crashing instead of resolving their current crisis, which is. surviving post-crash."*

Everyone remains quiet, trying to figure out what he actually means by this.

"On the other hand, those who survive always ask themselves these questions first - what do I need to do first? Do I make a shelter; how do I find food? How do I get help?"

My father interjects, "So that means if we are ever in a plane crash, I will make sure I have you by my side.

"Of course, eldest brother, nothing less."

In camaraderie, my father pulls my uncle's hand and grips it in a testosterone-fuelled masculine handshake as their wives wonder what that is all about.

***

I remember that dinner lesson well, somehow ingrained in my memory, with the delicious morsels of white flesh crabs.

Back on the riverbank, I sit up and make a small deep prayer.

"You are the only one true God. From you I beg for your mercy. Help me get out of this danger. Please protect me from Evil and keep me on the right path. Amen."

I have never prayed before; I have never prayed for my safety before. I shed more tears and as I stand on my feet, I can feel myself filled with great resolve. I convince myself that I am not really alone, for God is always with me, all the time from the beginning till now. He has not forsaken me. My tummy rumbles painfully. Food. Let's find food and then figure out how to get out of here.

3rd December

John: Null

Location: Melilas Village, Bumi

"Last night, you were completely out of it, dude," Adib wakes me up, as I grumble and complain in expletives.

"Yeah, Mister John - yeah I saw and heard," Mahmud joins the conversation.

"Oh my poor head," my head is pounding hard as I try to orientate myself.

Clearly, I'm not at home.

"Come on John, wash yourself and then let's head for breakfast - looks like you're gonna need a good cup of Joe, and not a cup of John!" Adib pulls me out of my sleeping bag.

"Mahmud, did you see something last night?" Adib asks.

"Yeah I saw the woman doctor running and tumble down and you guys bump into her," Mahmud replies.

"Really? Did you see something else?" Adib asks slowly and pausing in between the last words.

"Oh no, nothing. If you're asking me if I saw a ghost, then I'm the wrong person to ask."

Mahmud's words puzzle me, "Why is that, Mahmud?"

"Well, my mommy says I've got a seventh sense. So I'm all good," Mahmud replies grinning sheepishly.

"Sorry I don't get you, what do you mean by a seventh sense? That simply does not make sense," Adib asks.

"It's kind of like a sixth sense, where you can sense 'things', but I have the opposite of that," Mahmud replies, again grinning sheepishly at the end of each answer.

"Please, just talk properly - it's too early in the morning for this, Mahmud" I complain, nursing my poor, poor head.

"Yeah dude," Adib agrees.

"It's simple, OK? Ghosts don't see me and I don't see them. Actually, I never see any ghosts, I never feel anything, even when people tell me that the ghost is chasing them. They usually disappear when I'm there. Ghosts just stop happening when I'm around. It's my seventh sense - a gift," Mahmud again grins sheepishly.

"Oh, okay that sounds weird, but hey I respect that," Adib clearly looks confused by the whole conversation.

I get up on my feet, scratch my bum and head off to the washroom outside the hut.

Seventh sense, my ass.

On the other hand, I did see something chase Nurul, didn't I? Maybe it was something in my drink. Am I going to say now I really believe in Pontianaks? That's just impossible.

3rd December

Adib: Bunian

Location: Ingei River, Bumi

The bright morning sun has risen and the light bounces on the clear light brown river. Sparkles catch in my eyes and I love it. Blue black butterflies flutter around in the air around everyone as the whole expedition team lines up to get into the longboats.

The TV crew is busy making their money shots, whilst Yasmin does her coverage for the day. I see Ana with her posse of girlfriends taking photos of each other and then 'selfies' and 'group selfies' or 'we-fies'.

"It's no good to take a photo with only three people, otherwise you'll get a 'fourth' person in the photo," Eddie says to Ana.

"Well, let's have a look. See there's still just three of us here. No ghosts," Ana justifies.

"But you know you should be in our photo, because you know you want to, right?" Ana winks back. Eddie blushes and starts to stammer.

"And he's cute too," Dina rescues Eddie and proceeds to have their vain session of self-photography.

"You know, here's a couple of interesting facts. These longboats are similar to the ones at Kampong Ayer - you know, the Water Village. Although they are both open top boats, our boats are much longer - like longer torpedoes. Our boats are also different as they have flat bottoms, as the water can get pretty shallow here. From time to time, we might have to get out of the boat and push it into deeper water," Mahmud provides the tour guide narrative to the 17-year old caucasian orange haired student Sally Walls, whilst with gentlemanly etiquette helps her get into a longboat. He catches me staring at him, he winks back and gives me a thumbs up. Gosh, he's still wearing that Taylor Swift t-shirt from yesterday!

"*Life-jar-kat abery wan mus use life-jar-kat* OKAY!" I hear the El-Kapitan chef shouting to everyone, barely making sense if he had not been showing everyone the orange life vests to wear when getting on the boats. No one will ever dare mock him, his face projects nothing but the coldness of a stone carving.

The riverwater is surprisingly cold. I start to shiver, as I wade into the water and then step into the cramped longboat.

"Brrr, that was really cold," I say to myself.

"Looks like someone didn't take a shower today," says Mo, sitting cross-legged in front of me. His long legs can barely fit into the boat.

Before I could reply to him, Mo says "Don't worry I didn't shower today too - you know save water thing."

"Me too!" Zul who is sitting behind proclaims loudly.

"Me three!" I hear Matt, the footballer shouts out from the end.

Laughter erupts in our boat. I can see Nurul and John in different boats, they all seem happy and excited at the same time. I'm so glad John is feeling so much better. I see him entertaining a first year university student by the name of Hannah. No one can resist her perfect smile, with a matching set of dimples. I must confess I did have a crush on her once, and I would not be surprised if John will end up being very flirtatious with her. At least it will keep him from the other trouble he gets himself into. Behind us, two longboats steered by Mr. Ayang and El-Kapitan bring our supplies of food, equipment and base camp shelter materials. I can't help from noticing a chainsaw in each boat. Mr. Ayang told me that a few days ago, they pre-emptively chain-sawed the fallen logs blocking the river - it's more efficient this way. However, there may be new fallen trees, which would mean we would end up doing some manual work along the way.

As the boat glides across the river, I appreciate the surrealness of the fallen trees that lie on both sides of the riverbank whilst river otters play around in the water, indifferent to us. Everyone realizes that it is a beautiful day for a great adventure.

I could not help but notice that there's a half-naked man sitting by a large boulder. I can't see his face, his hair partially obstructing his eyes. He looks down and waves to me. No one else seems to see him. Not even Nurul. As we pass by him, I notice his half smile.

'*Bunian*': the hidden spirits that live in the jungle. "I sure hope that was a friendly smile," I say to myself.

He raises his right hand and gives a thumbs up. I do my best to reassure myself that that must be a good gesture and mutter a quiet prayer in my heart.

3rd December

Manis: Tenggiling

Location: Ingei Jungle, Bumi

Finding some low hanging *Salak* fruits, I tear off the thin snake-like skin of the fig-like *salak* fruit, its sweet nectar smell reminding me that I am alive. I bite on the sweet fruit, being so hungry I can't taste the usual mild acidic and sticky after-taste. Judging the sun's position in the sky, I figure out how to head north. Head north to civilization.

The sweltering heat of the tropical rainforest dries up my wet clothes, only to wet them back with my sweat, as I fight flies and mosquitoes that relentlessly attack me. I wonder if swatting them only seems to attract them to me. I jump across rotting and fallen logs and do my best to ignore the numerous leeches that feed off blood from my lower legs. From time to time, I would break low lying smaller branches, leaving it to hang downwards and then snap the lower half of that to point towards the direction that I will be walking to. In case, there's a search party, not that I am expecting one, they'll know I was here. More importantly they'll know which direction I am heading to. I remind myself that they will also know when I was here, by checking the state of branch - how dry is it and from the colour of the leaves.

I will live for you, Mama. I will live for everyone.

The gradient goes up again, I breathe hard against the humid air, my clothes sticking to me, slowing down my legs. I wonder if I should tear my khaki cargo pants into make-shift shorts but the thought of mosquitoes, flies, leeches and all kinds of creepy-crawlies going up my legs kills that idea. I end up having to stop. Panting hard, I bend down and rest my palms against my aching knees. As I stand up, I begin to notice this gigantic massive hardwood, its trunk so vast, I wonder how many people would it take to wrap their arms around it. If only I could climb it and then fly back home. I recite a little prayer for protection and guidance.

I take the time to reassess the direction I need to head to. I look at the sun's shadow and plot along the path of the shadow for 15 minutes, and that would give me a rough estimate of the east to west line. From there, I can figure out where north was. Somehow that would take it closer to Melilas village and I would figure out how to get there once I am nearby. I am so glad I regularly watch the Discovery channel.

As I prepare myself to endure a long walk, I notice a strange looking armoured-scale creature with a cute long snout crawling in front of me. It's a *tenggiling* or pangolin. This must be a good sign. Usually, a pangolin would roll itself up into a ball when you are near it or when you touch it but this pangolin seems to be indifferent to me. How strange. Looking at its path, it seems to be heading north as well. I follow the path of the pangolin, my companion saviour.

Following this small cat-sized armoured ant-eater; the pangolin, I follow it through the jungle.

"I'm going to have to give you a name." The pangolin pauses and looks at me. *Is it really doing that?*

"Oh, I guess you do understand me." I am starting to converse with my pangolin friend. I ignore the absurdness of the situation. The only name I could think of is Andie. No, I can't use that name. Think of another name. Andie. No, please think of another.

Andie. Andie. Andie. Andie. Andie. Andie.

"Andie then," My eyes well up and I start to cry, noticing how sad the pangolin's beady eyes are.

Turning its head, 'Andie' scratches the moist dirt with his claws and starts moving on. He must be telling me to get myself together and move on.

"Andie, I trust you will keep me safe."

***

It has probably been several hours since I have followed Andie.

Am I really putting my life in the claws of this pangolin? I must be losing my mind.

"Andie, wait. I need a rest."

The pangolin stops and climbs a tree. I notice the giant ants on the tree. It starts licking them off and eating them, and then claws a piece of bark off to reveal numerous ants in panic.

"I suppose I could try your delicacy," I try to convince myself that this is doable. Think survival.

I grab a giant black ant, its six limbs sprawling here and there, trying to escape from my clutches in futility. I look at the ant again, its much bigger than our house ants, the size of a AAA battery. I squeeze its head - it's jaws are no match for my thumb, and squish comes out soft gooey mush. Its limbs are still moving but I am pretty sure it is dead.

I can't believe I am doing this.

I throw the giant ant into my mouth, doing my best to think pleasant thoughts. Best to chew. No, no, no - just swallow. I could feel its legs still moving inside my throat as I do my best to swallow it. I pick some more giant black ants and ingest more than a dozen ants, hoping these ants won't poison me.

Think super-food.

Andie the pangolin jumps off the tree and looks at me and then starts moving in the same direction before our little break-time.

"Okay, Andie, I guess brunch is over."

I follow the pangolin, noticing we are going uphill this time. I feel safe with 'Andie'. I imagine that this is a walk in the park or a university sponsored walk.

Andie the pangolin stops, and starts walking around in circles. I look at it and wonder what is going on. I look ahead and only now do I notice that the pathway has ended. I can't see beyond the wall of vegetation.

"What is it, Andie? What's wrong?"

I go closer, and it rolls up into a ball.

What's going on?

I pick up Andie and it does not move, but looks at me as though smiling. Maybe I should just see what's on the other side of this tangled wall of vines. I can't see an opening through the vines. It is tougher than I imagine. I want to put Andie down on the ground, but he just seemed too comfortable in my hand.

"Shall I push through Andie?"

The pangolin winks at me. *It winked at me!* There's no possibility I imagined that. Or did I? I push my body against the vegetation wall. The wall does not give way.

'OK let's try that again," I am still holding Andie, we are doing this together. I take a step back, and propel my body with my left shoulder first into the wall.

The wall breaks. I hear instant snapping of branches and vines and instead of finding a jungle path on the other side, I realize that I have just pushed through and started to fall from a cliff to my certain end.

It is too late, there is nothing I can do, I cannot save myself. 'Andie' had tricked me. I should not have trusted a creature of the jungle. I wanted to live for you, Mama…

3rd December

John: Friend

Location: Drop-point Alpha, Ingei Jungle, Bumi

After a good two hours, we arrive at Drop-point Alpha, a white sand river beach. On any other given day, I would have loved to lay down here and get myself a sun tan.

Prof. Simon had mentioned that the river porters will bring supplies here and other members of the logistic team will bring it up to our base camp, a good thirty minutes climb up. I look up and I don't know if my knees can take that kind of punishment. Better go slow and steady.

The jungle is daunting. Trees grow with no rules and vines like I've never seen before, thicker than fire-hoses, defiantly tangle into everything - resistance is futile. What is most overwhelming is the jungle sound - no, I shall correct myself, it is the jungle traffic noise. It is incredibly noisy.

"You would think the jungle critters would stop in the presence of us people, but know one thing - this is their 'city'. I hear birds singing, cawing, shrilling, cooing, hooting, whistling, cackling, tweeting, chirping and...," I say out loud to myself, hoping someone would pick a conversation with me.

"Oh, oh, I know that sound. That's a woodpecker pecking into a tree and listen," Vol cups his right hand to his ear, "Can you hear that squawk in the distance?" he continues.

"Yes, I do. What do you suppose it is?" I ask with intent curiosity.

"I think it might be a rare Bornean peacock-pheasant, or maybe even a crested fireback pheasant!" Vol's eyes light up with so much enthusiasm, he sets me alight. I feel revived and keen to climb up and endure the pain of 49-year-old knees, worn cartilages will grind against each other without my immediate noticing.

A good ten minutes later, I notice how everyone seems to have zipped past by me. Adib slows down and waits for me, stopping frequently as I try to catch up to him.

As I catch my breath again, my knees feel as though small daggers have been inserted into them. I tell Adib, "You don't have to wait for me, just go on. I can see the Base Camp from here. They need you there. Besides the porters, the logistics guys will be going up and down so I'm pretty safe."

Mr. Ayang climbs up past us whilst carrying at least 5 backpacks and a trunk, as though there's nothing inside but fluffs of cotton wool in them. He just makes everything look so easy.

"Sure John, I expect to see you there in 10 to 15 minutes. Otherwise, I'll get the Special Boat Service to find you… and more importantly: NO, absolutely no partying on your own OK?!" Adib waves his index finger to warn me.

"Well, I'm glad I drank the bottle dry last night," I reassure him.

Adib still has his youth, as he seems to leap from step to step on this uphill pathway. I start taking baby-steps this time, but looking at Adib so far away makes me envious and more importantly sad about how so much youth has left me.

"BLOODY HELL! They should really build a bloody escalator here." I scream to myself.

"There's no electricity, so that's going to be a bit hard," I turn to my right and see a man who is clearly older than I am. I notice his warm smile and crooked teeth.

"Who are you? I don't remember seeing you on the team."

Maybe I should not have mentioned that last part, not here, not when I'm alone.

"Let's just say I'm a friend. I think you should hurry up, John Proctor. Coz' that woman's not really a friend of ours," the stranger's hand goes up and points past my nose to the distance, on my left side.

He knows my name.

I turn my head to my left and see a figure in white, standing in between the trees and the majestic liana vines. I can't seem to see it clearly, even though the trees seem quite clear to me. The figure just seems like a blur.

Must be this tiring climb tiring my eyes.

As I stare at it, I notice its feet are not touching the ground, floating a few inches above the jungle floor.

"That's crazy, it's day time - at least I'm not alone," I turn my head to the right and see that there is no one with me...

"Oh Lord!" With all my might, my body propels itself up the pathway, jumping in leaps and bounds uphill, taking me only 5 minutes to get to the top to the Base Camp.

3rd December

Nurul: Waterfall

Location: Ingei Jungle, Bumi

Our Base Camp has been built by the previous expedition groups - five wooden stilted longhouses as our state of the art jungle self-styled facilities, complete with its own zinc rooftops. Professor Simon and Shikin are busy designating the teams to their allocated work areas and delegating everyone's responsibilities. Now we've got to clean the place up and claim our sleeping areas - again on the floor. I start to miss my bed with its soft yet firm springy mattress. The logistics team are busy moving in the various but small research equipment into the longhouse in the middle.

"Hey Doc, can I bring you to the waterfall? It's beautiful there and we can take lots of photos there together," Ana comes up with her posse of girlfriends. I see Cindy and she's giving me the thumbs up. I simply find it hard to refuse anyone who does that.

"Ana, you've been here before?" It is my way of asking if she will get us lost in this jungle.

"Fourth time, actually. I will bring Johari as well, just in case," Ana, no matter how plastic she may seem, knows exactly what I am asking. She smiles and I smile back. I hope this isn't going to be like having high school 'frenemies' again.

***

We walk through an off-beaten jungle pathway. I watch my steps, making sure that there are no creepy crawlies on the brown leaves trodden pathway. This is when I realised the contradiction: I am awed by the beautiful tall trees, the persistent mesh of vegetation growing from tree to tree and down on the jungle floor, and yet I am terrified with each step I take forward. My thoughts drive me to imagine vengeful snakes waiting to strike my soft pedicured feet and the secret union of spiders working together to jump off every leaf in a synchronized and coordinated effort to attack and subdue me - Doctor Nurul, the home spider swatter. I fear they will finally avenge their perished domesticated smaller spider cousins.

Walking through the pathway, we stop for a while. Johari points to an ankle-deep pool the size of a large bathtub filled with soggy leaves, "The water inside that pool is very hot water by the way."

"Wah, this is the Ingei hot spring, isn't it?" Cindy laughs and then proceeds to take a photo with her white Canon digital pocket camera.

"Yeah, I'd recommend you clear the leaves out first before you take a hot bath. And yes, all the pools and small streams here contain hot water," Johari seems quite keen to show off his local knowhow.

As we walk further up the pathway, it becomes steamier and hotter than usual. There is another clear pool of water, which is pretty devoid of life and steam is coming off the pool. This is definitely a much hotter spring, and yet definitely prettier than the one before. There is a large flat rock protruding above the surface, right in the middle of the pool. I wonder if we should get up there and let others take our photos. I look at the steam rising off the water and shelf the idea immediately.

"I should really give each hot spring a name, you know one of these days I am going to turn this place into a proper hot spring for tourists, just like the ones in our neighbouring country, Malaysia... What's the name of the hot spring? Roaring?" Johari asks himself.

"It's called Poring hot springs and it's on Mount Kinabalu," Ana corrects him.

"Well, I definitely want to be there during the opening - Johari's hot springs!" Cindy playfully rubs Johari's shoulders.

"You can't touch me like that - I'm happily married," Johari takes out a clove cigarette, lighting it up and puffing away the sweet smell of self-destruction like nobody's business. Cindy is somehow upset that her shoulder rub was misinterpreted as flirting.

"Let's have a break here for five minutes - I hope you don't mind the smoke, Doc?"

"To be honest, I haven't given up on getting to meet a non-smoking Johari, you know," I walk away from Johari and head towards another smaller pool, whilst Cindy fills up her water bottle with the pool water and then tries to drink it.

"Oh yuck, this smells of rotten eggs. I can taste the sulphur," she complains. "Doc, do you think this could be medicinal?" I pretend I do not hear her.

Soon enough, we head out back towards our intended sightseeing destination, determined to see the Ingei waterfalls.

It has been two hours hiking up. My legs are growing tired and I want to give up and turn back. And as soon as that thought materializes, I hear the loud sound of water falling down. Everyone is excited and we all rush towards it. It's a sprint to the end. I am keen to beat Ana to the top. Who will see the waterfall first?

I push through overgrown vines, although wary of the possibility of spiders dropping down on me, I convince myself that I am invincible.

Majestic. I stand awed by the view of white water flowing down from a cave stream above, cutting the dark grey and brown sandstone. The cascading white water flows down like a series of mini-waterfalls, landing on each step before falling down into a pool that then becomes a river. I've never seen anything like this before in my life.

Forgetting safety, we all rush into the waterfall and start playing and screaming like children. Johari refuses to join us, no matter how much we beg him to join us. He just lights his cigarette and starts chain-smoking away. Secretly, I wonder if I should push him down into the waterfall and hope his cigarettes become wet and useless. I calculate the risk of an accident versus my all too noble and yet compelling cause and finally decide it is not worth the risk. Everything is perfect, rejuvenated by the waterfall of life, as pleasant childhood memories flood our minds.

Nothing could spoil this moment, I say to myself.

And then the screaming starts.

3rd December

Manis: Crash

Location: Ingei Jungle, Bumi

How could I have wrongly trusted my instincts?

My body is spinning; the sun blinds my eyes. I feel sick.

The pangolin has disappeared from my hands.

This is the end. I wait till I hit the floor of this cliff. It feels like an eternity; I am falling from a great height. This will hurt. I hit the jungle floor, feet first.

The heat and the cold. More cold going up my legs, and then I hear it.

Splash.

Before I could open my eyes, a mixture of air and water rush up my nostrils. I struggle to breathe but instead I swallow water. I crash into the river bed, but it does not hurt me. Pushing off the river bed, I am grateful that I landed in water.

Where am I?

Gasping for breath, I look around. Water splashing everywhere around me, bouncing on the water.

Is this the same waterfall? Why? Why am I back here? The pangolin is trying to kill me by either getting me to fall off a cliff or to lure me back to the demons.

I hear voices, from above. Is it the monsters or people? Adjusting my eyes, I can see what looks like people, girls like me. Is this for real? Looking round, I see Andie the pangolin struggling to swim across to the river bank.

How I could have doubted you, Andie? I rescue Andie and let him climb onto my back; not caring if his claws hurt me, and swim back to the river bank.

"Who is that? Are you alright?" I hear a distant female voice echoing.

"Who are you? Are you human?" I shout back, wondering if that is the right question to ask.

"What did you just say?" I can hear the puzzled expression in their voices, and realised they are not the monsters of last night.

"Help, help me!" I scream at the top of my voice towards them. I cry loudly, in disbelief, semi-choking in tears and breaths.

Someone jumps down from above and into the pool-river, and then another person jumps into the water. A man and a woman are swimming towards me. Up above, I hear intense voices, shouting and a few screams.

Is this a dream? Am I finally rescued? I lay down on my back and play victim. Andie curls up into a ball near my head.

Thank you, Andie.

3rd December

John: Eyes

Location: Base Camp, Ingei Jungle, Bumi

Adib is pacing up and down, he seems shaken. Something had spooked him.

"Where did they go? When are they coming back?" Adib keeps asking me over and over again. He looks very worried. Something is just not right with Adib.

"Adib, hey, don't worry - they have Johari with them - remember the smoking man who caught that turtle who now works for us… saving the wildlife? Remember that? He knows this place like the back of his hand. His people lives in this area. They're in safe hands," I assure Adib.

"John, something is just not right since we arrived here," Adib looks at me intently, a crease appears on his forehead. Now I start to worry that it might end up as a permanent crease.

"I know you don't believe in this stuff but something happened last night," Adib looks around as though he is making sure that he is not being watched. "Something came after Doc Nurul, you.."

I put my hand on Adib's mouth to shut him up.

"Adib, don't break the local taboo - I may be an Englishman, but I don't want any of this *cabul* business here in this jungle. I did see it. I saw IT, the thing-whose-name-we-won't-ever-ever-mention-in-this-jungle that was chasing after her."

"Really, John? You know people say that those things would go after to kill you, right?" Adib's eyes light up.

"I am still grasping this new concept by the straws," I explain to Adib.

"One other thing, as I was climbing the hill, on my own. I saw something and talked to someone who turned out to be not there in the first place," I confess to Adib.

"Adib, that's not even the worst thing, I saw a *Ponti-you-know-what* staring at me, on the way up! Yes, in the day-time. I know it sounds crazy but that's what happened to me…today!" I continue, finding difficulty in calming the pace of my words.

"Oh my God, this is crazy - a series of unnatural events happening at the same time - John, something had happened just before they left."

"No, no…What happened, Adib?"

Adib pauses, unsure if he wants to share his new revelation. "When I was alone just now at our sleeping quarters, I saw a small boy hidden in the roof who told me that danger is coming. And then he vanished by floating through the roof!"

I nod and formulate a plan in my head - find Mahmud. He is the only person, other than Johari who really knows this place.

"Have you seen Mahmud?" I ask Louise, who happens to bump into me.

"Yeah, he just left with Mr. Ayang and Mr. Patih, back on the boats to get more supplies from the village."

I curse out loudly.

"Why, John?" Louise asks.

"We need to get to the other group quickly, the ones that went off to the waterfall with the doctor and our guide," Adib answers, getting more upset with every moment.

"I can bring you there, I know this place well enough to find my way round, even if I am blindfolded in the middle of the night. Is there a problem? Should we tell Prof. Simon?" Louise asks.

"It's hard to explain. We have to go now," I look at my watch - it's already 3pm. We leave Base Camp and onto the jungle pathway to the fated waterfalls.

***

Two hours later, we arrive to find Johari and his group at the second hot springs pool.

"What took you guys so long?" Adib is almost shouting.

It is then that we all started to notice there's someone else new in the group. Her clothes seem dirty and torn. She had cuts on her cheeks and limbs. In spite of that, I can tell she is quite enchantingly beautiful.

"Wow, she's got really large eyes," Adib says out loud, seemingly in a trance upon seeing the unknown visitor.

"We all can hear you, Adib" I tell him. He blushes but continues to pursue his curiosity, "Who are you? Who is this girl? Is she real?"

"Of course, she's real and her name is Manis," Doctor Nurul protects her new patient.

"I think she had an accident in the jungle. She's dehydrated and not very talkative - let's just get her to Base Camp and figure things out from there," Nurul continues.

I am not the only one who notices that this new girl, Manis is holding a curled up pangolin in her hands. Adib looks at the pangolin, touches it and then takes a few steps back. "Why is this pangolin with you?" he asks, but no one answers him.

Together, we head down to the Base Camp. I begin to wonder what the apparition had forewarned Adib. The boy ghost said that danger is coming. Maybe it meant the love of his life has arrived. I feel an itch where my wedding band used to be on my ring finger. Yes, for a woman to reappear in a man's life, this could really be dangerous times.

3rd December

Adib: Calling

Location: Near Base Camp, Ingei, Bumi

"I barely know him, but I think El-Kapitan's a great guy," Cindy blurts out.

"How would you know that, Cindy?" Ana asks.

"Well, simply take a deep breath and smell that delicious food cooking."

"We all love the chef!" The women in the group declare in unison.

Mr. Vol appears from the shrubs and calls out to Louise, "I need to show you something quickly - something very interesting for us photographers. Can I grab you now before it gets dark?" I see Mo is with him.

"Sure thing," Louise nods and follows Mr. Vol downhill - possibly towards the river. I take little notice on how Mr. Vol seems quite fidgety.

Cindy looks at Nurul. "I think I will just go straight ahead with the girls, if that's good with you, Doc?"

"Sure Cindy, we'll be fine. just go ahead but spare us some food alright," Nurul stays close to Manis, knowing that although Manis needs to get to Base Camp, but it should not be at her expense.

"Yeah, don't worry I'll stay," I volunteer.

Everyone else except the kind doctor, Manis, Johari and myself flee off, rushing to Base Camp for what looks like an early supper. I start to notice how dark it is becoming. Manis seems a bit agitated. I reassure her, telling her that she's safe and that she is no longer alone. I could tell from her large eyes that she is not reassured. She must have been through a horror. All alone in the jungle, with no one to comfort her, except perhaps the pangolin. We head slowly towards base camp, at casual-stroll-pace. I want to ask her what happened to her, but I resist. Sally, the A-level student, runs towards us and accompanies the group into Base Camp.

"Aren't you guys late? It's gotten dark already," Sally looks quite concerned. I have never noticed anyone who seemed to be more caring for others than herself, a little angel.

And then that it begins.

The jungle starts shaking and a loud cackling fills the jungle. Rumbling and banging, so close, so near. I feel the pit of my stomach vibrate, twisting and turning. Is this an earthquake or worse?

Manis starts to cry, covers her ears and screams.

"Hurry, we must make it back." We all start running towards Base Camp, dragging screaming Manis with us.

"We must find safety! Not there. Away from here!" Manis screams hysterically.

We arrive outside Base Camp, our presumed safe haven and to our bewilderment, the jungle foliage and the towering trees around Base Camp shake violently. A force of harm is heading towards Base Camp. There is nowhere to run, nowhere to hide.

3rd December

Nurul: Hurry

Location: Base Camp, Ingei Jungle, Bumi

A tall dark entity appears in the middle of Base Camp, barely visible from the distance, the dusk light masking its movement, its limbs long and thin and to my horror, it has no face, no eyes, no mouth - just plain and pure evil. And then it shrieks an ear-piercing cry.

"Johari, come with me. We must save the others. Nurul stay here with Manis and Sally," Adib runs towards the danger with Johari. I could see the disbelieving of his own actions, courage has taken over his entire body.

Both Sally and I hold on to Manis, whose limbs are ice cold.

"No, not again. Did I bring these monsters to them?" Manis keeps muttering.

"Manis, what are you talking about?" I rub her arms vigorously to keep them warm, but in reality it was to keep myself calm.

"They killed my family. We must leave this place - the only safe place I know is behind the waterfall. We must go now!" I can see Manis is mustering all the courage in her.

"What about them? What about our friends?" I grip Manis' hand, begging her not to leave.

"They're already dead - it's the same thing that happened to my family. We didn't stand a chance. There's nothing we can do but run. We don't all have to die here. We must decide to live," I can hear the sadness and desperation in her stammering voice.

I cannot believe her words. I want to stop her, reason with her, but nothing. I am dumbstruck with this unreal reality.

"Come on, we don't have much time. Follow me back to the waterfall if you want to live!" Manis beckons us, but we cannot make up our minds, as we are unable to fully comprehend our new reality, a horror that should only happen in myths and horror stories. And with that Manis wastes no more time and starts running. She is sprinting for her life and heading back towards the waterfalls. I hear screams from Base Camp and more faceless shadow demons arrive, completely surrounding Base Camp. To my horror, they start picking up people, my new friends, throwing and hurting them. I shudder at the thought of the carnage that is happening. Is this for real?

"What are those things, Doc? It can't be real?" Sally's voice is trembling. I turn to Sally, who is frightened beyond words. She asks me, "What do we do, Nurul?"

"Run..."

We both run after Manis, the survivor of an unexplained ordeal. Questions fly through my head. Why is this happening? What is happening?

Sprinting to catch up to Manis, I shout to her "We're coming with you, Manis."

"What are those things?" I ask, in between gasps of breaths.

"I don't know. All I know is that they killed everyone, everyone in my family. They must be demons from hell!"

The jungle is a horrible place to be in. It isn't safe, it never was safe. I think of Adib, John and Johari, praying in my heart that they will be protected, somehow.

Was that a comfort thought? How could I run away from them, merely to protect myself? I know I would live a life of guilt, never being able to forgive myself, no matter how many times I can justify myself. I shouldn't run away. What am I doing?

Tears flow down my cheeks and as I wipe them with my fingers, running through this jungle, the light dimming, I see something from the corner of my eyes. Something is watching and following us.

3rd December

El-Kapitan: Succeed

Location: Base Camp, Ingei Jungle, Bumi

Dinner plans have been interrupted. There is screaming and shouting coming from outside the kitchen area. There is a familiar uneasy feeling, almost a sickening blood-curdling stench in the air. I pick up my *parang*, the same blade I had when I was in the army.

A dark ten-foot figure with long thin arms and legs, stands in the middle of Base camp. I shout *"Orang Tinggi!"* which literally means tall people, but no one is really listening. Everyone is mesmerised. Professor Simon is out with the others, unsure at what they are looking at. To them, this is not possible - this is the impossible. It, the 'Orang Tinggi' screams out a loud long cry, destroying any reason to believe it is a mere illusion. The panic sets in, and everyone starts yelling and screaming, running around aimlessly, trying to find shelter in Base Camp. Some run towards the longhouses, seeking shelter under the stilted longhouses. If only they knew.

Professor. Simon Muller and his best friend, Mr. Rani the forestry officer, scramble to hide themselves but it is too late. The demon picks them up by the heads. Struggling to escape, their feet frantically scramble in mid-air, desperately trying to pry off the demon's large hands, I hear their shouts for help. It unfreezes me. I move towards the demon, parang in hand.

I have fought them before. I will succeed. I will rescue them this time.

I hear the sound of bones cracking and then screaming from all around Base Camp. A liquid mush splatters on my face and over my chest. The two captives are no longer struggling; the demon crush their skulls with its bare hands. Bored, it drops the carcasses of both Prof. Simon and Mr. Rani on the dirt ground. A surge of anger and then rage consumes my heart.

Never again!

I did not hear Adib and Johari and the others shout for me to run away. I will succeed. I charge forward and jump up towards the demon. Chanting a few sacred words, I slash its torso with my parang.

I will succeed.

My body passes through the demon, just like passing through a shadow. My attack connects as I hear it scream in pain.

"How dare you, human? Who do you think you are?" The demon cries out.

I turn round to attack it again, moving side to side to avoid the demon's multiple and deadly kicks and punches. An upper cut slash on its torso, and a slash on its leg. The demon winces in pain, but my attacks are not stopping it.

I can hear the team members, hidden under the longhouses shout out and start cheering, "Kill it El-Kapitan!"

It seems they can all see this *'Orang Tinggi'* demon. They think it's a game. I will succeed. I will rescue them this time. Let me try something else.

The demon keeps trying to attack me, stooping down to throw punches and kicks but it is no use I am too fast for it. I run towards one of the longhouses and it starts to chase me. As soon as I am near the stilt beam, I jump up against the beam, twisting my body and propel myself, parang first to the demon chasing me. My parang connects with its neck.

The demon falls back onto the ground. There is no sound from it. I look at its head, it is nothing but a blank. Faceless and pitch black. Its body starts fuming and burning in small red flames.

"Hey demon, at least show me your bloody face when you die" I watch its body burn; not into ash, but into a red vapour that disappears without a trace.

"Everyone, it is over!" I raise my parang and hear cheers from the longhouse. I deserve this.

"HA HA HA, it is not over, human!" I spin round and prepare to attack, upon seeing a much larger demon. Before I could launch an effective move, this new demon punches my chest with its arm.

"HA HA HA - human, it is too late. You are now dead!"

3rd December

Adib: Others

Location: Base Camp, Ingei Jungle, Bumi

We all thought the demonic intruder was dead. Killed and vaporized into flames. And then another appears, this time a much larger demon. And we watch it punch our saviour, El-Kapitan, into the chest. More of these faceless demons appear, completely surrounding Base Camp. I can hear everyone gasp, whilst a few cry loudly. Our own hopes of salvation burst into flames.

We will all die here, in the forsaken jungle.

The demon pulls its hand out of El-Kapitan's chest. El-Kapitan does not move, but he does not fall. The demon starts punching furiously into his chest, each time its giant hand and arm passing through El-Kapitan. El-Kapitan turns round quickly and slashes his attacker with his parang. This new demon dodges the parang in the nick of time and jumps up onto the roof of one of the longhouses.

It starts to laugh, cackling beyond madness. "Welcome back Roslan! Roslan the crying captain! HA HA HA! How could I not recognise you after all these years? HA HA HA!" The faceless demon laughs euphorically.

Captain Roslan, El-Kapitan, does not reply, He is silent. His facial expression does not change in the *senja* light.

"It looks like you have forgotten what you have lost! We are going to make it hurt again! ATTACK them! Roslan is mine!" The demon maniacally screams his commands to his subordinates.

"Run, Run!" I hear Shikin screaming, dashing out from under the stilted longhouse and into the jungle. Her team mates follow behind her, whilst the demons try to catch them.

Zul and I had been smart to lay down beneath the stilted longhouse. We lay on the dirt ground, breathing erratically as we watch the events unfold before our very eyes.

"Why would she run out?" Zul asks me. I turn to him and see a long dark hand pass through the wooden longhouse floor above us and grab him. I pull Zul to free him from its clutches, only to see his spine and entrails ripped out from behind, blood dripping all over his body and on to me. This time, the wooden board floor cracks and bursts open. Another dark faceless demon is above us.

I look at Zul's face frozen in horror, he drops down onto the dirt ground, his hand still gripping tightly to mine. The demon drops down to the ground and stands up. Terrified, as I look up, I feel its evil intent penetrate into my head and every single bone in my body.

"Adib, run!" John shouts at me.

I jump away from the spot where I was frozen, missing a fatal kick from the evil demon.

"Run, Run!" I shout out.

"Where to? They've surrounded us!"

"Run the gauntlet," John screams out to everyone.

"What?" I scream.

"Just run in between them," Johari shouts out.

"No F-ing way!" I scream back.

I can see Shikin and her group are on the other side of Base Camp, dodging attacks from the numerous demons. As she approaches the edge of the jungle, a group of demons appear before her, striking her with such might, her body flies off and impacts onto a nearby tree, disjointed and broken. Instant death. I can see Dina screaming before another demon kicks her from behind. Her body tumbles down onto the ground several times.

Silent.

The three others in that group split up, two running to El-Kapitan whilst Ana runs towards me, nimble as a cat, sliding on the moist dirt floor to dodge the demon attacks.

Dark projectiles with black flames start coming out from some of the demon's hands.

Oh, just great - they can shoot us too!

On my right, I see the whole TV crew slaughtered. The cameraman's splattered body crushed by his own video camera. I cannot make out the rest of the crew, limbs severed and blood everywhere.

What do I do?

Mr. Biru is now by El-Kapitan's side, as two others Yusri and Eddie join him.

"John, our best chance is to join them. Stick together!" I don't know if John heard me.

"We have to get back to El-Kapitan. Captain Roslan is the only one who knows how to fight them," I yell out again to everyone, just as Ana heads towards me, panting and hugging me as though I could provide her protection.

"That's a bad idea," I hear a voice behind me, a voice I am familiar with.

I turn around and see an old man, sporting a white shirt and green pants, with a very warm smile and crooked teeth.

"Mister boat repairer!" I shout out and at the same time as John blurts out, "The ghost friend at the hill!"

"Who are you?" Johari asks.

"A friend. A guardian," The boat repairer smiles.

"Can you really help us? Can you save us?" Ana begs the old man.

"I will try my best, but we can't join them, and we definitely can't help them. Don't worry, he'll figure it out," The old man points to the group with El-Kapitan and smiles again. Demons start attacking us, but the old man blocks their physical attacks with his bare hands.

More demons head towards us.

"Run into the jungle and head toward the waterfall," the old man gives us our game plan.

Hannah, who no longer has her perfect smile, is not sure what is happening. One minute she is standing next to John and the next minute, she feels an ice cold sensation pierce through her abdomen. John turns round to help her, but becomes helpless when he sees she is becoming pale and unable to breathe, as she desperately holds her abdomen to find a warm wet sensation on her tummy, and then everything just pours out from her.

"John, run..." Hannah's body slumps down hard on to the dirt, eyes unblinking staring at the nothingness in between the trees of the jungle. Her killer, a demon, its hand clutching on to her bloodied liver stands before us, cherishing the moment. Our protector shoots out a bolt of white light from his hand, and with that, Hannah's killer dies immediately, bursting to red flames.

The other demons respond in rage and begin their onslaught. Without further hesitation, we run for our lives, as they relentlessly swarm and attack us. The old man blocks and shields us from the incoming demons. Dozens of black fire projectiles start flying towards us. There is no shielding us as I notice that these attacks are different, even the old man is avoiding from getting hit by these 'arrows'.

The tree line into the jungle is within grasp, and just as I enter into the safety of the foliage, I hear anguished screaming. I look back and see Ana. She has been hit by one of the black fire projectiles. Ana continues to scream as her back burns ferociously. The demons surround her and rip her head from her burning body. One of them chucks her head towards me. It lands near me with a soft thud and splash, then rolls a bit further to my feet. I dare not look at it.

I immediately look around me, it's just the four of us left: me, John, Johari, and our old man protector. More demons head towards us. We cannot outrun them.

"Everyone, please stand closer to me," says the old man.

Is this our final stand?

I look at Ana's head on the floor, her eyes closed, her face contorted in demise.

The old man's shirt glows bright white and then turns green, becoming brighter and brighter.

I shield my eyes from the bright green light. My head starts to hurt, like a sledgehammer's pounding on it.

3rd December

Nurul: Followed

Location: Ingei Jungle, Bumi

Dusk has turned into night. The only light we have is the LED torch lights Sally and I have. Running and holding them, the light beams dance in front of us as we take each step towards safety with the intention of living. I have lost track of how long we have been running through the now slippery and muddy jungle pathway but we are nowhere near the waterfall. We have not even reached the midway hot springs.

Manis is leading us. Sally and I can barely catch up to her. I am pretty sure she was the injured and dehydrated one. My body desires so much to stop and rest but I am so scared. Scared of the monsters, the demons that I must have seen somewhere before. But where?

Keep moving.

The night jungle can conceal whatever is hunting us and aggravates my fear of the hidden. There is a constant rumbling behind us and then there is the loud siren of the jungle night critters, a jungle city with its own deadly night life.

Soon enough, I start to notice the smell of the air has changed, is it the sulphur? Spinning round to my left I see the 'bathtub' hot springs Johari was showing off earlier.

"Hold on, what is that?" I say to myself.

There is a lady sitting inside the 'bathtub' hot springs. I cannot see her face. I stop and blink my eyes, and focus my light beam to the bathtub hot spring. There is no one there.

Sally does not stop for me. I sprint onwards to chase after the two, fighting cramp-like pain in my calves.

Up ahead, something stumbles down. A short scream, followed by a moan. Sally stops and searches the pathway ahead to see what lies ahead of us. The spotlight shakes as her hand jitters in terror. I finally catch up to her and use my torchlight to focus on what is ahead of us.

We see Manis lying prone on the floor, her body covered with leaves and mud. She is writhing in pain. I come up to her and assist her. She tripped on something and now has hurt her knee. I quickly examine her right knee and feel it with my hand as Sally provides me light.

"I am sure you've not broken anything," I reassure her. This is not a time to have a fracture.

"Can you stand up?" Sally asks. Manis stands up and walks with a limp. She knows she must continue the journey onwards.

"Pain is just in the mind," she mutters to herself.

She'll slow us down. Don't abandon her too. I won't abandon her.

We arrive at the second hot springs pool, but we cannot go forward any further. We cannot seek shelter at the waterfall as a sinister old lady stands before us...

3rd December

El-Kapitan: Together

Location: Base Camp, Ingei Jungle, Bumi

"Everyone stay together! If you can grab a pole or stick, do it but make sure these monsters don't touch you!" I shout to the five of us.

We turn our backs against each other, forming a defensive circular formation.

"I've got your back, El-Kapitan!" Cindy shouts out. She managed to get hold of a long piece of bamboo.

We are going to make it through. I will save everyone this time.

The demons surround us; they outnumber us at least two to one.

Mr. Biru taunts them, waving his parang in the air, "We're not afraid you. We will kill you all if you come near."

One of the demons charges towards Eddie, who is on my right and before it grabs him, I swing my parang towards it. Mr. Biru quickly leaves the formation to join the attack, parrying with his parang. Both attacks connect. We hear the demon scream in agony, but it does not die and merely retreats.

The demons close in on us. Even though they have no faces, we can feel their evil and blood-thirsty grin.

A larger demon taunts me, "Roslan, oh Roslan - you are going to hurt so bad, you'd wish you'd die a thousand deaths!" This time, five dark demons jump towards us. Cindy repels the demon with her bamboo pole but it passes through. Yusri joins the attack by throwing a stone at it, but that too passes through. As it tries to grab Yusri, I see Mr. Biru attack the demon, swinging his parang at it with all intent to harm it.

The other demons go after Eddie and me. Opportunistically, I attack both demons simultaneously, preventing Eddie from being attacked. They land a few punches on me, but these punches pass through me with no effect. They realise they can't really attack me. The demons take a few steps back.

"Oh Roslan, we can do this all night you know. You humans don't have the stamina. You are weak and we will crush you. Crush you like straws-dolls with our bare hands! Let's play around a bit more," the larger demon cackles out loud and then screams.

We return back safely into our defensive formation. We will not falter.

Suddenly, we are all pushed out by a great force from the centre. As I turn around, I see a demon appear from the middle of our defensive circle! It grabs Cindy, who tries to attack with her bamboo pole, but to no avail. I see Mr. Biru, rushing to save her. But I know she does not stand a chance. The demon pulverises Cindy's head with one blow, neck snapped and what was a whole head is somehow easily smashed like a broken watermelon; blood and brain matter everywhere. The stench of raw human tissue makes me nauseous. A mix of tears and rage fills me as I attack the demons with all my might.

Trying to gather everyone back into the circle formation, I rush back to our original spot, "Stay together!"

But no one listens. The demons kill us off one by one. A group of demons pounce on Yusri, ripping him limb by limb - his tortured screams echoing in my head, whilst Eddie is plucked by a demon and thrown high into the air like a ragged doll, crashing onto a longhouse roof, impaled by a broken supporting pole inside. Mr. Biru did not stand a chance either. The demons jump on him. His parang could not get them in time. They kick him. They kick the life out of his body, a human football being kicked from one demon to another. Eventually, he breathes and moves no more, broken and unfixed. The demons lose interest in soccer and turn towards me. I prepare my final stand.

And then it was just silence. Just me. And the twenty or more demons staring at me with no eyes in their faces. The demons start laughing.

"You see Roslan, your gift of immunity is actually a curse."

Who is that? What is that?

Behind the gang of demons steps out a gigantic demon. Different from the one that was taunting me from the beginning. It is a true giant demon compared to the others.

"Let's see how you hold up to this, Roslan the crying captain," booms the voice of the boss demon, pointing at me with its giant tree-size hands. Black flame projectiles shoot out from both hands and head towards me. The other demons rush away from me, leaving me with all intent and purpose to simply die.

Just kill me. I will not move. I accept my fate, my final end.

I feel the intense heat from the black flames as the projectiles hit me. All seven projectiles hit me dead spot on the chest. I writhe in pain as they pass through me, striking nothing but the earth behind me, black flames dying out and vaporizing on its own into nothing. I could sense the boss demon and its minions were disappointed.

"You may have survived, but the pain of living will be greater!" And with that the boss demon fades into nothing and all around, the other demons disappear.

My parang slips out of my hand and I drop to my knees. I look around and see the bodies of those I could not save. I start sobbing loudly.

Not again, I could not save them.

I slap myself hard on my right cheek.

Slap harder.

Why?

I slap my left cheek as hard as I can, but I do not wake up from this nightmare.

You should be dead like the others.

Why are you alive? Why are they dead?

I keep slapping myself, each single time much harder than before, to a point my body cannot take any more and collapses onto the blood-stained earth.

3rd December

Rahman: Azan

Location: Perwira High School, The Capital, Bumi

"It's late, father. Can this not wait till tomorrow?" My son plead, and makes a case about having to send his son to school tomorrow. The truth is I know that he feels out of place when it comes to my work-related acquaintances. The true nature of my work, my life mission.

"Rahmat, be a loyal son and be my driver. Someday, you'll be the man of the family and I do expect you to have grown some balls by then." I angrily scold him. I do not do more, for he is too old for me to smack in the head. It is enough that I have put him in his place. Maybe I should not have been so harsh on him. I get out of the car and before I close the door, I apologise to him, in my own way, which is a contradiction of myself, "Just wait here. I know you are strong and brave. I want to see that someday, preferably before I die."

Heading to a local school hall, I have been told that Azan would be here. He runs a night school of martial arts for the despondent. This should be interesting.

I walk through the corridor into the dirty and run-down school hall, paint peeling off and the flickering of the occasional fluorescent light bulbs, the synchronized shouting of the martial art *Silat* instructions and drumming becoming louder. The school hall cum night gym has cigarette smoke lingering, with groups of boys, men and girls playing cards in one corner, whilst another group of rowdy lads in tomfoolery, dance to loudspeakers pumping heavy bass rhythms - lyrics of fast sex and repugnant behaviour. In the middle of the hall, stands a young man teaching a ragtag group of men on how to use aggressive *silat* moves to strengthen attacks. Not the way how silat should be taught.

These students don't look like they need any defending. They look pretty stock, steroid-induced muscle bursting and bullish. All eyes stare at me. If I had known this was not such a reputable place, I would not have worn my white skullcap and white 'jubah' - the traditional white gown. I would have worn a pair of my old jeans and maybe a baseball cap. Of course, I wouldn't fit in either, as I'm too old to wear jeans, let alone a baseball cap.

"Dude, what do you want?" says the leader of the pack, a crew-cut hair, smoking, stocky man who seems to be watching his gang learn and train in Silat.

"I am here to talk to Azan," I answered, pointing at their instructor.

"He's busy - can't you tell?" the gang leader shouts out to me, flexing his chest muscles.

"It's OK, I'll wait," I reply, walking closer towards them.

Why is my body moving on its own towards them? Can't I just be patient? Just find a seat and watch them.

"Hey old man, are you deaf? I said he's busy. He works for me. I own him so he can't talk to you tonight," the gang leader starts marching aggressively towards me.

What is wrong with him?

I look around the hall; a sadness fills my heart - have we lost our next generation?

Where did we go wrong? Where did I go wrong?

"This is my F-ing school gym, my training ground, you bloody old man!" the gang leader swings his right fist to my face.

At this point, time and everything slows down. I look at his face, and wonder why - why is he like this? I ask myself: Where did HE go wrong? I dodge his swing, leaning backwards and as his elbow passes in front of my face. I push his elbow towards his face. His momentum spins him out of control and he falls on the worn cement floor. I can hear a hundred startled eyes stare at me, gasping in horror.

I am too old for this. "I don't want any trouble. I need to talk to him, it's urgent," I try to reason with the angry gang leader.

Humiliated, he stands up, throwing kicks and then punches towards me. Recalling from body memory, I move side to side, countering each punch or kick, with a punch to his limb. My centre stands, my stance is solid, my legs do not move except when adding momentum to each counterattack.

The crazy gang leader falls down onto the rough floor. He takes a bit longer to recover and stand up, there is blood on his forehead. Other gang members start to close in onto me.

"You're going to hurt so bad, critical-care bad, old man," a skinhead gang-member screams at me, wielding his metal chain menacingly.

The gang leader signals to the crowd to start their frenzy.

"I should really teach all of you your individual lessons, but I don't have time for this!" I snap punch the gang-leader in the neck, and he starts to choke. As he falls down on to his knees, I grab his right arm, twisting it behind him.

"You should have been taught this a long time ago. If I was your father, I would have been ashamed of you. I would have taught you this important lesson!" I shout calmly at my new captive. I grab his pinkie finger, extending it to the limits of his range of movement. He screams in pain.

"First lesson, always respect your elders," I extend his pinkie finger further to a point I can feel a crunching sound. He yells in pain, profusely begging forgiveness. The other gang-members are unsure of what to do next. They must be asking why this old man is so calm even in the face of overwhelming danger.

"You see you'd always think the shortest finger that you have is the most useless. It is actually the most important. You lose the strength of your grip if you lose this finger, especially if you want to ever wield a parang, or a dagger, let alone for your self-pleasures," I must calm myself and not enjoy this moment, do not take pleasure in this.

"Silat is never meant to attack people. It is always a defensive martial form. We don't really kick in Silat, Everything that we do is like in Life. It must be grounded to the Earth, to our *Bumi*, to our beliefs," I point out to the floor, widening my stance. The gang leader is on the floor, holding on to his precious broken little finger.

"Next lesson, everything we do should be driven by good intentions, not this. Not for hooligans. That's all of you here," I point my finger authoritatively at all of them, as they take steps away from me.

"I'll make you pay for this, old man," The gang leader is now back on his feet, pointing his index finger defiantly. Then he yells out to his gang to attack me.

"No one is going to attack me. I have not finished my lessons," I slide towards the bully gang leader, twist his body around, grabbing his offending finger, his arm behind his back again. He is locked in the kneeling position again. "Please Sir, forgive me. I don't know what I was saying!"

"Please don't interrupt the free lessons I am giving. Listen, you see God gave us this finger for a reason and the index finger was definitely not created so that we could go round threatening people especially your elders," I warn them, staring into the eyes of the gang members and straight into their timid and deviated hearts.

Without warning, I snap his index finger broken. He writhes in pain, screaming and crying with shame. The sight of him in such a pitiful state, demoralizes the gang and they start to leave the hall, leaving their 'glorious' leader without a gang to rule upon.

Azan comes up to me, "Who are you? And did you really need to do that? I had a good arrangement here. You're spoiling everything."

"I'm Rahman. Your uncle, Master Tuah, has asked me to take you in and train you," I introduce myself.

This 19-year-old boy with mild acne dons a printed T-shirt 'Keep Calm and Learn Silat' and I can't help from judging him. I judge him for his associations; I judge him for his choice of clothing; I judge him for the amount of hair gel he plasters to create gravity-defying hair spikes.

Hairstyles. It was easy in my time. You just part your hair on the right or the left. Or if you felt optimistic, you comb your hair by parting it in the centre. Why is life becoming more complicated with each generation?

"I got nothing to learn from you or from my uncle. None of that mumbo-jumbo has got anything to do with me," Azan rejects my handshake, packs his gym bag and starts walking out of the hall.

I could foresee how this conversation would end, so I say to myself to try something else.

"I notice you can't even teach them proper silat. All the forms are like copied from the Internet..."

Think fast, what's that internet TV thing your grandson talks about?

"...from YouTube! You are nothing but a joke for a Silat teacher, I can't even call you a Silat instructor. You are nothing but a loser and you will always be a loser. Your mother would be rolling in her grave, knowing that she had sacrificed herself for nothing. A loser son." I taunt him. I don't mean this; I hope the spirit of his mother will understand.

Azan stops, turns round to face me, the muscles on his arms tighten as his fists are clenched, locked in a familiar stance and his breathing is deep. In spite of his desperate need to stay calm, I could feel the storm of the century whirling in his hand. "Don't you dare talk about my mother."

"I can talk about anyone however I want to. Including your dead mom. It is now a free world, isn't it?" In my heart, I beg forgiveness from his mother's spirit yet again.

"Hey Mr. Rahman, do you believe in the Truth of Fists?"

His facial muscles tense up, showing ripples of fury from his temples to his cheeks.

"The Truth of Fists? Not really, but if it means I beat you silly and you end up listening to me, sure no problem. What's the chance of a 'nothing' like you beating me?" I taunt him further, wondering - maybe I should talk to my son Rahmat this way - Will it change anything in him?

As Azan drops the bag, time slows down, I look at his hand letting go of his bag and I see it falling to the ground and just before it reaches the ground, a mighty kick lands onto my torso. I fall down hard on the cement floor.

What was that? I am pretty sure he was still standing at the same spot. I look up and recover into my usual stance. He has moved but did he really move that fast?

Azan attacks me with a number of punches but none land on me as I block them, whilst other punches, I dodge with ease. He is fast but not too fast for me. I will wait for him to tire before I start my counterattacks. Let's tire him out and then teach him a good lesson. I can predict his movement, his attacks, counterattacks and the rests that he takes before each movement.

Azan takes a few steps back. He looks tired. I smile. I show him I'm not even breaking into a sweat. Without warning, Azan lands a powerful flying kick onto my chest. I did not have time to react and end up absorbing the full force of his attack. I wonder how he achieved that kick. I saw nothing. I did not see his flying kick at all.

Something is not right about this. I feel a strange sensation in my tummy. Taking a few steps back, I whisper a short prayer, quickly lick my index and middle fingers of both hands and then rub both fingers against my eyes.

I open my eyes; my vision seems blurry. No, it's not blurry. The school hall gymnasium looks clear. It is Azan, it is he who looks blurry. I walk closer towards him and it all makes sense. Where for others this would have been a wonderful accomplishment, but for me, for Master Tuah's legacy, this is the ultimate failure. I cannot help but sigh deeply in great disappointment. He has been using his *shadow* to help him improve his silat.

Oh Master Tuah, how this apple has fallen so, so far away from the tree.

"I bet you couldn't do that a third time, not from this distance. Not even if I close my eyes," I close my eyes and motion him to attack me.

I don't know how I know the shadow or the *karin* is about to hit me, it's simply instinctual. I immediately open my eyes, see his karin in mid-attack and grab its neck.

"No, please don't," Azan shouts, begging me not to hurt his karin.

"Please don't. I can change. I can do good things too," His karin begs me. A doppelganger meant to watch and deviate him.

"There is no place for a karin who help perform the wrong deeds," I chant a short prayer as Azan rushes towards me.

"I pass judgment. may God show mercy on you," I crush the neck of the karin with my hands.

Azan's karin dies instantly and fades away, burning into tiny red flames. Azan himself tumbles down trying to catch the fading red vapour flames.

"Why? Why did you do that? I needed him. He is my only true friend. I really needed him - now I am a bloody loser!" Azan starts swearing, yelling profanities. He gets up and starts kicking and breaking the chairs and the benches around him.

He really thinks he lost more than just a tool.

I allow him to vent. When he calms down, I approach him. "Keeping a karin knowingly is wrong, it is against our ways, our beliefs. You already know that. It is your family that has been upholding this law for generations, correcting those who deviate from this."

"I will take you in as my apprentice, and set you onto the right path," I put my hand on his shoulder, but he brushes it off.

"Enough. The gang you hurt was my ride home, so please just take me home. I never want to be an apprentice to anyone. Let me throw my life away," Azan sulks.

He really thinks that karin was his friend. Oh man, he got it in real deep.

I wonder what is going to happen to the Unit. We need five men to be part of the team. I visualize sad and grumpy Master Tuah and his diabetic feet, grimacing in pain.

Master Tuah, why did you leave things to rot to such a point?

3rd December

Nurul: Kebayan

Location: Ingei hot springs, Ingei Jungle, Bumi

A rather large breasted old woman with an inappropriate sinister smile block our path to the waterfalls.

Manis murmurs, "Kebayan!"

No, this is not possible.

The 'Kebayan' lady giggles with all evil intent as she glides effortlessly towards us. We run and scramble, screaming as she chases after us effortlessly.

I hear a voice in my head. "You were born from water, and it is water that will save you."

Yes, the Penan reminder.

"Head into the hot spring pool!" I yell out, missing by inches, the grasp of the Kebayan demon lady.

The water is scorching hot, much hotter than in the morning when we first arrived. Putting up with the pain, we clamber on to the large rock in the middle of the hot springs pool. The Kebayan lady does not go across the pool towards us. Instead she goes round the pool, trying to find a way to get to us, but she does not succeed.

"I just need some help. Won't any of you help a poor old lady like myself?" The Kebayan lady is a horrible actress. She points her finger at me, and then smiles.

All I want to do is scream at her, taunt her that she won't get any of us, but the fear clamps me down. How can this Kebayan demon be real? As a child, I figured out the Kebayan lady demon is simply a story to scare children, and make them aware of child kidnapping and trafficking. And yet, here is this demon lady from hell who wants nothing more than to end our lives.

"We will need to stay here till dawn," Manis suggests.

"At least that's better than being with that thing out there," I could tell Sally is glad she is finally able to rest and stay put instead of running around in the dark, dark jungle.

I look at the pool and wonder if I should drink the water, no matter how horrible it tastes.

"What are you doing?" Manis yells at me, as I stoop down to scoop the water into my hand. As I touch the very hot water, the smell of sulphur clears my sinuses and I could feel a sudden coldness by my feet.

The next thing I know is that the three of us are flying off the rock. I land onto the edge of the pool, soaked wet in hot water. I yell in pain. Next to me, Manis is screaming. I turn around and see the same demon that was at Base Camp standing on the rock, yelling profanities.

There is another scream behind me. Sally! Where's Sally?

She had landed outside the hot spring, and the Kebayan demon lady is coming after her.

"Run, Sally!" I yell out, as Manis and I run to rescue her. Sally is injured, she limps away from the imminent danger.

The Kebayan lady grabs her hand, Sally hits the demon lady with her other hand, kicking and screaming, but she does not get away. The Kebayan demon lady laughs as she pulls Sally in between her large breasts and she starts to disappear inside. I grab Sally's other hand.

"Don't let go, Sally!"

Manis grabs her shoulder and we both try to pull her out, this sadistic tug of war. Sally goes deeper and deeper into the Kebayan lady's body.

I start kicking her captor but the Kebayan just smiles, concentrating on her task of swallowing Sally into her chest. Sally's head is now inside it. Her screams become muffled and all that is left is her hand, now limp and lifeless. The demon standing on the rock starts laughing together with the Kebayan lady.

Is this a game to them?

This time, the Kebayan lady grabs my arm.

"Your turn to join Sally!"

"NO, NO, NO!!" I struggle to force myself from being pulled into the chest cavity of this demon lady. Manis has got my other hand and is puling with all her might.

I want to live.

Those were my last thoughts before I shield my eyes from a blinding light.

3rd December

Adib: Haven

Location: Ingei Jungle, Bumi

One moment we were at Base camp with our 'boat repairer ghost', the next thing I remember is a really bright green flash of light.

My head hurts and starts to spin, as I feel my body become lighter and lighter but then suddenly heavy. My feet crash into solid ground, and sinks a bit. It feels wet and muddy. There is a mild hint of rotten eggs in the air and the feeling of fear, anger and anguish surrounds me.

I look around. It is dark, but I see Nurul and Manis dance their death struggle against something I can barely make out - an elderly large breasted lady. A kebayan demon!

"I don't think so, granny," says the old man, our saviour boat repairer.

With a gentle swipe of his hand, the kebayan lady's hand is severed and drops onto the floor. She screams, holding on to her injured arm. Nurul is free, as Manis pulls her away from the evil kebayan.

Where's Sally?

A dark demon jumps in front of the boat repairer.

"Die traitor!" it screams.

The demon starts throwing punches at the old man, but none touch him as the old man dodges them, moving side to side and then slides under its legs. The demon is wondering where the old man went. It arches its back, clearly in agony and then its chest bursts open, as I see the old man's arm punches through it. The old man's arm glows white in comparison to the darkness of the demon's body. The demon goes limp and drops dead on the jungle floor, burning up in tiny red flames and finally disappearing into nothing.

"We won't let you get away, Jawad!" the Kebayan lady charges towards us, but more importantly towards Jawad the old man saviour. As she nears him, Jawad raises his knee, swivelling his hip and kicks her square on the neck. The Kebayan demon's neck breaks and she tumbles down onto the ground. A strong bile-inducing stench of rotting meat surrounds her as her body decomposes immediately right in front of our eyes.

"How come her body does not burn in red flames, like the other demons?" I ask. Of all questions to ask, at this time and in this place.

"She was human, or at least at one time in her life," Jawad answers me, turning round to count how many of us are here in the dark jungle. Night has set and although Jawad's body seems to glow green and white, Nurul uses her torchlight to see who has made it.

Once human, how is that possible?

"Me, John, Nurul, Manis and Johari - is Sally here?" I know the answer to that question but I have to ask again. I see Nurul clenching her fist, tears welling up and she is tight-lipped. I know Sally is gone.

Poor Sally. Poor everyone.

"Your name is Jawad and you are one of them, aren't you?" Manis asks our saviour. The look on her face shows sheer confusion. None of us here understand what's happening.

"Why is this happening?" I ask before Jawad could answer.

"Yes, I am Jawad. You should have asked my name first when we met and not before I had saved everybody here. That's just a bit rude, you know," Jawad answers.

Johari squints at Jawad and places his hand on Jawad's shoulder, "Hey, don't I know you from somewhere? I met you at a Chinese restaurant once and we had an argument about I-forgot-what."

Jawad brushes off Johari's hand, "Sorry we've never met before. But I know you, Mr. Pangolin-killer. In fact, other than Adib and John, none of us have met before. We don't have much time to chat. I need to get you all out of her and into safety."

Johari frowns, "I'm not a pangolin killer. Not anymore."

"Shall we head to the waterfall?" Manis suggests.

"No, they'd catch us before we can make it there," Jawad replies.

"Why don't you do that thing that moved us from Base Camp to here?" John is pretty sure that is the answer to everything.

"You are right, John Proctor. I have to move everyone to somewhere safe. To the safety of your home. To be precise: Adib's house," Jawad gestures for us to move in closer together.

"My house? Why my house?" I ask Jawad.

"Yes, why his house? I want to be in the safety of my own home now!" Manis protests, fighting sobs in between her words.

"It's the only human house that I have ever been to."

The hairs on my back stand up, as a chill goes down my spine.

"We've been watching over you for some time now, Adib," Jawad puts his hand on my shoulder. I can tell from his eyes that there is so much he wants to say and yet so little time.

"Once home, you will all be safe. Just stay away from the Ingei jungle. There's a war between our worlds. And this place here, it no longer belongs to Man. This is their last bastion; they will not bow down to any reason from any of you."

3rd December

Jawad: Home

Location: Ingei Hot springs, Ingei Jungle, Bumi

It is hard even for me to believe that I have finally allowed Adib to see me. He must have a lot of questions about his past and his future. There is so much at stake.

Making sure everyone is standing behind, I start the spell to transport us to Adib's house. I concentrate and recall from my memory a picture of Adib's house: the white paint, the wooden tiled floors and those horrendous cats that keep staring at me every time I am there. I remember a time when his parents were still alive, memories of him happier. I wish I could have protected his parents.

I pause the spell and turn to Adib. "When the time is right, I will tell you everything: the preparations you must make for things to come. You are the key to everything."

"What will come? Why am I the key?" Adib asks.

"The key to what kind of everything?" Manis asks curiously.

"Our salvation," I answer calmly.

At that instant, I feel an ominous presence. There is something coming.

"They're coming. I can sense them," I say to my human companions. I usher the humans to stand behind me, gesturing them to hold on to each other tightly and to stay close. I turn around and my feet automatically move into a defensive stance as I raise my arms ready to attack whatever is coming.

Doing two things at the same time is so much harder.

Concentrate - recall Adib's house.

A dozen demons materialize in front of us. They charge and start attacking. I close my eyes as they attack and find their attacks physically nullified by me. Although I cannot see with my eyes closed, I can tell their movements by reading their evil intentions. I sense an opening. Straightening the palm of my right hand and focusing my strength into it, I jab through to an attacking demon at its chest. I push through the outer layers of its chest; the outer shadows that protect its heart and crush the beating sensation enveloped within it. I open my eyes and see that the demon is dead and burning to oblivion.

"I've got more of that coming," I shout out. The other demons scream in rage as they furiously continue to attack me, trying to grab the humans behind me. I have trained devotedly all my life for this. I close my eyes again. I recall Adib's house in my head whilst at the same time, I karate chop a demon's neck to a point that it breaks.

Remember Adib's house. Remember his porch.

The demons continue to attack as I repel them; I find it hard to concentrate. This is more difficult than I thought it would be. I better kill them off first, and with that I cast a quick spell that materializes an old rusty spear. The demons do not stop, taking no notice of my spear.

Jabbing into their chests, as they pile themselves towards me, I ensure that one by one, the demons die. One larger demon, a sub-commander, slashes me in the shoulder, but not before I poke my spear into its faceless face and then pushing through beyond its head. It screams in agony, shouting profanities before burning into red flames.

"Finally, silence." I look back at the humans, who are terrified and yet awed by my ability to protect them. I look at my shoulder wound. It is not fatal, but it needs proper healing care. I stick the blunt end of the spear into the ground and close my eyes again.

Transporting myself is always easier than with a group to a faraway distance.

Meditating deeply, I recall Adib's stilted house: his porch, his wooden tiled floors and memories of him when his parents were around. I see my own children, my two sons playing with Adib. I recall my own house, my wife whom I have not seen since the day I fled my home to Bumi. I think of my family. I should really be there with them.

Oh no, stop... stop this. I got to think of Adib's house. What's wrong with me? Why can't I just concentrate on his house?

I try once again, but a deep loud voice booms from across the jungle foliage.

"I'm going to make you pay for your crimes, Jawad. You heinous traitor!"

I open my eyes and see a giant faceless demon barely hidden amongst the tall trees beyond the other side of the hot springs. It points its hands to me and fires black flamed projectiles, flying at great speeds towards me.

"Serigala, oh you insane psychopath! I can't believe they released you! These must be desperate times!" I scream at my former protégé; Serigala, the giant faceless demon, pointing my hands at it and countering by firing white arrows tipped with green flames towards it.

The projectiles from Serigala and my arrows hit and nullify each other.

"I have progressed so much more since we last met, my former master. Now take this!" Serigala the giant demon shoots out a barrage of black flamed projectiles from both of his hands again, but this time the attack is continuous.

I must counterattack him and get the humans away.

I release from my hands a larger number of white arrows to destroy his barrage. I know these are not as powerful as the ones with the green flames.

We must get out of here now!

I meditate in desperation, distracted by the presence of my former student.

Why would they release him and put him in charge of operations again? Have their plans been accelerated?

A pain penetrates my chest, followed by a number of other stabs of pain. I open my eyes and see my body burning in black flames, as the projectiles have hit me.

I must save them, even if it's the last thing I do.

"What happened? You've been hit!" Adib can see that I am injured and burning.

"Just stay together." The spell must work. A bright, white light envelopes us, protecting us from further attacks from Serigala. I can see the giant demon running towards us.

I calm myself as I try to extinguish the black flames on my chest. I recall memories of Adib's parents and my children playing with him when he was small. The pain of my injuries on my chest is horrific, the flames still burning away my chest. My breath is getting shallower, as I hear a loud rumbling of a giant storming its way towards us.

"We're getting out of here, Dorothy!" I shout to my human friends.

It looks like I will not make it alive, I cannot bring them to Adib's house. A deep sadness fills my heart. I see images of my wife and my two sons at my home, living their lives without me.

"Who's Dorothy?" I hear Manis screaming out, as the white light turns green and then much brighter than before, blinding everyone.

Our bodies become much lighter, and a feeling that our minds have floated away from our physical presence...

There is only one place to go. Maybe this is what has been fated.

Who am I to fight fate?

3rd December

Adib: Dorothy

Location: Unknown

Bathed and trapped in complete light, my head spins again as my body feels lighter, floating. I could feel a warmness inside, feeling stretched without hurting. I don't know how long this will last for but it seems to go on forever.

Eventually, my head starts to become heavy. My limbs feel as though weights have been attached to them. I can hardly breathe as the unseen surroundings squeeze my chest. I struggle, gasping for air but passing out.

It feels hot and bright and I hear birds chirping. I wake up and find myself on a dry dirt road. It is bright, a very bright day.

Was it not night only just now?

I look at my Seiko wrist watch, it's hands still moving - the chronograph indicating we are still at night; 8pm to be precise, and not in day time. I tap on my watch; it seems to be going faster than usual. The others are lying on the ground near me. I am the first one to stand up, as the tiny sharp pebbles stuck to my forearm start to fall off one by one.

"Is everyone here?" I ask.

Nurul, Manis, Johari and John are picking themselves up. A body lies in front of me, burnt. I think that is Jawad, or what remains of him. He is moving, barely, whispering softly and slowly, "Adib, you are a key, but not the only key. Find out why."

He points his hand to somewhere further up the road, "Tell her I'm sorry." Small red flames burn his hands and his entire body.

He saved us and now he is dead. We are lost, completely lost without him. I watch to give my respect to our saviour, as his body burns and evaporates into nothing on this beautiful yet tragic sunny day.

"What now, Mr. Key?" John asks me. In spite of what has happened, he has not lost his twisted sense of humour.

I look around and see on both sides of the road, tall golden grass being blown gently by the wind.

"I don't even know where we are. Anyone want to have a guess?" No one volunteers an answer.

"I think we should walk and see where this road takes us," I suggest.

Johari looks at me, "I guess that's a good suggestion. I'm with you, friend." He pats my back and then pats me again on the shoulder.

Manis puts her hand on her forehead, squinting in pain. "Wait, who's Dorothy?"

John takes a step back and then looks back at us, "This can't be real. I guess we'll just have to follow the non-yellow, no-brick road."

John laughs and looks at Manis, "Come on, Dorothy. Let's go!"

How can he seem so jovial after our friends have been killed by those evil demons? And now we are lost. We are completely lost and alone. If those monsters attack us again, there is no one to protect us. We won't survive another attack like that. Why did it happen to us? Why did we survive?

My mind goes back to the attack at Base Camp: Ana's decapitated head rolling to my feet, both her eyes closed tight. Why do I recall the vividness of this?

I pull myself together and snap out of the desire to give up. I clench my fists tight, as my own nails claw into my palm.

We head out together on this path to wherever, in this strange unknown land as I keep asking myself the same questions: Why am I a key? Are there other keys? The key to what exactly?

3rd December

Manis: Bujak

Location: Unknown

Walking on this hot bright day is tiring, especially since none of us have actually slept. It was only night an hour ago. We have no water; we have nothing to eat.

"Anyone got the time?" I ask.

Nurul the doctor, looks at her Gucci watch, "It's now 11."

John interjects, "Yup, 11pm according to my Timex!"

Adib looks at his watch, "That's not possible. I looked at my watch before we left - it was 8pm, we could not have walked for 3 hours on this road."

"I don't have a watch but I usually count my steps and I'm pretty sure we've been walking for about 1 hour 4 minutes to be precise," Johari exclaims, gesturing with his fingers.

Everyone stops dead in their tracks.

"Where the hell are we?" I ask everyone.

"Let's not panic. For all we know, we might still be sleeping in our tents and this is all just a bad, bad yet so-real shared nightmare that we will wake up from. But in the meantime; if I may strongly suggest, we should all just play along and see where this leads to," John fails to calms everyone.

"None of us were sleeping in the first place. We were supposed to have dinner. Remember, John?" The doctor reminds him.

"I have a theory, and its related to the Fermi-Hart paradox or popularly known as the Fermi paradox. What if those things that attacked us and the guy who saved us are….. hmmm, aliens, and what if this is their world? Their world is here on Earth, but just not visible to us until now. Or maybe not easily accessible," John starts his elaborate explanation, getting excited with each sentence.

"Stop it, John. We don't need this now," Adib is clearly upset with John.

"Let's just head out and see where this path takes us. I am pretty sure Jawad wanted us to go here. He brought us here in the first place. I'm heading this way," Adib walks on, indicating he does not care if we follow him or not.

I run up after him, grab his arm and push him on the chest. "Hold on, Mr. Key. There's no need to be rude to any of us, you know. I can throw a tantrum too if I want to."

Adib pauses and tries to say something but doesn't. He stays quiet.

"We've lost so much..." I cannot finish the words.

"I'm sorry, Manis. We all need each other. This is not the time for any of us to fall apart. Come on, let's go," Adib waits for the rest to catch up.

The dry dirt road slopes down, and we see a number of houses down below. There is smoke coming out from the chimney of one of the houses. It looks like a small farm. Johari gestures for us to run into the field on the side of the path. We lay down, hiding and watching the settlement below.

"It looks like a small farm," Adib then points out to the other houses and on closer observation, we see the other houses are rundown and abandoned.

"I don't think anyone lives in any of the other houses," Adib continues.

"Look, look, there's a woman coming out of that house," I point out, barely holding down my excitement and fear.

In the distance, we can see a middle-aged woman bringing out a bucket of clothes to hang on to some clothes line.

"I don't think she lives alone," Johari point out to the different sizes and shapes of the clothes.

"She doesn't look like an alien. What do we do now, Mr. Key?" John asks me.

Adib punches John in the shoulder, "Will you just stop it?"

We did not notice the golden grass behind us rise up. And then two spears protrude from the mounds behind us.

The sharp spear points nudge at Johari and John.

"Ouch, what the..." Johari and John yell out in pain.

As I turn around to see, the sun blinds my eyes, I can only see two large shadows, holding spears in their hands.

Is this the end?

"This is the end for you - we don't let trespassers live!"

EMPAT

4th December

311 | The Last Bastion of Ingei

4th December

Azilah: Hitam

Location: Hilaga City Locked Archives Hall, Hilaga City, Ifrit

I rub my hand across the long wooden table, situated between two giant bookshelves. The soft grooves run against my palm - soothing and distracting me from the overwhelming thoughts about the woman in the mirror and her bright glowing blue eyes. A green ancient book lays open, halfway revealing too much and too little at the same time. I look around and gaze upon the unaccountable number of books and shelves in the Hilaga City Locked Archives Hall, essentially a library that holds the key to our past.

She had bright glowing blue eyes and she did step out of the mirror. She did pull me up. She did talk to me. I did not imagine it. I could not have imagined it. I should have told Master Selym, but I chose not to.

"Azilah, listen to your heart. You know who you are. Do you know who you should be?" Her voice keeps echoing in my head, even as I try my best to concentrate on looking for clues in the green book, The mysterious Amanah treaty.

Do I know who I should be? Is that even a question I should be asking. I am a loyal Hilaga servant. I can't concentrate any more. I have tried my best to read the treaty, the minute details have bored me. I convince myself that to get back to my current task I need to start by summarising on what I have read so far. I know that the Amanah treaty has a small portion about peace requirements amongst the three warring parties - to be precise, it is a war between only two parties - the humans and Azzah citizens against Hilaga. There's a significant portion of pages dedicated to the lengthy protocols on communication between Azzah, Hilaga and the humans.

The only thing I had found on inter-world travel is that only four people are allowed to perform such travel. The first being The Great Conjurer Jawad of Hilaga. Maybe he could talk to us and help us. He is from Hilaga, though no one really knows where he is and what he does. He no longer represents Hilaga City Supreme Council interests. I wonder why.

The second person has a name written in an ancient language that the people in Azzah used to use. Unfortunately, I cannot read it. The only symbols I can decipher are those that represent fearless and brave. Whoever this person is he or she is likely to be alive as the city of Azzah no longer exists.

I look at the third name, but the name has faded away, the ink a mere shadow of a shadow on the aged paper. I hold the page against the light but nothing. No clue whatsoever on whom this person is. How inconvenient.

The fourth named person is only titled as the human leader of the Gergasi Clan. Why have I heard of them before? How come they have the ability to travel between our worlds? The humans have inferior technology and yet this person from the Gergasi Clan can travel to Hilaga without using our MATA portal.

Strangely enough, a large chunk of the Amanah treaty is about resource sharing - on how the three groups are to work together on a large ancient meteorite found in Azzah which they have called Sikar. Most of this is written in Azzah scripture and seems very technical with drawings and ancient numbers. I skip through these pages fast, flipping through fast and yet as carefully as I can.

An interesting page titled Sikar and Humans catches my attention. One particular line intrigues me and I can feel my heart beat much slower when I read the line over and over again: "the presence of humans disrupt the function of Sikar in this world. The humans have known this long before which is why they have very little interest in any study on Sikar and harnessing it…"

Is Sikar what I think it is? I ask myself.

"Azilah, looks like you found the Amanah treaty!" I am startled by Keeper Azran, to a point that I nearly jumped out of my chair.

"Sorry, I don't mean to creep up on you like that, Azilah."

"It is not your fault, Keeper Azran. I've just been lost in my thoughts, reading this book."

"Yes, we have been trying to find it for some time. It must have been waiting to reveal itself to you, Azilah. You must be very special indeed," Keeper Azran smiles wryly.

I don't respond and nod in appreciation to his kind words.

"Azilah, have you ever heard of The Biru Prophecy?"

I recall a moment in my childhood, so vivid that I cannot tell the difference between this memory and the present. A silent conversation at the old Great Tree with both my parents. I cannot hear the words from my parents, and I cannot hear my own words. I look at their hands, gentle swaying of their hands in the air, a ritualistic hand dance perhaps. I do not remember it well. I snap out of the memory.

"Yes, The abolition of the Noble Houses."

Keeper Azran half smiles, "No, Azilah that is not really the prophecy."

"Well, what do you think is The Biru Prophecy?"

"It's not for me to tell you. You are supposed to know for yourself, Azilah," Keeper Azran walks away from the table. I fold my arms in protest. I can't believe he just mind-teased me with that conversation. It is probably the only entertainment he gets in this dull place with these dusty, dull books.

Keeper Azran heads to the centre of the Locked Archives Hall, and gather with the other dozens of Keepers. They chant a short prayer together and bid each other goodbye. Their faces previously almost emotionless, now strained and tearful - as though, this is their final goodbye. They slowly disperse and solemnly disappear in between the rows of bookshelves.

Is this their ritual and then carry out business as usual? Live and say their final goodbyes each day, believing that today is their last day of their lives?

I tell myself to get back to reading the Amanah treaty book. The more I read the more intriguing it becomes. If only I could read the Azzah scriptures. I read whatever I could translate or guess-decipher. I find out that the humans' ability to negate the Sikar effects and properties has resulted in an agreement to a new protocol to ensure that humans do not enter our realm. I wonder how many people in Hilaga know about this.

I am about to read the next page, when an intense tightening sensation all over my body overwhelms me. A sudden white flash, I cannot see anything but the white light. Instantly, I shield my eyes with my hands, but it does nothing to protect me from the blinding light, so bright I can see the bones in my hands, transparent. The overwhelming light fades a bit, still filling the entire Locked Archives Hall and then passes through the walls of the Hall. The walls become briefly transparent and I can see the City outside of this building. The white light disappears and then reappears each time as bright and blinding and then disappears again through the walls. My head throbs in pain, as the blinding flash occurs for a few more times - I counted a total of five flashes. I wait in the silence, whilst my vision slowly turns from blind white to blurriness with persistent white patches on the edges. I become disorientated. What was that?

There is a low and faint rumbling in the sky. I wonder if it is a thunderstorm? I look up but I can't see through the stained glass windows near the ceiling. The rumbling does not seem to stop. The floor starts to shake. The walls tremble, as tiny cracks form and deform with each heart-wrenching tremble.

And then it happens. An overwhelming ear-splitting roar, I cover my ears tightly, as I watch from below, the large stained glass ceiling windows shatter, a deadly rain of the most beautiful rainbow glass shards. Ghostly and violent white dust swoops in as thunderous shock waves hit everything in the Locked Archives, knocking down and breaking the bookshelves. The books fly out violently out of the shelves, like birds flying in disarray and in fear. My own body is thrown away from the table and I tumble several times onto the floor. I quickly try to pick myself up, my feet feeling semi-jelly, coughing bitter dust out of my mouth.

What had just happened?

There is total and complete darkness and the room has gone very cold. Am I blind? Did I hit my head so hard that I have become blind?

Think quickly. I reach for my pockets and find an emergency light orb. I squeeze the soft cold orb hard, its yellow amber light slowly glows in my hand, becoming brighter and brighter. I hold it above my head as I scan around me; the knocked down bookshelves and panicking Keepers trying to find each other, whilst some have already started picking up the books. They shouldn't have bid each other goodbye. Sometimes it's just asking for it.

My training tells me I must prioritize. I examine myself and reassure myself that I am not seriously injured. I must find the Amanah treaty.

To my surprise, the Amanah treaty is still on the table, with the last page unturned, whilst my chair and all the other surrounding tables and chairs lay broken to smithereens. Not a scratch on that table or the book. Now is not the time to figure out why. Next priority is to find Master Selym.

I shine the light towards the sleeping quarters' entrance and rush off towards it, jumping over the debris of broken bookshelves and tattered books. I hear a Keeper shout at me not to step on the books.

Is he serious? Prioritize. Ignore them.

I push through the doors to the sleeping quarters. It is even colder, immensely cold, fog appears with each breath. There are so many people here, at least a dozen in strange attire. They all look injured.

"Is everyone alright? Is anyone hurt?" I shout out to this group. As I shine my light orb to examine them better, to my horror, I see distorted pale faces, some have white cloth stuffed in their mouths. They swarm me. They are not my people! They are phantoms of our own past!

4th December

Nurul: Earth

Location: Unknown

Shielding my eyes to see what is apprehending us, in between my finger I can see the two figures, completely covered by golden straws.

"Stand up, and move now!" A voice booms out from the taller straw entity.

"You will face judgment from our leader; and if deemed fit, you will all be executed!" shouts the slightly shorter straw entity.

As I stand up, I notice the two straw figures who are no taller than my shoulders, are brandishing rather sharp spears.

Nudging us with their spears, we marched down a path towards the house with the smoking chimney.

"Don't even think of running. We can throw our spears and accurately pierce your heart with our eyes closed!" They warn us.

Johari tries to make a run, but the taller straw figure effortlessly swings his spear and hits him on the head with the blunt end of the spear. Johari is knocked out cold, and starts to bleed from his nose.

I check on Johari, feeling his pulse and scalp. He is still alive. We should plan and coordinate an escape. I look at Adib, but his eyes do not meet mine. How are we going to tell each other on what to do? I try to formulate an escape plan, but nothing materialises. I look at Johari again. He is still unconscious. I better check him again, once we get indoors.

"Please don't hurt us," I plead. "We will listen to what you tell us to do." That's good - gain their trust and sympathy.

The taller straw figure grabs Johari and throws him on his back.

These short guys are tough and strong. This is not the time to make a mistake. I notice Adib is very quiet and un-engaging. From the look of his eyes, I can tell he is analysing the situation. He will figure out a plan.

We approach the timber house, smoke gently rising out of the chimney. The straw creatures push us into the house and the doors slam hard behind us.

Johari is flung onto a table; his head makes a thud as it hits the table. He clearly isn't receiving the best post-head-injury 'neuro-care'.

I look around for exits. There is a large wooden door at the end of this room, which looks like a living room and dining room. I see a large old wooden table in front of us, and what looks like a sofa set in front of it, covered in over-sized square-pattern quilts. The quilts remind me of a time when my own grandmother made a quilt blanket for me, with custom pieces salvaged from unwanted fabrics.

The lady of the house, a rather stern-faced lady with black curly hair, moves towards us. Her steps are loud, thumping on the wooden floors, followed by loud creaks after each step.

My heart starts beating fast. My instincts tells me I should be afraid of this woman. Very afraid. Is she just like the Kebayan lady?

She looks at Johari, who is starting to wake up. She wipes the blood from his nose, rubbing it in a continuous gentle swirl between her fingers, whilst clearly in a state of bewilderment.

"He's not from here. Did you do this, Jawad? Where is he? Jawad, where are you?" She shouts towards us, and then lock her sights on to Adib. Adib seems undaunted, shaking his head from side to side. She starts to scream in a language we have never heard of and weeps.

"Ma, what's wrong?" The taller straw figure goes up to console the weeping lady of the house. He puts both hands on his head and the straw head comes off to reveal the face of a fair-skinned young boy, with large dark eyes and mild facial hair.

This boy is probably 12 years old. I can't believe he captured us.

"Ma, what is it? What's wrong? Shall I put them away?"

The other straw figure pulls off his head gear to reveal another fair-skinned boy, slit eyes with a mischievous look on his face. He goes over to Johari and looks at the blood dripping from his nose.

"Hey Eedi, look, his blood is different. It does not turn to a red vapour. It turns into a brown clay!"

The shorter boy grins and looks squarely at us, "You're not one of us. You're humans. We love humans!"

He jumps up, "Actually, I've never met a human. My father used to talk about humans. I never thought we'd ever meet one and definitely not in our village!"

"I'm Eeqil, son of Jawad the Great Conjurer, the guardian of 'Amanah'" Eeqil jumps up to shake our hands.

It is a great relief to be welcomed instead of being on the verge of an execution.

Their leader, the woman of the house, leaves the room through the door on the other side.

"Let Ma be on her own. She needs to get some fresh air," the taller boy says to the shorter boy.

"I'm Eedi. Welcome to the ruined city of Azzah. It's really a village now these days. But it's our home," The taller boy hugs us.

"I apologise for our behaviour, earlier. We thought you might have been Hilagaan border guards in disguise," Eedi says apologetically, doing his best to ignore the fact that his mother is indifferent to us, lost in her own world of sadness.

"Did you say you are the son of Jawad?" Adib asks.

"Yes, I did. Have you met him?" Eeqil pounds his chest with his small hands.

"He saved us and brought us here," Adib chooses his words carefully.

"My father's amazing - he is the only one who can transport himself and people to-and-fro our worlds! Wow! That is just amazing! I'm going to write this in my diary!" Eeqil is jubilant.

Eedi looks back to make sure that the other door is properly shut.

He whispers to Adib, "I know my father is not alive, otherwise he would be here." He bites his lower lip and lowers his head, "Please don't tell Eeqil what happened. Not today. It's his birthday today."

Eedi musters a fake smile, pushes the pain deep into the recesses of his heart.

"Let's eat and welcome you properly to our city of Azzah," Eedi welcomes us again with hugs. As he hugs me, I can feel warm tears flow down on my shoulder. He does not want to let go.

I pat on his back. I want to soothe him with kind words but nothing comes out, so instead I hug him tighter. Today, we have lost people we care for, lost ourselves in a world which does not belong to us.

The Mother re-enters the house. Having regained her composure, she walks silently to a cupboard to reveal a chocolate cream birthday cake.

"What? No candles!" Eeqil complains.

"Sorry brother, there were border guards manning yet another road block to the town."

"Well, how old are you Eeqil?" I ask.

"I'm 70 years old today!"

Did he say seventy?

"Got his first arrest warrant this week!" Eedi interjects.

"It's not fair, damn border guards. I'm still a baby, you know!" Eeqil moans, pretending to blow out imaginary candles on his birthday cake.

"A handsome baby. I hope you remembered to make a wish," Mother smiles down and kisses him on the head.

He can't be seventy. He barely looks like he's 6 years old. Everyone in the group is stunned.

"How old are you, Eedi?" Adib asks. I suppose one of us had to ask.

"I just turned 125 years old 3 months ago," Eedi replies.

Manis gasps upon hearing. We all stay quiet. Best not to ask too much for now. We won't ask 'Mother' how old she is.

How do we get home? What's happening back home?

"Adib, I'm going to say you're the leader of this group, so I'm going to delegate you this task. Please ask them how do we get home," I whisper to Adib.

"Not now. We should get to know them better. Earn their trust," Adib reasons.

"Are we safe here?" John eavesdrops and interjects.

"I feel safe with them, this is Jawad's family after all - the man who sacrificed his life to save us," Adib whispers back.

"Adib, you know he wasn't a man, he's one of them. Whatever they are." John pauses to reflect upon the gravity of the situation. "Yes, I guess you are right. We should be able to trust them."

"Let's rest tonight and find out more information tomorrow," Adib walks away from us, and heads towards Eeqil and starts some casual banter.

"I'll check up on Johari," I won't stand idly by.

Johari is nursing his headache. "Hey Jo, how are you?"

"Headache boss. That damn kid hit me. I can't believe that kid hit me hard. A kid, I tell you. Wait till I get back on my feet. I'm going to punch him in the head and see if he enjoys that." The good thing about being a clinician is that I am assessing his Glasgow Coma Scale whilst listening to him.

"Ssshhh, just rest and don't think about it," I reach for a tissue in my pocket and wipe the blood dripping from his nose. I look at the piece of tissue and notice the red blood is no longer there. It's turned to brown earth.

4th December

Adib: Ruin

Location: The Ruined city of Azzah

"Happy birthday Eeqil! I can't believe you are 70 years old! Do you know how old I am?" I ask the younger boy, who is actually as old as my grandfather.

"I don't know, I've never met a human before. What's your name human? I forgot to ask. Actually, it's your fault, You should have introduced yourselves first," Eeqil grins, points his index finger at me and then picks his nose with that same finger. I do my best to look away, without being too obvious.

I decide that I should be diplomatic and try not to correct him. "Well, you are right. I forgot to introduce myself. I'm Adib," I then point to the others and introduce everyone in the group to our hosts.

"I know your kind don't live that long, not like us - but then age is only a number," Eedi, the elder brother joins in, and passes a warm light brown tea drink to me.

I sure hope it's just tea.

"Since you are friends of father, you better stay with us. Besides, there's nowhere safe to go here, not with the Hilaga border guards patrolling in our city."

"You know we just got here and we are still processing a lot of information. Where exactly are we again?"

"You're in the ruined city of Azzah. By right, this place here is supposed to be Batin Village of Azzah, but then there's nothing really left of Batin or Azzah."

"Nothing left but us," Eeqil corrects his brother.

"So you can say Batin and Azzah are the same place," Eedi continues.

I try to summarise his points in my head, "Batin village and Azzah City are the same place?"

"Yes, the problem is that most of the villagers have been evicted and their houses are in the process of being demolished. We're the only residents left in this village! We're essentially the last real residents of Azzah city," Eeqil seems proud as he emphasises that they are the last residents in the village and city.

"Evicted? Ruined City? Batin Village?" I am so confused.

"Batin house... that's it! We should name our house Batin House. I can see it on a sign board: Welcome to Batin House," Eeqil starts jumping up and down in excitement of his new idea.

"No, don't even think of that. You're already in trouble with the authorities," Eedi puts out the flames of his younger brother's plan.

"Hold on, guys. Why is this city ruined?" I ask. I better ask my questions one by one and slowly.

"There were two cities in this world, Azzah and Hilaga. There was always war between the two cities, struggling for territory," Eedi pauses and sips his drink and then looks at me and the mug I'm holding.

I better not be rude and politely start sipping. I notice he is watching me as I take a small sip - Ooh! this is a very sweet warm tea.

"My father's actually from Hilaga. He's a great powerful warrior-conjurer, until he met and fought with my mom," Eeqil, his dark small eyes light up as he moves up closer to me, keen to add to the story-telling.

"Actually, the story is that they met each other several times on the battlefield as sworn enemies. Each time both survived, vowing to fight each other to the death every single time. One day, during the bloodiest battle of the war, they challenged each other to a duel. Both sides stopped fighting so that they could watch them duel," Eedi continues his story, occasionally staring at the mug in my hands.

"They fought for several days without resting, without sleeping. Eventually, they found they had more in common and fell in love," Eeqil excitedly starts weaving his own story.

"What do you know about love? You're just 70 years old," Eedi is clearly annoyed with Eeqil's constant interruptions.

"Well, the girl that you fancy does not like you back, so both of us can't really say we know anything about love, can we?" Eeqil puts his finger below his right eye, pulls it down and sticks a tongue out.

"I'm not going to comment on that. It's a working progress. This girl Zara really likes me; she is just a bit shy."

"Okay, so your father and mother were from different cities and they fell in love when they fought each other during the war? Did I get that right?" I make a mental note. "So where exactly are we again?" Manis asks but no one answers her.

"Yes, that's right," Eeqil reassures me, leaving Manis unanswered.

"Anyway, back to MY story, when they realised they had fallen in love with each other, they could not fight each other and both sides had no more will to fight and created a peace treaty agreement: the Amanah," Eedi eyes Eeqil, hinting to him not to interrupt him. Eeqil gestures the zipping of his mouth.

"Both cities united to form one nation. I don't know what exactly happened but in the War of Peace, our people were tricked and Azzah was absorbed slowly, building by building, house by house, family by family." The sombre look on his face reveals the depth of tragedy.

"Hilaga has expanded and taken everything but us and a few other villages."

"War of Peace? What do you mean by that?" I ask.

"There has always been war, even during peace time. I think the worst of wars are the ones that you can't see - the silent war of peace. It happens slowly. People are killed slowly, as their way of life and freedom are taken away from them whilst they are unaware of it. The worst thing is that many give up their freedoms willingly, not understanding the consequences."

I look at Eedi. He is so intense. His words reveal himself as a mature thinker.

"You've been talking to Uncle Tikus too many times. I'm telling Ma. You know she doesn't want you to talk to him," Eeqil heads off towards the stairs.

Eedi catches him by the ear, "I'll whip your sorry ass if you do that. You know I will, right?" Eeqil nods.

The last villages of Azzah city?

A wave of tiredness hits me. I hope I've not been drugged.

Eedi notices I am feeling sleepy. He grabs my mug quickly. "It's my father's mug, a special gift to him. Can't have you breaking it."

Eedi escorts me upstairs. I feel so tired and yet have enough attention to admire the carvings on the solid wood stairs. The curvy repetitive carvings feel familiar to me, and yet I am sure I have never seen them before. I notice there are many bedrooms upstairs, more than enough for the rest of us.

"You can sleep here, Mr. Adib," Eedi motions to me to move quickly into the bedroom. I notice the large round window by the bed as I allow myself to fall on the soft mattress. It is unbelievably softer than my own bed. I smell the faint scent of flowers from the mattress. As Eeqil closes the door, I see Manis going into the bedroom across mine, she turns around and smiles at me.

I adore her large eyes - yet again - I start wondering if she is the type who is vulnerable to crying; that she would need someone to always be with her, or perhaps her large eyes means that she is someone who stands on her own feet and would never need anyone like me. Maybe being independent means she wants to be with someone who is strong-willed like me. Who am I kidding? Me strong-willed? Never mind that. Just cherish the moment.

What a beautiful smile.

The sea of tranquillity.

4th December

Azilah: Phantom

Location: Hilaga City Locked Archives Hall, Hilaga City

Their wretched and pained faces pale white, grey and blue, a few of them are still wrapped in pre-cremation white clothes.

This can't be!

It is only now when I realize again who they are that the stench in the air hits me.

They're phantoms of my people! Ghosts in my world! Impossible.

They start swarming towards me. I start to panic, as I become breathless - suffocated by both their stench and the impending threat they potentially pose.

"Stay away from me. I am not intending to hurt anyone. I just want to find my master." I grip my fists hard, one hand squeezing the light orb harder as the orb responds and brightens, my hand translucent in the bright yellow light.

The horde of spectres move aside, giving me an unobstructed pathway to the sleeping quarters.

"Master Selym!" I shout out. A lady ghost with white cloth plugged into her empty eye sockets and her oral cavity points to a room on the right.

I rush through to find Master Selym on a bed, holding his pillow tight - muffled voices. Is he shouting?

"Master Selym!" I pull the pillow away from him.

He jumps out of the bed, towards me, hitting me with his knee in the chest as I fall back onto the floor. I see the dark blade of his Kerambit dagger in his hands, ready to plunge into my chest. His eyes look wild, with a glint of red. In reflex, I grab his hands and fling Master Selym across and over my shoulders, before falling onto the floor. As my light orb drops onto the floor, Master Selym lands on his feet behind me. I watch as the orb spins its flickering yellow light towards his feet.

"Master Selym, it's me Azilah!"

"Sorry Azilah, I had a strange dream. What's happening here? Why did you enter my room and why is it so dark in here?"

"It's dark everywhere, Master Selym. Something bad happened. I am not sure what it is. Did you not hear the sound and the shock waves? The Locked Archives Hall is badly damaged."

"Are we under attack? This must be a takeover," Master Selym starts to talk to himself.

"Takeover, Master?"

"Lord Jahat, we must protect him. He is the only person that is in the way of the Hilaga City Supreme Council. If this is a power grab, then it would be the work of the Hilaga City Supreme Council. We must hurry and protect him."

Master Selym runs out of the sleeping quarters corridor, now empty, no ghosts, no phantoms and through the ruined Locked Archives Hall. There are no lights working anywhere. My light orb illuminates the area around, as I catch a glimpse of the Amanah treaty book still at the same place. Now is not the time to deal with it. We rush out of the building. It is pitch black, the skyscrapers are dark and devoid of all light. Only the stars seem so much brighter in the cloudless night sky.

We have never had a blackout, What is happening here? Hilaga City Supreme Council? Why would they destroy everything to stop Lord Jahat? A thousand questions are in my head as I run silently, chasing after Master Selym through this narrow alley back to the main road.

The ground crunches with every step we take, broken and shattered glass - we crush our broken dreams to tinier glass fragments as we rush towards Hilaga City Hall. We must protect Lord Jahat.

As we approach the dark road, there is nothing but chaos. Many citizens are out in the streets, holding out their own light orbs, stunned and murmuring whilst pointing to the light-less tall buildings. Everywhere else, a mass of panicking dark shadows rubbles in the distance, occasional light flickers revealing the helpless citizens, some in their nighties, some in their night duty clothes, trying to make sense of the loss of power in a city that has always had constant power and light. "Hilaga is the light of the Universe", I start to recall the political slogan some time ago. I ignore the constant tapping of the glass windows high above me.

Master Selym and I push through the crowd into the Hilaga City Hall entrance. Master Selym pushes frantically at the elevator controls but to no avail. We are trapped on the ground floor. There is no way up.

"What now, Master?"

"There is a secret emergency mechanical elevator built in the corner. Hurry!"

After breaking off a hidden panel, we both step into a wooden elevator, that has a wooden switch handle with a bright red arrow engraved into it.

"How did you know about this secret elevator, Master?"

"Lord Jahat secretly commissioned for it. I personally eliminated the workers who built it."

A cold ice sensation runs down through my spine, as I find my place in the one corner of the small cramped elevator.

"It only goes up to one place, Azilah. Hold on to something!"

Master Selym pushes the wooden handle up, and we are both catapulted up at incredible speeds. I hold on tight to the sides of the walls of the elevator. They should have built handrails to hold onto. I do my best to stop my stomach contents from propelling up too. The elevator stops abruptly, as both of our bodies are flung to the roof of the elevator and then we fall hard onto the floor.

Master Selym groans, as he picks himself up. He knew this would happen. Master Selym pulls apart an outer door with his bare hands, revealing the 50th floor hallway to us.

"Come on, Azilah. Search for your strength now!" I stagger up and catch up to him. We run towards Lord Jahat's office. It is hard to miss, it's the one with five Hilaga City Hall guards, armed with unsheathed daggers, standing hesitantly in front of the door.

"TRAITORS! You will all DIE! Lord Jahat is our true leader!" Master Selym shouts, withdrawing both his bladed weapons.

I take out my dagger, and yet I am unsure on what I am doing. Are they really traitors?

"Hilaga is the Light Unto this World!" In the dark, I can see Master Selym jump towards the first two guards, they didn't have time to defend themselves, as Master Selym's daggers cut both their throats instantaneously. He was so fast, I did not see the daggers make contact, simply the sound of gurgling and crimson fiery sprays of their blood lighting the hallway.

Two other guards rush towards Master Selym, their battle-cry muffled quickly by Master Selym's kicks to their abdomen followed by stabs through their mouths. Both guards fall ungraciously, slumped on the carpeted floor.

"I surrender. I don't want anything to do with this. I am only following orders. Please." A guard pleads for his life, but before he could say anything else, Master Selym decapitates him quickly. As he turns to me, I see his eyes glow fiery red, "Hurry!" Master Selym kicks open the doors, revealing a large, spacious office filled with intricate ornaments and keepsakes, illuminated by many tiny light orbs glowing yellow and orange. Lord Jahat, seated at his table, maintains a calm posture, and yet, I see beads of sweat trickling down his face.

"Selym, I knew you'd come. It seems the Hilaga City Supreme Council must be responsible for this. If only I had my youth, I would have killed them all with my bare hands. They are supposed to kill me, but they hesitated," Lord Jahat wipes sweat from his face with the table cloth and then hands it to Master Selym.

"That was their mistake, Lord Jahat." Selym wipes cleans his daggers.

"Is this a takeover? A coup?" I ask stammering, wondering if I have a right to ask such an open question.

"Yes, a coup. They've been planning to remove me from power, they must have become impatient. I can't imagine any better time than now to act. I am the most popular now, and I have the greatest number of supporters. But still, how did they cause such a massive blackout? I had confirmation that even our backup power generators are no longer functioning!"

"My Lord, it seems the Hilaga City Supreme Council believes that to win, they must destroy everything first. 'Scorched City Policy'."

"Yes, it seems that way. I am truly disappointed. I was expecting to play a lot more games with them."

"What's the plan, Lord Jahat?"

"Let us head towards the Hilaga City Supreme Council. We have our loyal people there. We will make a few stopovers and rally some of our most loyal troops."

"Someone like Serigala would be useful right now. I can see why you brought him out," Master Selym suggests.

Lord Jahat smiles, as though congratulating himself for his master stroke and then realises that Master Serigala is unlikely to have made it back to Hilaga.

"The blackout - Serigala is still in Bumi - the entire unit is still there."

"You still have us, Lord Jahat."

"Yes, Selym the Great. The people will rally behind you. We will emerge victorious. Selym, I want them all dead. You understand? The Hilaga City Supreme Council, them, their followers, their children, every single last one of them. Tonight, the games come to an end."

4th December

Manis: Faith

Location: Batin Village, The Ruined City of Azzah

I rest on this soft, soft bed in a strange house, in a strange land, surrounded by human and Bunian strangers who are now friends. The only friends I have left. This house belongs to the Bunian family of Jawad's, who died protecting us. Why did he have to die protecting us? I stare at the ceiling, and then realize how the different irregular wood pieces fit in perfectly to create this beautiful ceiling. I remember memories of my mother, my siblings, my father and then my nephew; Andie, and his family. I pray for their souls; may they rest in peace.

What will happen next?

God, please protect me and keep me safe, wherever I am.

***

The thunderous sound of falling water. I am back at the waterfalls, hiding in the rock recess behind the curtain of water. This can't be, I am supposed to be safe now. Why am I here again? I feel the danger lurking beyond the waterfall. The giant demonic shadows moving across the screen of water.

"Don't worry. I'll keep you safe," I turn around to see the pangolin, whom I have named 'Andie'. Andie had saved me whilst I was lost in the jungle. He kept me protected, when I was alone. Did a pangolin save me, or is it a friendly jungle spirit, or perhaps God's sent saviour?

"Andie, is that you?" I ask the talking Pangolin.

"My name's not Andie, but for you Manis, you can call me anything you want," the pangolin squeaks.

"What's going to happen to me? To us? Will we be safe? Will we ever get home? Will we be stuck here forever?" I ask a barrage of questions, ignoring the fact that I am speaking to a talking pangolin. I must be going mad.

"There's nothing to worry about. Life is like a river and you are a leaf, floating down the river that has already decided where to take you. Know in your heart that you are nothing but the leaf, and everything will happen the way it has been fated. Trust in Him," The wise pangolin moves closer to me, and huddles next to me, its hard scales rubbing against my arms. How I wish I could have armour like that and just roll up away from all this danger.

A large water rat suddenly appears swimming towards me. I shudder in terror; fearful the water rat would bite me with its giant sharp teeth.

The pangolin stops me from screaming, "Don't worry, he's a friend. He's actually going to help you." Sure enough, the rat climbs on to the rock wall and rests next to me.

"You must trust the path that has been set upon you, for it has already been written since the beginning of time. For that is the true test of the faith in fate," whispers the rat into my ear, its whiskers tickling my ear.

"Who are you? Why are you talking to me, er... Mr. Rat? Sorry what is your name?"

The giant rat strokes its long whiskers dry, "Manis, you'll know my name when we meet. In the meantime, we'll protect you here," The giant rat's eyes seem more reassuring. I look at the rat, it does not look that bad, that menacing or disgusting. I put my hand out, holding in mid-air and the rat nods in consent. I stroke the giant rat, its fur feels warm and cold, like stroking a wet yet warm ragged towel.

"Never question fate..." Andie whispers as we both watch the rumbling shadows of the giant terror flickering on the silver screen of falling water.

4th December

Rahman: Break

Location: The Capital, Bumi

"Rahmat, drive us to your cousin's dine-in," I tell my son who looks increasingly uneasy.

"It's already midnight, father," Rahmat replies hesitantly. I look sternly at him and he knows that our relationship is based on pure autocracy.

"Look Mr. Rahman, I'm not in the mood to eat," Azan tries to decline.

"The least I should do for you is make sure that you've had your dinner before I send you home. Otherwise, I am sure your uncle would be very unpleased with me," I insist.

Your uncle would be beyond being unpleased; he'd be furious if he had known you had been using your Karin to further your personal gains. In ancient times, you would have been executed.

"My nephew runs a decent 24 hours dine-in, selling local fast food. Here you won't find fries, instead you'll find rice with fried chicken and a spicy chili paste or fried noodles. A very simple menu, with only two choices. He consulted me once, asking me if it was a good idea to have just two choices in the menu. I simply replied to him that it is like how we choose to live our lives; you only have two choices: light or darkness."

My son instinctively knows the 'drill'. Rahmat walks slowly to the cooler fridge, picks up canned drinks and starts fidgeting and tapping into his mobile phone in the corner, giving me some time to talk to Azan.

"You have some good Silat moves, even without the Karin,"

"It was not fair. You had intentionally provoked me. I would have been better if I had a calmer mind."

"Being calm is never about having the right conditions. It is always about the right conditioning," I pause and tread carefully. "I wonder who taught you those moves," I know the answer already but let me hear it from him.

"My mother, before she died. Everything else was picked up here and there, and yes from the internet and YouTube," I can see the shame and anger swirl in his mind.

"Your mother was my student, until she decided to start a family. To have you. It was a great honour to have been a teacher to her, even if her training was not complete. It was my opportunity to repay your uncle Tuah for guiding me." The waiter interrupts our conversation and places our food: spicy chili chicken rice for Rahmat and as for Azan: fried chicken noodles marinated in soy sauce. Rahmat comes back to our table, takes his food and sits away from us.

"I know I need to do something important, something meaningful in my life, but all venues are closed for me. I can't exactly go to college any more. I have no interest in school any more. Other than Silat, I don't know what I should be doing. And I definitely don't want to do the things that you guys do," Azan replies. I resist the sweet aroma of his fried noodles.

"Azan, why is that?"

"Look around, it's the 21st century. Only crazy people talk about the spirit world. I don't want people to think that I am...." Azan pauses, clearly looking for the right words so as not to offend me, "an exorcist or spiritual practitioner of some sort. I want to fit in society, get married without anyone thinking I am some weirdo! Don't you get it, Mr. Rahman?"

"And this is coming from someone who had a pact with his Karin," I try to reason with him.

"That was different, no one else but me knows. He was my only friend, my only true friend, and you killed him. He didn't even get to plead his case. He was good to me," Azan loses his appetite, throwing his fork on to the table.

A thought passes through me. No, I will not slap him for that insolence. He is not my son. And he needs a more gentle guidance. I thank myself for having grown to be a more mellow man.

"Azan, I hope after you rest tonight, you will think about it. My team needs you. There is so much I want to show you. I can help you find your true bearings in life again. Don't fight it," I advise Azan but all he does is cross his arms in contempt, his eyes staring into the distance, refusing to look at me.

"Just take me home, old man," I feel Azan's defensive walls are up and I know there's nothing I can do tonight. I won't give up on him. I am so glad that I am a persistent man.

4th December

Azilah: Distrust

Location: Hilaga City Hall, Hilaga City

Using a hidden lever hidden underneath the control panel of the emergency elevator, Lord Jahat controls the descent of the elevator to the ground floor. No surprise plunge, slow and gentle. I hate the thought of crashing onto the ground floor. When we reach the ground floor, the first thing I notice is the crowd in the streets being much more noisier and rowdier than before - a swarm of angry bees waiting to attack anything and everything on sight.

As we step out of Hilaga City Hall Building, the crowd of despondent citizens rush towards Lord Jahat, as Master Selym and I struggle to push them away. Hands grabbing out to reach Lord Jahat, pleading for help in this dark unforgiving night, their loved ones trapped in the very buildings that had been our pride and jewel of Hilaga progress. The screams and wails intermix with the constant banging and tapping on the glass windows of the buildings above us. Our own technology is now our downfall. If only we had known and had been prepared. We should have made sure each building had their own mechanical emergency elevator like the City Hall building.

Lord Jahat manages to climb on to Master Selym's broad shoulders. He gestures with his hand for the crowd to calm down and listen. The humid air smells of burnt plastic and ash; and yet poses no challenge to Lord Jahat who captures the complete attention of his people so easily.

"Citizens of Hilaga! A great crime has been committed by the Supreme Council! In their struggle to maintain their power, they have done the unthinkable! We will punish them for this act of self-hate and self-sabotage. We, the citizens of Hilaga are not their expendable pawns. I, Lord Jahat, will make sure their blood will burn these streets bright red! Who is with me?"

The crowd thirsts for blood as they throw their fists into the air, shouting out their loyalty to Lord Jahat, "The Supreme Council must die!"

Hopelessness. He can stoke the flames of anger so easily to quell all sense of futility.

"Hilaga is the Light unto the World!" Lord Jahat shouts out to the sea of angry and determined faces illuminated by moving light orbs, shouting in chorus with his words. The wailing of the lost drowned out by the chants for blood.

"We march to the Supreme Council! Bring any weapons you may have! Hilaga is the Light unto the World!"

Lord Jahat's mob grows by the hundreds, and then by the thousands, as we march in unison, stomping feet, united towards the Hilaga City Supreme Council building.

"Azilah, whatever happens, Lord Jahat's safety is our priority - we protect him with our lives. I ask no less from you than that. We cannot afford to make a mistake now." Master Selym squeezes my arm hard, and I acknowledge my oath to Lord Jahat.

We arrive at Martavig road, a wide eight lane road that separates us from the 'Tessenk' - the official name for the Hilaga City Supreme Council Building. It is a horse-shoe shaped building with a narrow entrance that leads to a spacious tiled walkway in the middle. Few people have been allowed to step inside, the building full of so many secrets by secretive people. The building should be dark but everywhere inside and outside the building there are tens of thousands of light orbs. I can make out the shadows of the figures holding the orbs inside the windows of the Tessenk. These must be the soldiers who are loyal to the Supreme Council. On the walkway, there are thousands of yellow light orbs on the ground and three large wooden throne chairs. There are two figures seating on two of the chairs, whilst one is clearly empty. On each side, there are three figures standing, each holding a banner. The light is too dim to make out whose banners those are.

Lord Jahat motions for the mob and his own loyal soldiers to stop, whilst he formulates a plan. I know he does not want to walk into a trap. It seems the Supreme Council has been prepared for this. I guess that proves the Supreme Council were the ones who had started the coup.

Master Selym makes hand signals to his Units, whom I am not familiar with - to spread out and try to flank the enemy.

One of the figures sitting on the chair stands up and walks towards us, escorted by one of the banner figures. Who is that?

Lord Jahat starts moving towards them, telling the crowd to stay put - the thirst for blood can wait. Master Selym and I keep very close to Lord Jahat, we try to synchronise our steps with Lord Jahat's footsteps which seem to pick up pace as we get closer to the mysterious figure. We will protect him even if it means we forfeit our lives.

When we are close enough, I recognise the figure, the female who was sitting on the chair. I don't recognise the person carrying the banner, but he sure looks menacing, tough and much taller than Master Selym. His torso and limbs seem to bulge out of his clothes. He seems unmoved, undaunted by the danger of our angry mob and soldiers, whom at a moment's notice could tear him apart limb by limb.

"Sara, it's over. Your takeover plans, the people will not accept it. When the Supreme Council becomes weak, the people become stronger. Make it easy for us and I will make it easy for you."

"Oh hello Jahat! What happened to all the pleasantries? We used to be so civilised and so much more intimate than this," says Supreme Council leader Lord Sara, a grey haired woman whose council robes do little to hide her slender body. She leans close to Lord Jahat and gives him a quick kiss before embracing him passionately. She melts his old heart for a while, before Lord Jahat pushes her away.

"Sara, aren't you a bit too old for this? We have gone beyond kiss and make-up. Do you understand the repercussions of this?"

"Jahat, we are never too old for anything. Let's get some things straight. We have always been prepared for all eventualities including your mad lustre for power - any excuse to get rid of The Supreme Council. I think we should talk in private. Let's avoid further difficulties for our people."

"It would be easier to get rid of the Supreme Council right here, right now."

"Oh Lord Jahat, you have much to learn. Look closely at the banner that is with me now," Sara points to her banner-man. "You don't recognise it, do you? But it seems Selym here recognises it. I apologise if it brings rather bad memories. "It seems Master Selym has been staring at the person carrying the banner all this time."

"Ehsom? Is that you? Aren't you supposed to be dead?" Master Selym's voice is barely audible as he points towards the banner.

"Yes, Selym - I had some very special missions that required for me to pretend to be dead. It's good to see you again. I wish it had been under better circumstances. I would hate to kill you with my own hands."

"That banner is the 101!" Master Selym cannot believe his eyes. "My father founded and led the 101." He corrects himself, "I meant our father, Ehsom."

"Sara, the 101 has been disbanded for a long time. What's the meaning of this?"

"Although, your 'mob' and your soldiers outnumber us, our soldiers are the elite of the elite. *'Crem de La Crem'*. They are highly trained and skilled killers - with real battle experience. They have pledged their loyalty and their lives to defend the Tessenk. It's not just the 101. The Tebnihs, The Nama Unit and the Kidon Unit are all here. I don't even see that beast of a soldier of yours here. I heard he is still stuck on Bumi. You and all these poor people you have manipulated to confront us will die in vain before you step foot onto the Tessenk grounds. I promise you that."

"Sara, I could just kill you here and see what happens." Lord Jahat can barely smile, as he searches Sara's eyes to figure out her plans.

"I am expendable. In the event of my death, and No. 3's death, No. 1 - Lord Nathan will take over as a singular council entity. We have prepared and made far-reaching detailed plans for all eventualities. He is not here. He is with the rest of the 101, far away from us. You have no idea who we are, what we are capable of. We are true patriots, who would burn this City down to the ground and kill every person and child to save it. I don't have to tell you what will happen if you try to destroy the Tessenk? Do I, Lord Jahat?"

 "So Sara, you expect me to simply walk away from all this, this attack and the ruin you are causing to this City?"

I hold on to my dagger tightly. My heart starts to beat erratically and I do my best not to show my fear. I expect the situation to worsen at any moment now.

"Selym, your blue-eyed student seems too green for this," Ehsom comments to Master Selym, who refuses to respond.

"Jahat, this is not our doing. We did not cause this blackout. It serves us no interest. We ourselves want to find out what has happened, but we cannot do this divided. The City must stand united. Jahat, you have the power to unite us and together Hilaga will be strong again. Let us put aside our differences for now and launch a proper investigation."

"Another ploy to buy time, whilst your Kidon units try to figure another way to assassinate me. Like the ones you placed in City Hall."

"You wouldn't have noticed our Kidon assassins. I assume you killed the City Hall guards watching you. They must have panicked and acted on their own. They must have followed our outdated protocols for these things."

"That's a shame about your outdated protocols," I hear the sarcasm in Lord Jahat's voice.

"One of them was my nephew, Daun - he was quite a caring and gentle Hilagaan - I thought spying on you was one of the safest jobs I could give him. This would break my sister's heart. She would never forgive me for this." Sara's face remains emotionless, giving away nothing as she speaks - I can't tell if she is trying to manipulate Lord Jahat or is in mourning.

"My condolences to you and your family." Lord Jahat clears his throat, "As for the blackout, I will need proof before I believe anything you say. I did promise all these people that your blood and all those that stand with you would burn on these roads bright red."

"Jahat, we don't have proof. Only our history points to something similar, but never on this scale."

"Stop playing games, Sara." Lord Jahat snaps at Sara as the mob rumbles with restlessness and impatience.

"Jahat, how could you forget? The attack on Hilaga City by the Gergasi Clan."

What clan is Supreme Council Lord Sara talking about?

"Tuah and those Humans," Master Selym whispers.

4th December

Serigala: Failure

Location: MATA Portal, Ingei Jungle, Bumi

I was sure I had killed my former mentor Jawad the Great Conjurer. And yet I saw them disappear before my very eyes. Retreating to the MATA Portal, my soldiers are still in their shadow demon shape. I know most soldiers prefer to be in their own real flesh and form, but I quite like being this monstrosity - a giant shadow faceless demon in the human world. There is nothing like the excitement of the surge of power and the crushing of humans in their fragile bodies - meaningless ants with only one purpose: my entertainment. Pure thrill.

"What do you mean that MATA does not work?" I fume at the twelve demons left in my unit.

"The portal is closed, Master. We have been trying to use it for the past few hours, but it will not open. Someone must have closed the portal."

"That's not possible. One does not simply close the portal. It cannot be closed. It has always been open, there is no mechanism to close it," I push one of my underlings aside.

"What do we do, Master? We cannot be in this form for long. We need to nourish ourselves," says a shadow demon underling. He is so much smaller than me. Even at 10 feet, he is only up to my ankles.

They will serve me well. Today was a bad day. We had huge casualties. I should go back and create a larger number of casualties on the human side.

"Come here everyone, we need to have a discussion."

The other underling demons cautiously move towards me.

"Clearly, something has happened since my former mentor created his own portal and I strongly suspect he has created a portal to our world."

The other demons gasp in horror and murmur amongst each other. "Is that really possible?"

"Oh yes, I've seen him do that before. It was a lesson he had promised to teach me... never mind."

"Master Serigala, if he did bring humans to our world, it would disrupt our own MATA portal."

"And much worse, they would damage the City itself. Let us not worry about that. If only we had killed them all before they escaped to our world."

My underlings drop to their knees, "Please forgive us, Master Serigala. We have failed you. Please let us redeem ourselves."

I motion them to stand up, "Yes, you have failed me. I will give you all the chance to fight back. We lost the battle but it is the war that we must win. Winning a war is about inflicting the most damage to the humans to a point they can never recover. Let us reflect upon this moment and figure out the next step in our action plan. Is that understood?"

"Yes, Master Serigala." My underlings stand up. I can see their relief. I wonder if I have been too unforgiving in the past. I should try to be an inspiration to those I lead. Be more... What is that word?... Compassionate. Yes, that is the trend now. Leaders must show or at least pretend to show compassion for their followers. I reach out my hand to one of my more senior troops. "Whatever happens, we will be in this together, even for the long run."

"With the MATA portal down and the humans there, does this mean we are stuck here forever?" Another underling demon asks.

"Yes, unless our people can figure something out, or they kill the humans there."

"How long can we survive in this world, boss?" the same underling demon asks.

"Not long. I will ensure that your fallen brethren has not died in vain. That's why I must thank you for the sacrifice you are making today."

"What sacrifice, boss?" another underling asks.

"Hilaga is the Light Unto the World!" I laugh as I immediately grab the necks of two of the demons, snapping it and absorbing them into my body, black on black - shadow melting into shadow. The other demons are in shock, unable to comprehend what is happening. Dark projections from my giant form grab all ten of them, crushing their shadow bodies before absorbing them into me.

I hear their cries of help and cries for the names of their loved ones.

No one can hear you. That's just pathetic. Please die with some dignity. Help me help you make Hilaga great again.

Their absorbed bodies will sustain me for months enough time for the MATA portal team to figure out what to do.

The bonds of weakness can only be broken with the strength of resolution.

This is a good time to visit an old rival and make him pay for what he did. With renewed energy, I disappear from the jungles and materialize near an apprentice's house.

A human subcontractor.

4th December

Burut: Contractor

Location: Junjungan Village, Bumi

It is way past midnight. The hairs behind my neck stand up for no reason, my tummy feels knotted and my hands feel tingly. I know something big is going to happen tonight. It feels like it has been a long time. I have taken too long a break this time. *Dayang, how I have missed you?*

I look at myself in the mirror and ponder upon my lonely life. I pick up my late wife's hair brush and brush my own shoulder length hair. I stop and look at her hairbrush and then glance at the doll, sitting in the corner of my bedroom. An effigy of my late wife. Every day, I ask her for forgiveness, kiss her and tell her how much I really loved her. I then put her hands on her lap, just the way I want her to be. An obedient wife. She should have always been obedient. I made 'her' myself using her old clothes, stuffing from pillows and of course, her actual hair which I managed to cut before she was buried. It was dangerous but I made the effort to cut out her heart and embalm it, placing it in the effigy to keep the essence of her presence with me.

Why did she have to be so curious? Why was I so careless? She was a true gem, now lost. She was my soul-mate and now I live my life in these empty rooms.

I brush my long hair harder until all the entangled becomes untangled. The strength in my strokes will smooth out the undesirables. I allow my hair to cover the scars on my neck.

I sure miss her. Anyhow, I hope tonight's gonna be a big night for me.

Lately, these contracts have been a bit harder to fulfil.

"Burut, I have a job for you," A familiar voice booms directly into my head. I step out of my bedroom balcony and see a giant shadow demon towering beyond the rooftops. The streetlights illuminate everything but him. To unfamiliar eyes, the demon would appear as a shadow that passes by and disappears in the darkness.

I bow down, "Yes, Master Serigala. I am your loyal servant and I am very pleased to be able to serve you. Let me prepare myself."

I walk back into my bedroom, walk towards the effigy of my wife, leaning down to kiss and smell her hair, I whisper; "I loved you, I really did. I will always regretfully love you."

I note to myself that I need to add more hair conditioner on her hair to make it smell good again. She would always joke about how we both had long hair and that was why we were meant to be together. That was just so silly. She had no idea the horrors I had committed. Regret, that is all that I have when I think of her.

Heading towards a large old closet which has been custom built by myself into the wall of this house, I take off my clothes and enter the closet. The closet is roomy, purpose-built to provide me comfort. I thought about putting a refrigerating unit previously but it was just too complicated for me to figure out. I could not risk hiring workers for this sensitive job. Sitting down cross-legged, I pull down a lever on my left, which opens a secret hatch on the roof, the gentle night breeze flows down around me. I take a deep breath in and inhale this cool ash-tinged air.

I should really talk to my neighbour who keeps doing these night backyard burning. He thinks no one knows. But I know and if he doesn't listen this time, then I will have to add him to my list.

In some ways, I am so glad that no one lives here but me. It is easier this way. No more vulnerable witnesses.

I close my eyes and chant forbidden words that do not belong to this world. My body becomes lighter and I feel myself begin to float. I open my eyes, and stare at the stars twinkling brightly in the cloudless night sky. My neck starts to hurt; it feels like it is burning and then it starts to hurt really badly. I hold myself back from screaming, whilst I push my arms against the walls of the closet and tell myself that for every good and amazing experience comes a lot of pain first. My head rips away from my torso. I have become free, free from the prison that was my body. Now my head levitates a meter above from the rest of my body, though still connected through my entrails.

Concentrate, I'm nearly there.

I must be careful at this point so as not to cause damage to my own body. I put a few thoughts into myself and feel my small intestine disconnect from the large intestine. Now I am free to fly.

My head, me, the 'Babalan' flies up the large closet, through the connecting duct to a special opening at the roof.

"Woo hoo!"

No matter how many times I see this, I continue to appreciate the beauty of the city's edge in the horizon, lit with all kinds of incandescent, LED and fluorescent lights. I feel the wind blowing against my face, neck and hanging appendages. This is true freedom for the privileged few like myself.

"Burut, hurry up! Don't you dare make me wait!" the towering demon yells at me.

I fly towards the giant demon, my Master Serigala.

I hope he does not want me to do yet another pregnant woman. It is a messy and such a lowly job. The people get so upset when I kill pregnant women. They search more vigorously and always end up accusing innocent people. I should consider myself a professional. I have got enough years of experience for higher class kills.   I want to say all this to Master Serigala, but his leadership style isn't really what you call 'flexible'.

"Hi Boss, you look great tonight. I see you look much bigger than usual. Are you alone? Where are the usual others?"

"Enough chit chat, Burut. I have got a tough job for you. Once the job is done, I will be indebted to you and I will reward you extremely well. Come, let's go."

I never get to choose the jobs. I'm supposed to be a freelancer, but this 'client' never lets me have a say.

Master Serigala grabs me - the flying head - with his giant shadow hand and brings me closer to his torso.

He seems to be in a hurry.

We disappear into nothing, coldness seeps into every part of my skull as we reappear in a suburb near the Capital. I thought I heard a dozen voices screaming just before we reappeared. It gives me a real chill down my 'neck'.

I should get him to teach me this trick. It would be very useful for getaways.

Master Serigala points to a house near the centre of the suburb.

"Burut, I can't enter that house. It's protected by a powerful 'guris'. Do what you must to get the old man out. Even if it hurts you, I can heal you. Once he is out, I will take care of him. As for the others, they are yours to do as you please," he commands me. I obey without hesitation, flying faster than ever to the house, hurling myself towards an upstairs bedroom window. With my special eyesight, I can see the protection spell around the house.

"Oh boy, this is going to hurt me! Whatever Master says, Burut does!"

I smash my head towards the lower corner of the upstairs bedroom window at full speed. My face and hair burns as the window breaks. With glass fragments embedded on my face and the pungent smell of my flesh burning terrifies me, I scream in pain. Instinctively, I quickly roll around on the carpet to extinguish the flames on my face and hair. I assess the dark room, which I can see as clear as day.

The occupant in the room is now awake, standing and wondering what broke the window. She looks at me and screams in terror. I have seen this so many times before, the reflection of me in their eyes, the terror of the body-less head, the very same look of shock, fear and impending death. Without hesitation, I hurl myself towards her abdomen, and bury my sharp large teeth with great speed and strength, ripping her skin, the adipose, her guts ... and best of all her liver. I will need a good liver! She tastes so fine, her flesh so soft and nourishing. Her screams are no more as her body falls back onto the floor with a loud thump, with me still embedded into her, still gouging upon this wonderful feast. It does not take me long to devour her entire torso.

I could use a napkin right now, as her blood and bits cover my entire face, and half burnt hair. I roll around again the carpet to wipe the blood off. My burnt face is healing fast and my mangled and burnt hair is growing again - smooth and long.

Let's feast again.

I float towards the door and using my forehead, I pull the door lever down and then bite the metallic door handle and pull the door open.

I hate the taste of metal. At least this one is not a door knob.

Entering the corridor, I hear footsteps, someone is coming up the stairs, a sweet and uncertain female voice calls out, "Hey Salmah, what happened? Why are you screaming in the middle of the night?"

By the time she comes up the stairs, she sees me in all my glory and gore. I rush myself towards her and bite her neck hard. She tumbles down the staircase on to the halfway landing, knocking off a small table and picture frames. I keep gnawing hard through her neck and rip her carotid artery, warm spurts of her life drains onto my face and my mouth. I hear a crunch as her neck snaps. I keep biting on it anyway.

Never miss out on a good meal.

I look at her torso and wonder if I should devour the goodies in her now. I just love this job. Mission first, I'll eat her later. She's not going anywhere, in any case. A broken glass photo frame catches my eye. A portrait of the family I have just reduced, and yet they look quite familiar. To be precise, the old man in that photo looks very familiar. I ponder and then it comes to me as a sudden and urgent realization.

No, not THIS house. Not him. His deep and hoarse voice startles me.

"Who's there? What's all this noise?" Comes out an old man from the living room. He sees me and runs towards me. Yes, I know who he is, and he has seen my face. He will come after me at my house.

No, no, no why him? Why his house?

As much as I would like to kill him now, I am no match for this man, not Guru Tuah.

Master Serigala, why did you send me to do this job?!

"Die, Babalan!"

I glance back and see a blue glow coming from his hands.

"Holy crap!"

Bolts of lightning come out of his hands and nearly hits me. I see an apple-size burning hole in the wall, where the lightning bolt struck. I feel the heat of the near miss on my face.

I must get out of here.

Two more lightning bolts come out, as he tries to shoot me down. I fly desperately, hitting and knocking down wall picture frames, and bouncing against the walls of the house.

"I'm sorry, I didn't know it was your house. I didn't mean to kill your family. It's a mistake."

Tuah shoots out a volley of three lightning bolts.

Quick I must get out of here! Why do they have to put iron grills on the ground floor windows! How am I going to get out of here? I'm going to be dead if I get hit by one of those lightning bolts!

Four lightning bolts barely miss me and yet they've singed my entrails. With luck, I manage to spot a small glass window above the front door. I have no choice, I fly straight towards it, shattering this small window. My face and hair starts burning again, the horrific smell of my burnt flesh again! A double guris! I try to fly out towards the night sky, but instead I crash land on to the driveway, tumbling until I end up on the manicured moist lawn.

Not again! I'd better be rewarded well for this job.

Guru Tuah opens the door and runs towards me.

I'm going to be finished.

"I am finally gonna be able to get my revenge, Tuah!" Master Serigala's voice is a relief to me, as he appears just by my head.

"In the nick of time, Boss!"

"We'll see about that," Tuah raises his hands, and shoots so many lightning bolts at one time, it looks like a flashing river of lightning in the night sky.

Master Serigala does not move, he nullifies the attack with his own attacks of black flame projectiles: the Dunar attack.

"Humans age so much faster with time. I look at you, and pity your body that has been ravaged by disease. My vengeance is now complete. I killed your sister some time ago and now the rest of your family inside that house is gone. All that is left is just you! Die Tuah, Die!"

Master Serigala prepares a large Dunar black flame projectile, taking his sweet time, looking at the old man's despondent look on his face.

He releases the Dunar and it flies towards him, but does not hit him. Something had pushed the Dunar away. Someone pushed the Dunar away.

"Rahman, you came just right on time. To be honest, I wouldn't mind dying in its hands right now. I'm too old for this."

Rahman walks towards Tuah, as his son Rahmat follows closely behind, doing his best not to look at the giant shadow demon. Azan does not follow; he gets out of the car and just stares at the unbelievable sight of a demon giant: Master Serigala.

"You will die with your Guru Tuah too! Hilaga is the Light unto this World!" Master Serigala fires a few large Dunar projectiles. Rahman's arms start to glow bright white and he shoots out one single lightning bolt, devouring the Dunar black flame attacks with ease. Rahman's attack is so incredibly bright, the whole neighbourhood basks in the light, confusing the neighbours to think it is daytime. The lightning bolt hits Master Serigala, just before he disappears into nothing. Azan runs up to Tuah, and then leaves him to run into the house. He screams and yells in anguish.

Rahman, Tuah and Rahmat stand together staring at me. Although I am in pain, burnt and wounded, I do nothing. I cannot fly. I dare not fly.

Maybe they did not see me, maybe I look like an old coconut on the grass. I should play dead. I just stay still until this is over. Why didn't Master Serigala take me with him?

I start to panic as I know they have already seen my face. I'm a dead man one way or another. They'll find me, find my body and burn me. What do I do? I must get out of this country tonight.

I see Azan running out of the house, I can see his rage-filled swollen red eyes, tears flowing down his cheeks. He stares at me; I dare not move. He goes to the garage, picks up a spade and runs towards me.

"Please don't hurt me. I'm sorry. I'm just following orders," I plead as I roll around trying to lift myself off the ground and fly away, fly away to my own freedom.

I must get out of here now, I can do this. All I have to do is just fly high enough above that fence and land in the ditch. I can figure it out from there.

I keep thinking about getting hold of my passport. Where did I place my passport?

With all my strength, I propel myself upwards.

Yes! I am flying again. I must make it over that fence. Positive thinking is all I need.

A loud clunk. I did not see it coming, as I fall back down on to the grass. My head hurts bad. That boy hit me with the spade.

"Please, please I can make it up to you. Don't kill me. I am human too, just like you."

Azan steps on my appendages and brings the spade down fast and hard onto my poor head.

It's just a setback, I can heal, I can heal, I say to myself.

"Please don't hit me! For God's sake, that hurts! Please forgive me. I am so sorry. I didn't mean to kill your family. Please show me your compassion. Please. Please." I yell for mercy, in between hits. "Look kid, I am just following orders. I did not want to do this. I was forced to take orders."

Why won't this boy listen?

He hits my head repeatedly. I scream in pain, begging him to stop. The pain is too much that I become numb, caught in between fleeting moments of consciousness and flashes of memories of why I had chosen this path. I see a figure running towards me, maybe one of them will stop this kid, reason with him to spare me.

I just wanted to fly. I wanted to be free.

Glimpses of my late wife, and the look on her face, in complete disbelief before I ended her life. Why did it have to come to that?

I look at the other figure — it turns out to be a shadow of the rest of my body - waiting. I hate it when my mind plays tricks on me.

The last thing I hear is the tragic crunching sound as he bashes my skull broken and my brain matter splatter out onto this otherwise beautifully manicured lawn.

4th December

Rahman: Dendam

Location: Tuah's house, The Capital.

Azan is busy smashing the Babalan - the evil flying head into smithereens. He yells non-stop. I see some of the neighbours coming up to us.

I raise my right hand up and usher them away:

"Sorry, nothing to see here. Just a problem with our electric circuit. Go back to your homes, where you'll be safe. You did not see anything here."

I know they saw what they should not have seen. I pray no one has taken a video of this, the last thing we need is a viral video of us fighting a demon from a parallel dimension.

Tuah collapses on to the driveway. The strain has been too much for him. We all rush to him.

"Azan, you are the last of our family. Learn from Rahman before it is too late. They will also come after you.

Someday, you will remember this day, when you punish them and wipe them out," Tuah looks at Azan, and holds his hand.

"Rahman, here's my dying wish: Teach him what I could not, what I cannot. Be there for him. I see that this is what has been willed. Promise me."

"Guru Tuah, I promise, if God is willing."

"Uncle, we can take you to a hospital now," Azan pleads.

"No, no hospital. Better to die at my own house. At least the Hilagaans will know I outlived all of their assassination attempts... tell me who has the last laugh? There is no god but Him..." Tuah takes his last breath, his vacant eyes stare at me, he looks like he is smiling with full expectations that I would uphold my promise. I close his eyes and hold him in a tight embrace. Tuah, you have been such a wonderful mentor to me. How could I ever measure up to you?

My heart feels heavy as I remember his words and our last conversation: "Never promise anyone anything when they are dying. You'll end up regretting it."

How ironic, I thought.

"Please forgive me, Uncle Tuah, for all my wrong-doings." Azan trembles as he kisses Guru Tuah's hand and then his forehead, refusing to move away from him. I have to make sure that none of us will ever regret taking Azan as my student.

Police cars arrive, flashing blue lights illuminating the dark house of tragedy. This is most inconvenient. I make a phone call to a member of the team, who happens to be a high-ranking government official.

"Merah, I am the bearer of sad news. Guru Tuah and most of his family are dead," I pause as I gather my courage and then utter one word to him, "Hilaga." There is silence on the other side of the line, then Merah mutters 'indescribables' to himself.

"The police are here at Guru Tuah's house. Please deal with the police. His nephew Azan is with me, and he is now a member of our team."

"Rahman, I also have bad news. There's been a tragic development with an expedition group in the Ingei Jungle. Let's not talk about this on the phone. We shall talk when we meet." The deep voice on the other end of the phone is so typical for a high-ranking bureaucrat - always attempting to be authoritative, in the worst of events.

I hang up the call and look around me. I am still having difficulties at accepting what has transpired for the past few hours. I look at Azan, tears fall from his face, grimacing in anger. I know there is no other place now for him, but to be with me. Let vengeance be the best motivator for him. For now...

The LIMA team is complete. There is no more time to waste.

End of Book 1

About The Author

Aammton Alias is a practicing medical doctor. For the past 16 years, he has worked in a variety of hospitals, hospices and intensive care units. Eventually, he settled down as a family physician in a lovely, small town.

Although others only see him by the boundaries of the definition of a medical doctor, those who know him well know that he is NOT confined to that description. He is a passionate advocate for those who seek his help, and his compassion has made him an activist of various causes. He is also a writer, a poet warrior, an entrepreneur at heart and most importantly, he is a family man.

http://www.about.me/aammton

You can reach him via Twitter @Aammton

PREVIEW of Book 2

The Well Of The Seven Kings

SARIN: Gemat

5th December

Location: Air Force Base Bravo One

Boots. Six pairs. We sit tightly in the metal black bird as it hovers above the ground, loud vibrations shake the cage, but not our cores. It is a routine now for the 5th Recon Unit - 'The Prowling Tigers'. An air crewman in the cabin with his over-sized green helmet nods and thumbs up the pilot, and then starts to close the doors of this Sikorsky S-70A 'Black Hawk' helicopter. I look at the different faces of the team, snort and spit out the most vile and viscous of phlegm through the helicopter door, watching it land on to the landing pad below. The air crewman looks at me, but my cold stare stops him from making comments.

He wouldn't understand. The unspoken rituals that us warrior men, must make to ensure the safety of the troops we lead. Every man here has his own ritual: things that need to be done to dispel bad luck and ensure safe passage.

Sergeant Menawan; a smooth-faced tracker, sits in front of me. He is grinning with no apparent purpose whilst fiddling with a black string tied around his left wrist, a talisman to ward away evil spirits. I do my best not to look at it. He is from the 'Dusun' indigenous tribe, a pagan whose family still practise the dark arts of shaman-ism. I press my hand onto my own chest, feeling the outline of my own silver talisman. Protect me from the unseen evil.

The Black Hawk helicopter soars into the air and we fly over patches of sporadic and unchecked urban development, orange and white houses below like mosaic pieces, crisscrossed by never-ending black asphalt roads. A battle to claim as much of the green and turn them into the illusions of the dream called progress.

Lance Corporal Azim is sound asleep whilst another, Corporal Jagau - our heavy weapons specialist, seems at ease reading a book.

"What's the dumb book you're reading?" I shout out to Jagau. The helicopter blades chopping and thundering through the air, makes me barely audible. If only they gave us onboard radio sets. I hate budget cuts.

Jagau shows me the cover 'Be the One Percent: Unlock Secrets to True Success, Real Wealth & Ultimate Happiness' and gets back to reading. I smile away, hiding my concerns for this soldier. Pep talk perhaps later or a career counsellor. Private Kilau, on the other hand, is happily listening to his music via his earphones. He smiles at me. Kilau is always smiling and cheerful, no matter what his situation. I reminisce the time I heard about his women troubles, especially when his wife rammed her car to his car when she saw him with his secret girlfriend. I often wonder how he got his wife to accept him back. Perhaps the secret is to smile away our troubles.

Fifteen minutes later, I can see through the helicopter window the houses are no more, it's all green and trees all around. Another thirty minutes before we land. I close my eyes and recollect the conversation earlier with the commander of the base.

***

"Sarin, this is Dato Kassim." I shake hands with the elder but confident man, lowering my shoulders slightly to show my respect for this man of great stature. His title Dato, is like being knighted by the Queen, except it is not the Queen of England that 'knights' him.

I could not help from noticing his sparkling diamond encrusted platinum ring, square with a dozen smaller twinkling diamonds in formation. He must be a businessman too.

"I have been informed that my daughter Dr. Nurul Kassim has disappeared in the Ingei jungle. Something terrible has happened to the expedition team," Dato Kassim pushes the rims of his designer sunshades. Real men take off their sunshades when they talk to other people, it is disrespectful not to do so, no matter his stature.

"There are already soldiers from the Third Battalion encamped there," Dato Kassim's index finger in mid-air and half-pointing towards me, "But I need the best. Please, Captain Sarin. Lead your team and find her. She means the world to me." I turn to the Commander, who nods in acknowledgment.

"Prepare your team and meet at Hangar J in 30 minutes. You will be briefed there."

"Yes, Tuan Sir," I salute the Commander.

"Dismissed."

"Captain Sarin, bring her home safely and I will make sure that you and your men will be taken care of, as a sign of my gratitude."

"Don't forget me too," I hear the Commander laugh as I close the door behind me.

Ingei. Why? Is this the same thing that happened with my old Unit?

***

The sudden jerking of the helicopter interrupts my thoughts as we are thrown by unforgiving wind. I look out and see dark overcast clouds. I tap the on-board communication system.

"Pilot, how soon are we landing?"

"We can't land at the LZ. The winds just came up out of nowhere and pushing us against the landing zone."

"Land us safe, pilot."

"That's always the plan, Captain Sarin."

The helicopter tilts 45 degrees on its side, as it goes round its original landing approach. Through the window, I see the tall rainforest trees almost touching the helicopter. Of course, this is a mere illusion, the helicopter is not that near. I wonder why can't the pilot just land vertically, since this is a helicopter and then remember the landscape and the tall leaning trees, which can sway uncontrollably in strong winds. There's only one way to land this helicopter. I grip the side of the hard ABS seat as I realise another more dramatic way for this helicopter to land: a crash. No, we won't crash. The pilot is very experienced.

The Black Hawk helicopter completes the circular approach and levels out. I look ahead and through the windshield in front. I see the clearing, the landing site. Let's land safe.

A white shadow of a giant hand of rain water and wind pushes the helicopter back and the helicopter loses altitude, dropping down as I feel my stomach content float up half way up my throat.

Did I see a large hand pushing the helicopter? Can't be.

The helicopter rocks backwards unsteadily, and before we fall further with this metal black bird, the pilot surges power into the helicopter blades. The Black Hawk responds and we soar up and backwards to safety.

Sergeant Menawan curses, "Looks like the Bunian people don't want us to be here." He leans forward and to our shock, he pulls the helicopter door open and shouts into the wind a familiar Dusun spell to ward away evil spirits. Water splatters into the helicopter as the air crewman closes the door, avoiding eye contact with Menawan. Too scared to look for confrontation with a mad Ranger.

The helicopter tilts 45 degrees on its side, trying the same approach again. Third time lucky, I pray. As we level out again to the same landing zone, Menawan pulls the helicopter door again, and shouts out unimaginable expletives into the wind. Wet thick leaves blow into the helicopter cabin, swirling inside covering out eyes and slapping our faces.

"HEY BUNIANS, I WILL SLAP YOUR FACES WITH MY BLOODY UNDERWEAR IF YOU DON'T LET US LAND!" Menawan screams maniacally. Everyone stares at Menawan in disbelief. What the hell is he on?

As though in response, the wind and the rain abruptly stops, allowing the helicopter land on to the grassy clearing more forcefully than expected.

I grab my gear and jump out of the Black Hawk helicopter as my men follow suit. In the corner of my eye, I see the pilot giving the eye at Menawan, as the air crewman sweeps the leaves from the cabin with his feet, his own expletives inaudible with the thunderous sound of the helicopter blades.

Hunching down, my men and I run across the moving sea of tall grass to safety along the tree line ahead. The helicopter soars back into the air. We are now on our own.

"Welcome back to Ingei, Captain," Sergeant Menawan taps me on the shoulder. *What does he know about my past?*

With our full gear, we march to our rendezvous point nearby. We are to meet up with the army regulars, a platoon from the Third Battalion army.

There I will meet with my former Captain, my former mentor, my former saviour. Former Captain Roslan. The Cursed Captain. Maybe he will tell us a different story about the killings of the Ingei expedition team.

My Other Books

If you enjoyed this book, try reading my other books:

Be The One Percent: Unlock Secrets to True Success, Real Wealth & Ultimate Happiness

Bob is ONE of the 1 Percent, the ones who have found UNLIMITED WEALTH, TRUE SUCCESS & ULTIMATE HAPPINESS. I have known Bob since I was a child. There was always something about him, but I could not figure it out. He seemed liked any other ordinary person. In fact, he kept a low profile, except to close friends and family. It was only recently that I realized Bob is not just special, he is EXTRAORDINARY, knowing the Secrets of Life and much more.

There are many other 1-Percent persons who passed through my life and yet I did not notice until now.

Let us take that journey together.

BE THE 1 PERCENT

Ask yourself these questions:

Do you want UNLIMITED WEALTH?

Do you want constant stream of SUCCESS?

Do you want to be completely and truly HAPPY?

Learn the Secrets of the REAL 1 Percent.

The 1 Percent are far richer & powerful beyond measure.

They live amongst us unnoticed, with the Secrets of Life known to them.

Living with True Success in all forms, Real Wealth that neither taxes nor burdens & have achieved the Ultimate Happiness. They live in full Abundance, whilst the rest of us 99% still live in scarcity. Their hearts contain the secrets to nullify the intent and the anger of those who seek to harm them. Life is easy & fulfilling, like a beautiful dream. Would you not want to be one of them?

Included towards the end of this book are 12 SIMPLE PRINCIPLES to practice and uphold as you begin your new journey to your new life

http://www.book.b1percent.com

The King And The Minister

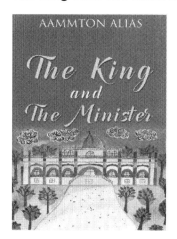

A beautiful children's book about a story of a wise minister who has some important advice for the King. Will the King listen? Will the advice prevail? Suitable for preschool children to read on their own and/or for bedtime reading. Illustrations are made from original watercolour paintings.

Kids age 6-8 will also love this book

Available at http://www.king.b1percent.com

The Vessel of Our Writing Dreams: Where Do Our Ideas Come From

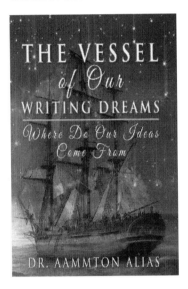

We are the vessels of our dreams, our ideas and yet where do our ideas come from? Is it simply a mesh of neurons blasting out until a printout comes out? Do we even own these 'ideas' that we claim to originate from us?

How do we ensure that we continue to both learn and project new ideas? Do we immerse ourselves in an inspirational environment? Did you know that when you shine, you give others permission to do so themselves?

Dr. Aammton Alias shares his personal experiences and odd non-linear stories to help you find the answers to these urgent questions.

Available at: http://www.vessel.b1percent.com

LET ME GO! How to Get Off Unwanted WhatsApp Chat Groups For Good

Being in a social media chat group can be quite useful and entertaining. On the other hand, having too many groups can be quite a pain in the butt – everyone underrates the stress of maintaining a presence in social media chat App groups...And what about those who you are keen to avoid are in the same chat group as you? Leaving a group without saying anything is considered sacrilege. What if they won't let you leave? You leave the group and then they keep inviting you back. You can check out anytime you want, BUT YOU CAN NEVER LEAVE! Do you have to block every person in that group to have your peace? Here are 1001 - funny, witty, intoxicating and annoying - ways to leave your social media chat groups!! Have you heard of Nuke Options? Do you want to know how you can Troll & Spam like a Pro?! Available at http://www.wtfrak.b1percent.com

Now Everyone Can Write And Publish A Book In 3 Days

Everyone dreams of writing a book and having their book published. Somehow, it seems like such an impossible dream.... hold on... here is a book to help you write your first book in 3 days!! There is no hype about this. It is simply a tested and proven pathway. If you don't believe me, simply check my other books and their publication dates. In this plan. Learn how to figure out what you can write about IMMEDIATELY! You can choose to write an eBook and if you want you can convert this into your first printed book, with almost zero money down.

This express book writing and publishing technique involves writing your eBook for Amazon Kindle and then getting it self-published into a printed book. It is so easy to write a book now these days, I keep telling friends, family and yes, strangers that if you can talk about something, you can definitely write about it. What are you waiting for? Available at: http://www.write.b1percent.com

23788032R00233

Printed in Poland
by Amazon Fulfillment
Poland Sp. z o.o., Wrocław